THE DUKE'S DARK SECRET

BOOK FOUR IN THE ASTLEY CHRONICLES

COURTNEY MCCASKILL

HAZEL GROVE BOOKS

THE ASTLEY CHRONICLES

THE ASTLEYS OF HARRINGTON HALL

The Astleys of Harrington Hall

Edward Astley IV, Earl of Cheltenham
Georgiana Astley, Countess of Cheltenham

Edward Astley V, Viscount Fauconbridge, age 27
Harrington Astley, age 26
Anne Cranfield (née Astley), Countess of Morsley, age 24
Caroline Greville (née Astley) Viscountess Thetford, age 20
Lady Lucy Astley, age 19
Lady Isabella Astley, age 19
John Astley, deceased at age 2
Frederick Astley, age 14

First published in 2023 by Hazel Grove Books.

The Duke's Dark Secret Copyright © Courtney McCaskill, 2023.

Excerpt from *Let Me Be Your Hero* Copyright © Courtney McCaskill, 2023.

Excerpt from *My Favorite Mistake* Copyright © Courtney McCaskill, 2023.

Paperback ISBN: 978-1-63915-018-2

Kindle ISBN: 978-1-63915-019-9

e-book ISBN: 978-1-63915-020-5

This is a work of fiction. Names, principal characters, events, and incidents are the products of the author's imagination and have no factual basis. Any resemblance to actual persons, living or dead, or actual events is purely coincidental.

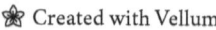 Created with Vellum

PROLOGUE

Gloucestershire, England
October 1802

he pounding at the door was loud enough to wake Cecilia Chenoweth from a dead sleep.

She stumbled from the bed and clung to the mantelpiece until her vision swam into focus. Still, the pounding continued. She threw on her dressing gown, managed to light the oil lamp, and rushed to the front of the house.

Ceci peered out the front window and saw a local farmer, William Nash. She could guess the reason he had come well enough. Her father, John Chenoweth, was the local rector, and when a woman struggled so mightily in labor it seemed unlikely that the babe would survive, he would be summoned to perform a hasty baptism, sometimes in the middle of the night.

She fumbled with the key. Strange. She had not realized that Mrs. Nash was in the family way.

She pulled the door open. The farmer's face was grave. "Please come in, Mr. Nash."

He made no move to enter, instead glancing over his shoulder, where Ceci could just make out a farm wagon in the moonlight.

She cleared her throat. "I'm sorry to say that my father is not here. He left some hours ago to attend your neighbor, Mrs. Anderson, in her confinement. Which I am guessing is what brings you here..."

The words died on her lips. She peered into the darkness. "D-doctor Stuart? What are you doing here? Should you not be attending Mrs. Anderson?"

"Lower him down," Dr. Stuart said. "*Gently.*" That was when Ceci noticed two of Farmer Nash's sons reaching into the back of the wagon.

As Dr. Stuart stepped into the lamplight, Ceci gasped. He had left off his jacket, and his shirtsleeves were rolled up to his elbows.

They were splattered with blood.

"Mrs. Anderson... is she... is she..." She couldn't seem to form the words.

"Mrs. Anderson is fine," Dr. Stuart reassured her. "Her labor was long, and we were worried for a little while there. But she finally bore a healthy girl two hours ago."

"Two hours ago?" Ceci shook her head, still muddled with sleep. "But if it was two hours ago, where is my... my..."

Just then, a great groan came from the yard as the Nash boys lifted something... no, *someone*... from the back of the wagon.

"Papa?" Ceci gasped, stepping forward.

Dr. Stuart stopped her with a gentle hand on her arm. "We need to get him inside."

Ceci led the way in a trance.

Dr. Stuart took charge. "Clear the dining table. We'll lay him there."

Ceci hastily moved the candlesticks and salt cellar to the sideboard, then snatched a pillow from the front room. The Nash men maneuvered her father through the door. Farmer Nash carried his feet, and his sons each lifted a shoulder.

Her father's face was a portrait of agony. As the Nash boys laid him on the table, a horrible sound came from his abdomen, part sloshing, part grinding of bone upon bone, and her father cried out.

"Papa!" Ceci rushed forward, tucking the cushion beneath his head. She took his hand, startled by how cold it was. "What happened?"

"He must've taken a fall from his horse on the way back from attending Mrs. Anderson," Dr. Stuart answered. "I found him lying by the side of the road when I headed home an hour or so later. Given his injuries, he most likely got kicked or trampled. It takes a lot of force to fracture the pelvis."

"Fracture the pelvis?" Ceci had never heard of someone fracturing their pelvis before, but it sounded serious. "What does one do for a fractured pelvis? Can you set it, or—"

Dr. Stuart's expression was a mix of exhaustion and sorrow. "There's nothing I can do. Such a fracture can't be set, and he's bleeding on the inside. Quickly, from the look of things. I'm so sorry, Miss Chenoweth, but I must advise you to make your final goodbyes while you still can."

"My final goodbyes? You mean he's... he's..." The room swayed. Farmer Nash took her upper arm in a steady grip and guided her into the chair one of his sons had pulled up behind her.

Her father couldn't be dying. He just couldn't. He was only forty-six years old and was in excellent health. Although Ceci knew all too well that tragedies happened every day—

her mother had died of a fever when she was just two years old—she had always assumed her father would be around for decades to come.

The two of them had always been a duo, for as long as she could remember. She had no siblings, and all four of her grandparents were dead. Her parents had both been only children, so she had no aunts, no uncles, no cousins. If her father died...

I'll be all alone in the world.

"*Ceci.*" Her father's pained voice pulled her from her daze when nothing else could've.

She leaned forward. "Yes, Papa?"

"So... so sorry, I—" He broke off with a gasp.

"Oh, please don't!" She smoothed the sweat-soaked hair back from his brow. "There is nothing for which to apologize. It was an accident."

"N-not that. Your mother. I—" He sucked in a wheezing breath.

"My mother?" Ceci frowned. Why on earth would he bring up her mother at such a moment? It wasn't that they never discussed her. Ceci loved hearing about her and would pester her father for stories, most of which she had heard dozens of times.

But her mother had been dead for nineteen years. What could possibly be so pressing in this, of all moments?

Her father's breath was growing more labored. "Should... should've told you the truth."

"The truth? What truth? What are you talking about?"

"It wasn't—" Her father broke off, gasping. "She didn't—"

"Papa?" she whispered. He tried to answer but couldn't make a sound. Ceci could not bear to see her beloved father, who had for so many years been her protector, her guide, and her confidant, in agony.

Her father was trying to speak but nothing came. "It's all

right," she said, dabbing at her eyes with the sleeve of her dressing gown. "Whatever it is, it's all right. I love you. I love you so much. That's the only important thing."

Her father shook his head, and, with a tremendous effort, lifted a shaking hand to his heart. The torment produced by this motion was plain upon his face as he slid two fingers between the buttons of his shirt and began to sift around.

What was he doing? "It's all right, Papa." Ceci tried to gently take his hand, but he continued searching beneath his shirt. "Just… just rest now."

His face had gone gray, but she marked the moment he found what he'd been looking for. She watched in astonishment as he pulled out a strange key dangling from a chain.

"What's this?" She had never seen this key before. But how was that possible? How could she not know about the existence of an item dear enough that her father apparently wore it each day, hanging just over his heart?

He pressed it into her trembling fingers, and she leaned forward to peer at it. It was gunmetal grey, so dark it looked almost black in the candlelight, finely wrought but with a design that sent a chill up the back of her neck. A black snake wound its way up the length of the key's shaft before swirling its head around the flat plate that formed its grip. The plate was engraved with an elegant script. "Number four," she read aloud.

She started to set it aside, but her father pressed the key into her hand. "You want me to keep it?" she asked.

Her father nodded.

"It's important?"

His nod was fainter this time.

"Is it something to do with Mother?" she whispered.

His eyes had lost their focus, but he jerked his head up

and down. He wrapped her fingers around the key and held them there.

Then his hand went limp, and although his eyes were open, Ceci knew he could no longer see her.

She buried her head against his chest, letting her tears run into the linen of his shirt.

There were voices after that. Comforting murmurs she scarcely heard. A steady hand on her shoulder guided her to the sofa in the front room. She watched in disbelief as Mr. Nash and his sons carried her father's limp body back outside.

Someone pressed a cup of tea into her hands. By the time she finally stirred herself to take a sip, the tea had gone stone cold, and light was breaking through the dining room's windows.

CHAPTER 1

London
September 1803

Standing beneath a crystal chandelier in Astley House's glittering ballroom, Cecilia Chenoweth forced a smile to her lips and tried to look anywhere but at the man standing a few feet away.

It didn't work particularly well, as the man she was determined to ignore was Marcus Latimer, the recently elevated Duke of Trevissick. He was widely regarded as the most handsome man in London, being in possession of pale golden hair, frost-colored eyes, an elegant fencer's physique, and the sort of cheekbones that made sculptors weep.

He also happened to be the particular man Ceci pictured when she hugged her pillow as she drifted off to sleep at night.

But making eye contact with him was entirely out of the question.

The problem dated back to the first moment she had clapped eyes upon him. It had been one year ago, and she had just arrived in London in order to attend the wedding of her dear friend Caroline Astley to Henry Greville, Viscount Thetford.

Ceci had been taking tea with Caro in the morning room, and Caro had said something very, very funny, as Caro was wont to do.

Unfortunately, Caro had dropped this *bon mot* at the precise moment two simultaneous events occurred.

One, Ceci took a sip of tea.

And two, the most handsome man in the world came strolling into the room.

This wretched convergence of events meant that Marcus Latimer's first impression of Ceci was of her snorting tea out of her nose.

It still made her cheeks burn, recalling his look of derision.

Was it possible to recover from such a humiliating incident? This was not one of those rhetorical questions— Ceci desperately desired to know how it could be done. They both served on the Board of the Ladies' Society for the Relief of the Destitute, a charitable organization founded by the Countess of Morsley back when she had been Lady Anne Astley, so Ceci had to attend board meetings with him on a regular basis. Even after the passage of a year, the mortification had not lessened one iota.

So, speaking to the duke? Unthinkable. Making eye contact? Horrifying.

But Ceci found it difficult to keep her gaze from straying in his direction. Like some bright, golden treasure at the British Museum, he could not help but draw your eye.

Retreating to the opposite side of the ballroom would have made ignoring him easier, but alas, that was not an option. This was a subscription ball being held on behalf of the Ladies' Society, and Ceci had a job to do tonight: organizing the charity auction. She therefore could not stray from the long table upon which the articles to be sold were displayed.

And, frankly, she had no desire to leave the table, at least, not this close to the beginning of the ball. This was due to the fact that she had managed to wear a hole in the sole of one of her dancing slippers.

Dancing slippers were notoriously flimsy things, and it wasn't uncommon to wear a hole in one during the course of a full night of dancing. She had been very careful to shuffle her feet as she made her way over to the table, and so long as she could conceal the hole until the second half of the ball, no one would think anything of it.

Still, she was nervous that someone would notice. If you looked at her foot from precisely the right angle, the fraying was visible even when her foot was flat on the floor.

Perhaps she should have mentioned it to Georgiana Astley, the Countess of Cheltenham. She knew Lady Cheltenham would have bought her a new pair of slippers. After her father's death last year, the Astleys had taken Ceci in, as she had no living family. This was awkward, but necessary, as it was considered improper for a young, unmarried woman to live alone.

But, upon looking into her father's financial affairs, Ceci had been shocked to discover that she was destitute. She could not understand it. Her father had made a good living. Ceci knew the church post he'd held for most of her life brought in twelve hundred pounds a year, as well as free use of the rector's cottage. Although her father had enjoyed a few indulgences—books, the best coffee ordered in from London, and sheet music for his daughter—they had lived frugally. Why, he had always told Ceci that when she married, she would have a dowry of a thousand pounds or so!

The point was, Ceci should have inherited *something* upon his death. But she had not, and without a farthing to her name, the imposition upon her friends was a thousand times worse.

Not that the Astleys seemed to mind. Lady Cheltenham had offered to buy Ceci an entire new wardrobe at the start of the Season, an offer Ceci had gratefully but firmly refused. She was determined to make her own way, not be a burden on her friends. And she was starting to have some success in this regard. The many hours she had spent at the pianoforte over the years now stood her in good stead, and she had managed to attract fourteen music students. The pay wasn't great, but after the lessons she had scheduled tomorrow, she should have enough saved up to get her dancing slippers resoled.

Everything was going to be fine. All she had to do was keep her feet concealed beneath the edge of the tablecloth for the next two hours and not look at Marcus Latimer.

How hard could it possibly be?

As he examined a Kashmiri shawl that would be auctioned off later in the evening, Marcus Latimer struggled not to look at Cecilia Chenoweth.

As always, it proved to be a difficult task. Even in that hideous, high-necked monstrosity of a gown in a color that artists probably referred to as *doleful beige*, he could scarcely keep his eyes off her.

Her finest feature was her eyes. They were huge. Brown. Slightly wide set. And *still*. She was the very definition of a sloe-eyed beauty.

And saying that her eyes were her finest feature was a significant compliment because Cecilia Chenoweth had a figure so delectable that she could make a burlap sack look seductive. Every inch of her was luscious, the *beau ideal* of a pocket Venus. Her breasts were particularly magnificent. Full. Round. Large enough to overflow his hands.

Not that Marcus was ever likely to lay his hands upon the likes of Cecilia Chenoweth. It was plain that he made her uncomfortable.

He wasn't sure what he had done. He had been *relatively* well-behaved. He wasn't one of those men who went around pawing and grabbing. He didn't need to—ever since he came of age, he'd had his pick of the most beautiful women in London. Hell, he hadn't even made any sordid innuendos!

At least, he didn't *think* he had. He supposed that, when one was as prone to making sordid innuendos as he was, it was possible she might have overheard something not intended for her ears.

Marcus would probably never know why she couldn't bear to look at him, much less speak to him. But look at him she could not, and he tried to honor her wishes by leaving her alone.

But it was difficult to ignore her entirely. How could he possibly be expected not to notice the most stunning woman in the room?

But he was trying to be good, damn it, so he fixed his gaze upon the shawl neatly folded upon the table. It was a rich Prussian blue with a colorful floral border at each end. Such shawls had to be imported from the Himalayas in India, and typically cost about as much as a carriage. This one was particularly fine, and the color was rare. It would suit his little sister, Diana, splendidly. Marcus had in fact just returned to town, having left as soon as his father died in order to fetch Diana, who had been raised in the far reaches of Yorkshire by their great-aunt Griselda.

The shawl was easily worth five hundred pounds. Marcus decided he would bid a thousand, as he had been planning to make a donation to the Ladies' Society anyway.

His mind made up, he prepared to go off in search of a decent glass of wine when a shrill voice pierced his thoughts. "Is that a *hole* in your slipper?"

Frowning, he turned his head. It proved to be Araminta Grenwood, the waspish daughter of a viscount. Miss Grenwood had spoken loudly enough that fifty heads had turned to see what the fuss was all about.

Marcus flinched as he realized that those fifty pairs of eyes were not merely trained upon Miss Grenwood, but also on her intended victim, Cecilia Chenoweth.

Cheeks aflame, Miss Chenoweth was standing so close to the table displaying the auction lots that her slippers were entirely concealed by the tablecloth. "I think you must be mistaken, Miss Grenwood," she said in a tremulous voice.

Miss Grenwood seized a fold of the tablecloth and drew it back. "I'm not! It's no use shuffling your feet. I can see it from here." Triumph glittered in her beady eyes. "Well, it's a good thing you're so occupied overseeing this hodgepodge. It's not as if any man would be seen dancing with *you*, anyway."

Something in Marcus snapped. Although his brain knew that Miss Chenoweth's fondest wish was to avoid him, his legs carried him down the length of the table in three rapid strides.

His hand snapped out. "Come, Miss Chenoweth."

Her gorgeous brown eyes met his, filled with a mix of terror and confusion, and Marcus felt his heart give an unexpected thump.

But she did not move to take his hand.

That was when it dawned on him that she truly did not understand that he was asking her to dance. Which was perhaps unsurprising. Marcus scarcely ever danced, because when he did, the gossips of the *ton* tended to get carried away. If he danced the opening quadrille with someone, then by the Sir Roger de Coverley at the close of the ball, it would be considered an established fact that his partner was the next Duchess of Trevissick. It was tiresome, and Marcus preferred to avoid the whole bloody business.

But his usual reticence explained why Miss Chenoweth stood there, frozen. "May I have the next dance?" Marcus clarified, unable to keep a trace of annoyance from his voice.

"Oh!" Her gaze shot back to the floor. "Th-thank you, my lord." She flinched as she recalled that he had just inherited a dukedom, and she had therefore used the wrong form of address. "I'm sorry, that is to say, Your Grace. But I couldn't possibly—"

"Of course, you can." Miss Chenoweth's particular friend, Caroline Greville, Lady Thetford, came striding up, her eyes filled with poison and fixed upon Miss Grenwood. She wrapped an arm around her friend's waist and ushered her around the table, ignoring the panicked look Miss Chenoweth shot her. "She would like nothing better than to dance with Your Grace. Isn't that right, Ceci?"

"I... er..."

"There!" Lady Thetford exclaimed, seizing her friend's hand and placing it in Marcus's outstretched palm. They were both wearing gloves, but still, he felt a tremor run up his arm.

The viscountess glared directly into Miss Grenwood's scowling face as she said, "Miss Chenoweth is *absolutely delighted!*"

Marcus wasn't so sure about that. But at least she did not remove her hand from his.

Before they went to join the dance, he stared Miss Grenwood in the face for a full beat, then pointedly turned away without saying a word of greeting. It was the cut direct, the worst insult he could dole out toward a lady, and a silent testament to what he thought of her remarks.

Miss Chenoweth allowed him to lead her to the top of the set and proceeded to stare at the floor for the entire duration of the country dance they shared.

CHAPTER 2

The following day, Marcus found himself ensconced in the ducal carriage, on the way to Astley House, home of the Earl and Countess of Cheltenham and their many children. On the seat next to him lay a bouquet of perfect, blush-pink hothouse peonies.

Seated across from him was the reason he had asked Lady Cheltenham if he might call upon her today.

"Are you nervous?" he asked.

His little sister, Diana, tore her gaze away from the window. "I am," she admitted. "I haven't much practice in meeting new people, nor in mixing with polite society."

This was a rather spectacular understatement. But Marcus was careful not to let a trace of concern show on his face. "Don't worry. You will learn everything you need to know. And these are our friends."

It was true. Marcus could count on one hand the number of people he truly considered to be his friends, but Edward Astley and his mother, the Countess of Cheltenham, numbered amongst them.

Yet even friends could cause hurt, unintentional though it might be. Marcus would not permit anyone to hurt Diana. Once, fifteen years ago, he had failed to protect her.

He had vowed that he would never fail her again.

Today would be a test, to see if it was possible for Diana to be accepted in high society. And if even his friends, the Astleys, could not pass it...

Then he didn't know what the hell he would do.

The carriage drew to a halt, and he handed Diana down. It was time to face their fate.

The Astley butler, Yarwood, showed them to the morning room. The room was packed, which was perhaps unsurprising, given that last night, Marcus had asked Lady Cheltenham if he could call on her today to ask for a particular favor. Such a cryptic remark was bound to pique anyone's curiosity. In addition to Lady Cheltenham, Marcus's good friend, Edward Astley, Viscount Fauconbridge, was in attendance, along with his new wife, Elissa. His friend's wretchedly annoying younger brother, Harrington, was there, as well as the Astley twins, Lady Lucy and Lady Isabella. Rounding out the party were Lord and Lady Thetford, which was not unexpected as the viscountess had been Caroline Astley before she married Henry Greville.

Everyone was there. Except...

"Where is Miss Chenoweth?" he asked.

"She is in the music room," Lady Cheltenham replied. "She is expecting a piano student."

"Ah. I see." It was customary for gentlemen to bring flowers to their dance partners the following day, hence the peonies.

Marcus felt a pang of disappointment. He found he had been looking forward to seeing her reaction to the flowers.

Then again, Cecilia Chenoweth was continually

disappointing. She hadn't so much as glanced at him while they were dancing last night, and although he thought she had thanked him upon the country dance's conclusion, whatever words she had uttered had been spoken so softly, he couldn't be entirely sure.

This was the source of his regret. No matter how sumptuous her figure, how could he imagine himself engaged in flirtatious banter with a woman so meek she couldn't string together the words *good* and *morning*? How could he picture himself seducing a girl so fainthearted she couldn't even look him in the eye?

Well... to be fair, he had *pictured it*. Oh, he had pictured it.

But he knew it was nothing more than a fantasy because the woman he saw in his dreams, the sophisticated temptress? She didn't exist.

Lady Cheltenham was awaiting his response. "These are for her," he said, brandishing the peonies.

"May I, Your Grace?" Yarwood stepped forward and took the flowers. "I will see that they are placed in some water."

Marcus nodded his thanks. He cleared his throat as he turned to face the assembled Astleys, who were regarding him expectantly. "As you can see, the reason I asked if I might call upon you today is because I wanted to introduce you to..."

He turned to gesture to Diana, only to discover that she had not followed him into the room. He leaned out the door and found her lurking behind a potted palm in the entrance hall. He took her hand and drew her forward, whispering, "None of that, now. It will be all right."

Once Diana made it into the room, Marcus released his sister's hand. Every eye was fixed upon her. He tried to view Diana as they would be seeing her, as if she were an ordinary girl and not the most important person in the world. They would see a young lady of middling height and slim figure, with delicate features and the same pale blonde hair and light blue eyes as him. Her plain white gown was made from a very fine muslin, one he had personally selected and sent to her. But, as it had been assembled by the local seamstresses of Ilkley, it was not cut to the latest fashion, and the fit was not nearly fine enough for the sister of a duke. At least the gown was improved by the rich blue Kashmiri shawl draped around her shoulders.

And, although it was something he scarcely noticed anymore, he knew the Astleys would also see that Diana wore only one glove. The reason she was only wearing one glove was that she had been born without a right hand, and her right arm ended halfway between her elbow and wrist.

He also knew that this would not come as a surprise, precisely. He was given to understand that there had been a storm of gossip following Diana's birth, and the entirety of the *ton* already knew that the wicked old duke's daughter was missing one hand.

But there was a difference between knowing something like that theoretically and seeing it in the flesh. And there was no telling how people might react. The thought of people gaping at his sister, even insulting her, filled Marcus's gut with a vicious rage.

But these were his friends. They would make Diana feel welcome.

Wouldn't they?

The room was so silent you could've heard a butterfly's wings. Lady Cheltenham slowly rose to her feet, then crossed the room.

She came to stand before Diana and clasped her hand. "You, of course, are Lady Diana. I'm sorry," she said, fishing a handkerchief from her pocket and dabbing at her eyes. "It's just that you could not look more like your dear, dear mother. You both favor Lydia, as I'm sure you must know." She turned to face Marcus. "You simply must have a portrait made of the two of you." Lady Cheltenham steered Diana so that she was standing beside him, posing them together. "Only look how handsome it will be!"

Across the room, Lady Thetford surged to her feet. She stalked over, her hands balled into fists. "Your Grace, I know it is not my place to insist, but..." She trailed off, gazing at Diana longingly. "You are going to let me assist in the planning of Lady Diana's wardrobe. Aren't you?"

"Indeed, that is why I have come today. You see—"

Lady Thetford cut him off with a cry of delight and began circling Diana. "Apple green, lilac... any shade of purple, really... and mazarine blue. Yes, she must wear *mazarine* blue to her debut ball. That will look *divine*. La, we will have to be very particular about shades of yellow..."

Marcus cleared his throat. "In addition to Diana's wardrobe, I was hoping that you, Lady Cheltenham, might help prepare her to make her debut. Due to the death of our mother, Diana has not received as much instruction in the ways of society as is befitting the sister of a duke. But I can think of no one more qualified to guide her."

Lady Cheltenham snorted but somehow managed to do so elegantly. "I wish I could share in your confidence. How fondly I wish someone would come along and teach Izzie the fundamentals of deportment."

Lady Isabella smiled broadly, clearly taking this as a compliment.

"But of course, I should be happy to help Lady Diana prepare and to sponsor her as well. Let's see, she will need to learn the latest dances, and she probably won't be used to dining with quite so many removes."

"Allow me to clarify," Marcus cut in, as Lady Cheltenham did not seem to appreciate the magnitude of the challenge she was facing. "Thirteen years ago, it became apparent that the old duke was not capable of providing a suitable home environment for a young girl."

This was the euphemistic way of saying that his deceased father had been an abusive piece of scum and had Marcus not managed to remove Diana from his household when he did, he was convinced she would have shared the same fate as their mother.

He continued, "My father made things... difficult. In the end, only one of my relations was willing to weather the duke's wrath and take Diana in. My great-aunt Griselda."

The countess's face paled. "Wait. Do you mean to tell me that Lady Diana has learned everything she knows about proper comportment from *Lady Griselda Saxe-Mecklenburg?*" She turned to the butler, rubbing her temple. "Yarwood, fetch a glass of the 1782 Latour."

"Thank you," Marcus said as the butler hastened toward the sideboard. "I would love one."

"Pour one for the duke as well," Lady Cheltenham said, plucking the glass from Yarwood's hand as he passed and downing half its contents in one gulp.

A ghost of a smile stole across Diana's lips, and for the first time since entering the room, she spoke. "I see you are acquainted with my Aunt Griselda."

"Do not mistake me, child," the countess said, setting her glass aside, "I am a great admirer of your aunt. But when it comes to choosing someone to teach a young lady the ways of decorous behavior..."

"Hers is not the absolute first name that comes to mind," Marcus supplied. "But do not mistake me—I will be forever indebted to Aunt Griselda. And although deportment is not her forte, Aunt Griselda did impart upon Diana a number of qualities that I know will stand her in good stead."

It was true. Aunt Griselda might be the family eccentric.

Whenever he pictured his great-aunt, she was striding across the moors, her long legs clad in trousers, a pack of the brown and white speckled pointers she had brought with her from the Continent trotting at her heels, smoking a pipe as she shot pheasant out of the sky.

But Aunt Griselda possessed an unwavering self-confidence that, in Marcus's observation, the world stripped most women of. Marcus had made a point of traveling to Yorkshire several times a year to visit his sister, and under Aunt Griselda's guidance, he had watched Diana transform from the shrinking child whose main goal in life was to squeeze herself into a hiding place where her father couldn't find her into a spirited young woman. Although she was still on the taciturn side, especially in unfamiliar company, deep down Marcus knew that Diana understood her own worth. That was the gift Aunt Griselda had bestowed upon his sister, and he would not exchange it for any amount of social polish.

"Well," Lady Cheltenham said brightly, "at least we have plenty of time. This Season is all but over, but you are both welcome to stay at Harrington Hall for however much of the winter you like. By next year, Lady Diana will be ready to make her bow."

"I had something different in mind," Marcus said. It was undignified to tug at one's cravat, but he was sorely tempted as he came to the most challenging part of his request. "As the Season is all but over, the last opportunity for Diana to be presented at Court will take place in six days' time. That evening, I will host her debut ball at Latimer House."

"Six days?" Lady Cheltenham blanched. "Is such haste really necessary?"

"It is." Marcus had heard the whispers saying that the reason Diana had been sent to an obscure corner of

Yorkshire was that his father was ashamed of her 'deformity' and had hidden her away.

Marcus neither knew nor cared whether the old duke had been ashamed of Diana's arm. It was patently untrue that he had wanted to send her away. His father had specifically enjoyed having a ready supply of victims to terrorize, and Marcus had been forced to resort to some truly deplorable tactics to convince him to give Diana up.

But Marcus was not ashamed of his sister, and he would not tolerate anyone saying that *he* was now hiding her away. It was bad enough that she'd spent the last fifteen years living on the edge of the wilderness where her only sources of amusement had been books, the sorts of sporting activities Aunt Griselda favored, and the bleak moors that surrounded them.

Now that his father was finally rotting in hell where he belonged, Marcus intended to give Diana the life she deserved. She would have the finest wardrobe of any woman in London. She would spend her days shopping and driving in the park and her nights at balls, parties, and the theater. She would be received in the highest circles, and she would see the wonders of London, Britain, and, as soon as travel to the Continent was safe again, Paris.

Lady Cheltenham was waiting for him to elaborate, so he said, "The timing is unfortunate, I will admit. But there is too much time during the long winter for tongues to wag. It is therefore imperative to demonstrate that Diana will be joining the very highest ranks of society and that she will be accorded the full respect due to the sister of a duke."

Comprehension flared in the countess's eyes; she knew the ways of society as well as he did and understood the importance of setting expectations yourself, rather than letting the gossiping biddies of the *ton* set them for you.

"Very well, then. Six days. We will have to set an aggressive schedule, but we will find a way."

Lady Thetford rose to her feet. "The dressmaker will need to begin immediately and will no doubt charge an outrageous sum to complete Lady Diana's wardrobe with such speed. How fortunate we are that money is no object!"

The corner of Marcus's mouth twitched. "Indeed, it is not. But try not to let them rob me blind, won't you?"

"I will head to Madame D'Aubert's right now and explain the urgency of the request. We can begin discussing silhouettes and selecting fabrics. If you will bring Lady Diana 'round in an hour or two, she can have her measurements taken."

"Very good," Marcus agreed. "If it is not too much trouble, Aunt Griselda could also use a few things that are presentable."

Lady Thetford wrinkled her nose as she smiled. "Consider it done. I look forward to making her acquaintance, just as I look forward to getting to know you, Lady Diana."

Thetford stood and offered his arm to his wife. He paused to bow over Diana's hand. "Lady Diana, it is a pleasure."

The two of them departed. Lady Cheltenham had seated herself at a writing desk in the corner and was muttering under her breath whilst scrawling out a list of everything Diana would need to learn in the next six days.

From across the room, Lady Lucy waved. Diana hesitated, then approached.

Lady Lucy smiled warmly. "I am given to understand that you have been living in Yorkshire. Is that correct?"

"It is," Diana said softly.

"What is it like there?" Lady Lucy asked.

"Well, Aunt Griselda's house is quite remote. The closest

town is Ilkley, but that is a good twelve miles away. Our house overlooks Ilkley Moor—"

Lady Isabella gasped. "Ilkley Moor? Did you truly live on *Ilkley Moor*?"

Diana glanced about, bewildered. "I—I—yes."

"Izzie writes Gothic novels, you see," Lady Lucy explained. "She is therefore fascinated by moors, caves, haunted castles… any place that's eerie."

"Oh," Diana said, brightening, "I love Gothic novels!"

Lady Lucy patted the settee beside her. "You do?"

Diana gingerly took a seat. "I do. Having grown up in a place so isolated, I've always done a great deal of reading."

"Was it not difficult to get books up there?" Lady Lucy asked.

Diana laughed. "Surprisingly, no. Every month, Marcus would buy all the latest titles and pack them up in a trunk, along with some tea, some sweets… anything he thought we might like. And he would send it to us in one of the ducal carriages."

"Marcus?" Lady Isabella frowned, looking perplexed. "Oh, do you mean your brother?"

"Of course," Diana said softly.

Lady Isabella peered at him suspiciously. "Somehow, I did not think of him as having a first name. Or, at least, of anyone using it."

Marcus took this as a compliment. He was a duke, not everyone's chum. But Diana smiled softly. "He's not nearly as terrifying as he'd like you to believe."

Lady Isabella's response was to narrow her eyes. "Hmm."

"Ooh," Lady Lucy said, "have you read the latest from Evangeline St. Vincent?"

Diana's eyes brightened. "Do you mean *The Haunting of Gravesend Reach*? Isn't it wonderful? I've read it three times."

"What did you think of Lysander?" Lady Lucy asked.

"*Lysander?*" Lady Isabella leaned forward, her expression arch. "Don't you mean the Duque de Mondragon?"

As one, the three girls began giggling... No, cackling... Gackling, which, of course, was not a word, but seemed the most apt description for the sound emanating from the three young women.

Once the gackling had died down, Lady Lucy smiled at Diana. "Won't you stay for tea?" She glanced up at Marcus. "Is that all right?"

Diana turned to him, eyes beseeching.

Marcus nodded. "Of course." Because this was what he had hoped for, just as much as he had hoped Lady Cheltenham would agree to shepherd Diana into society: that she might strike up a friendship with some of the Astley girls, particularly the twins, who were around her age.

But he had absolutely no desire to spend the next hour listening to the three of them debate the dubious literary merits of this Duque de Mondragon.

He turned to Edward Astley. "Perhaps we could have a drink in the library."

His friend stood, along with his wife. His eyes were apologetic. "I'm afraid we have tickets to the British Museum."

A timed reservation was required to get into the British Museum, and it could take weeks to get a ticket. Knowing Fauconbridge and his new wife, who were both bookish in the extreme, this would be one of the highlights of their time in London.

Marcus held up a hand. "Say no more. Enjoy your visit."

Harrington Astley rose from his chair, an insouciant grin on his face. "Well, Trevissick, it looks like you're stuck with me."

Marcus scowled. Surely he did not expect him to sit down

and enjoy a drink with the man who, during their days at Eton, had once put a litter of baby weasels in his bed?

"I believe I can find a way to occupy myself in the library for the space of an hour. *Alone.*"

Harrington laughed, having expected nothing different.

Across the room, Lady Isabella whispered something that caused another round of gackling to break out.

Marcus hastened out the door.

*M*arcus waved off Yarwood's offer to show him to the library. He was a frequent enough visitor to Astley House to know where it was and where Lord Cheltenham kept the brandy.

He made his way through the crimson parlor, its walls lined with Italian paintings. Straight ahead was the library.

He had just laid his hand upon the knob when the sound of a chord being struck upon the pianoforte came from the music room to his left.

Marcus froze. It was a minor chord, its very discordancy the key to its haunting beauty. But what had the hairs on the back of his neck standing on end wasn't the notes so much as the air of command with which they had been played.

A series of softer chords followed, then another accent. Without realizing his intentions, his feet drifted away from the library toward the open door to the music room. He listened to the dynamic peaks and valleys, perfectly executed and dramatic in their contrast, and recognized the piece as Beethoven's "Eighth Piano Sonata." He had heard it in concert not a month ago, although whoever was playing it now was far superior in their interpretation of the music.

The notes trilled into a delicate arpeggio as he reached the doorway. He stopped short, recoiling in surprise.

Because seated at the pianoforte, in profile to him, was none other than Cecilia Chenoweth.

Was this the same timid little rector's daughter who did nothing but stutter and stammer in his presence? The girl who was so meek she could not even meet his eye?

He could scarcely countenance it. Yet there she was, so absorbed in the keys that she did not mark his presence. In a way, he shouldn't be surprised. Everyone said she was a rare talent on the pianoforte. He had also heard dozens of snide remarks about how since her father's death, she had been forced to lower herself by offering *piano* lessons—said in such a tone you could be forgiven for assuming this must be a euphemism for selling sexual favors on the corner of Piccadilly and St. James's. Even Marcus, whose list of prominent attributes did not include the word *kindhearted*, found this a rather callous statement to make about someone so recently orphaned.

Her right hand floated down the keyboard again in a delicate flourish. She was definitely good.

But the real test was about to come.

She paused dramatically, and then the tempo suddenly increased as she entered the technical section. She dropped down to a mezzo piano then slowly began to build, ratcheting the tension higher and higher before suddenly dropping it down again. Marcus felt rather than heard her crescendo and was startled to find that his heart rate had kicked up along with the tempo.

He held his breath as she came to a particularly challenging series of runs, but they were as clear and sparkling as a brilliant-cut diamond.

It wasn't merely her technical proficiency, although he would describe that as flawless. Cecilia Chenoweth had a visceral understanding of the piece. She knew when to back off, when to crescendo, how to wring every ounce of emotion from the keys. The passion with which she played was visible on her face, and as she threw her head back, exposing a creamy expanse of her neck, Marcus found himself gripping the doorframe with white knuckles.

She was *magnificent*. He, who had attended hundreds of professional concerts over the years, featuring the finest musicians in all of Europe, had never heard anything like it.

Who *was* this girl?

He listened, rapt, until she hammered out the final chords with a flourish, then he broke into applause.

Miss Chenoweth shrieked as she spun to face him, eyes huge, one hand flying to her heart. Her chest rose and fell as if she'd been sprinting, and he fancied it was not from her exertions at the keyboard.

He stepped into the room. "Beethoven, Miss Chenoweth? How scandalous."

She gazed up at him, her sloe eyes wide with terror. Gone was the passionate, confident performer. She was once again the shrinking little vicar's daughter, cowed by his mere presence.

He wondered if she could even manage to form an answer.

Just when he was ready to give up, she drew in a breath. "I am sorry to have offended your delicate sensibilities."

Had mousy little Cecilia Chenoweth just delivered a retort? Would wonders never cease? "I haven't a single delicate sensibility, as you surely are aware. And thank God for it. Otherwise, I would have been shocked, absolutely shocked, by the sight of you thrashing about—"

She drew herself up primly. "I was not *thrashing*."

"You were so far gone that near the end, I am fairly certain you slavered upon the keys."

She raised her chin. "I most certainly did not."

He leaned forward. "I can see a drop just there, upon the middle C."

She narrowed her eyes at him before inspecting—then wiping—the offending key. "Although I would not presume to call myself an expert on Beethoven—"

"You should, if that performance is any indication."

"—my personal opinion is that if the performer is not flailing madly and foaming at the mouth, they're not even trying."

That startled a laugh out of him. "I am inclined to agree, but still, it is shockingly unladylike."

"You prefer something ladylike, do you? Shall I play you 'The Battle of Prague?'" she offered, referring to a particularly vapid piece he was subjected to at every home musicale.

"What you should play," he said, giving her a pointed look as he flicked his coattails out of the way and seated himself upon a plush orange silk chaise longue, "is the 'Moonlight Sonata.'"

She stared at him, as still as a fawn crouched in the tall grass hiding from a wolf, as if a single blink would spell her doom.

He raised an eyebrow expectantly.

Shaking herself, she turned back to the keyboard.

Marcus settled back into the cushions of the chaise. "Moonlight Sonata" might not have the furious intensity of the piece she had just played, but it was considered every bit as inappropriate for a young lady. Blazing with dark passion, "Moonlight Sonata" was anguish made exquisite. Its emotions were considered to be both too intense and too melancholy for young women, who were expected to be unrelentingly cheerful, to be vivacious to the point of vapidity.

Having grown up in the worst home environment imaginable, Marcus knew firsthand that the world could be a very dark place. He therefore found the interminable merriment most young ladies had been schooled to display nauseating. Which was not to say that he sat around wallowing in his despondency.

But he had come by his darker emotions—anger, grief, shame—honestly. Those feelings were not *wrong*, and he had found that when they did rear their ugly heads, it was far more effective to sit with them for a time than to try to push them into the shadows and wish them away.

And so, Marcus had a keen appreciation for the "Moonlight Sonata."

And he had to wonder... Cecilia Chenoweth, an exquisite talent who had grown up motherless, and was now fatherless, too?

What could she do with such a piece?

He gave a flick of his wrist, gesturing for her to proceed.

CHAPTER 4

*C*eci was having the strangest afternoon of her life.

She was spending time with the Duke of Trevissick.

No. That wasn't quite right.

He was spending time with *her*.

Intentionally.

Considering that the expression Marcus Latimer normally assumed whenever his gaze fell upon her could be best summarized by the words, *isn't that a pity*, this was a shocking turn of events.

And not only was he voluntarily remaining in her presence. Suddenly the Duke of Trevissick, the man who had always regarded her as dull and pathetic, found her impressive. Because she was certain that he did.

It was an almost incomprehensible reversal, and she wasn't sure how to feel about it. On the one hand, anything was better than the pity with which he had looked at her last night after Araminta Grenwood had giddily pointed out the hole in her slipper.

Yet she feared the inevitable letdown when he decided

she wasn't half as interesting as he had supposed.

She had no idea how she was going to speak to him when the music concluded. But that didn't matter at the moment, because right now she was playing "Moonlight Sonata," one of her very favorite pieces, and one she had been playing more often of late. Her emotions following the death of her father had been something of a jumble. Of course, she felt the things one would expect—sorrow, loneliness, grief.

But, if she was being honest, there were times when she felt angry at her father. It turned out that the reason he had died with scarcely a farthing to his name was because he had hired a veritable army of investigators to look into her mother's death. Going through his papers, she had found drawer after drawer of their reports, none of which revealed anything of value.

Ceci was angry that her father had pursued the case with such a blinkered obsession that he hadn't spared a single thought about setting money aside to make sure his daughter would not wind up destitute should something happen to him. As it was, all her father had left her was a box of strange documents and a mysterious key to an unknown lock.

But her bitterness also stemmed from the fact that he had kept something so significant from her for so long. It was clear that he believed her mother had died by foul play, not a fever, as he had always maintained. She could understand concealing such a harsh fact from a girl of six. But she was one-and-twenty—old enough to have been told the truth.

And mixed up with her sorrow and anger was a sad sort of confusion that was difficult to put into words. They had always been so close, and her trust in her father had been absolute.

Now, she was left wondering if she had ever known him at all.

Ceci might not have the words to describe this mess of

feelings, which fluctuated by the minute. But she did have Beethoven. And no matter how tangled and confused her emotions might be, "Moonlight Sonata" managed to encompass them all.

As she sank into the music, everything else fell away. She forgot about her humiliation last night at the ball. About the fact that the man of her dreams had asked her to dance not out of desire, but out of pity. She forgot about the fact that Madeline Sherborne had failed to appear for her pianoforte lesson today, and this meant she did not have the shilling she needed to fix the holes in her infernal dancing slippers.

She even forgot that Marcus Latimer was in the room.

When you were playing Beethoven, you were allowed to wear your heart on your sleeve, to be impassioned to the point of being overwrought. You were *supposed to*. Which was, of course, why young ladies were not permitted to play certain works of Beethoven.

But here she was, playing one of those forbidden pieces. And when it came to the pianoforte, Ceci did not play anything by half-measures.

After striking the mournful final chords, she let them linger in the air. Slowly she became aware of her surroundings.

The Astleys' rosewood pianoforte.

The orange and white music room.

The Duke of Trevissick, seated nearby.

She hesitated a beat before turning to the chaise, nervous to see his response.

What she saw made her recoil.

Because Marcus Latimer, the man who never had a single hair out of place, whose posture was always as upright and starchy as his meticulously arranged cravats, lay sprawled against the blood-orange cushions of the chaise.

His right foot was on the floor, but his left boot dangled

in the air. He had thrown an arm across his face, which made it difficult to gauge his reaction.

He groaned and rubbed his forehead. "Incandescent," he said, sitting up. He gave a single tug at his exquisitely tailored chocolate brown coat and it settled into place without a single wrinkle. Abruptly the ordinary man who had needed a moment of repose was gone, and the immaculate duke had returned.

His gaze snapped to hers. "Why have I never heard you play before?"

The question was sharp as if it were somehow her fault. "I honestly do not know. You are a frequent guest at Lady Cheltenham's gatherings, and she always asks me to play."

Awareness flashed in his pale blue eyes. "Ah, but Mr. Nettlethorpe-Ogilvy is inevitably in attendance as well. I am therefore forced to flee the music room, lest I be subjected to *the bassoon*."

Ceci bit her lip. "Mr. Nettlethorpe-Ogilvy has improved significantly in the past year, and—"

"He is atrocious," he said with a note of finality. "That still does not explain why I have not heard you play anywhere else."

Ceci gave a humorless laugh. "I am not invited to play anywhere else. The last thing a hostess wants is for her own girls to suffer in comparison to the penniless daughter of a country vicar."

"Well, you should be forewarned that I intend to request you by name at every gathering going forward."

Ceci's cheeks warmed. "That would cause gossip."

He shrugged a negligent shoulder. "And?"

She felt annoyance simmering up. Spoken like a man, a rich and titled one, who had the liberty of not giving a fig about what people were saying behind his back. "As an unmarried woman, I must be careful."

"Ah, but you won't be unmarried for long. Are you not all but betrothed to Archibald Nettlethorpe-Ogilvy?"

Now her cheeks were truly burning. "You have been misinformed," she said quickly. "Mr. Nettlethorpe-Ogilvy has not made me an offer of marriage."

The duke looked baldly skeptical. "But he is courting you."

He was. He had formally asked permission to court her three months ago. There were a number of reasons that she should have welcomed this news. They were friends. She knew with absolute certainty that he would make an exceptional husband. And, while she was desperate, he was rich.

She should have been ecstatic.

Instead, she had just… frozen.

She had done the rational thing and stammered out an awkward agreement, and Mr. Nettlethorpe-Ogilvy had not seemed put off by her stilted response. After all, who knew? Perhaps with time, her feelings for him might grow.

Sadly, in the intervening months, her feelings had not grown a hairsbreadth. She simply could not imagine Archibald as her husband.

The duke was awaiting her response. "Yes, he did ask to court me. But that does not necessarily mean a proposal will follow."

"Of course, it does. I know Nettlethorpe-Ogilvy. He wouldn't have asked to court you unless he was gravely serious about marrying you."

Gravely serious. Not exactly the romantic sentiment to set a girl's heart aflutter. "I would never assume—"

"Do you mean to accept him?"

She sputtered in protest. "I do not even know how to answer that, considering he has made me no proposal."

"When he asks you—"

"Who even knows if he means to?"

He rolled his eyes. "Fine. *If* he were to ask you, what would you say?"

She swallowed. This was one of several questions that kept her awake at night, tossing and turning in her bed. Given the chance, would she marry a very good man, but one she knew with a growing certainty that she would never grow to love? Would she sacrifice the possibility of making a love match for the security she so desperately needed?

The silence stretched on as she weighed her words. Finally, she said, "I daresay that only a great fool would turn down so fine a man as Archibald Nettlethorpe-Ogilvy."

She had expected him to gloat at having been proved right. Instead, a sour look stole over his features. "See? You have nothing to worry about. Your impending nuptials will absolve you of any scandal. And I shall be able to hear your perfect rendition of 'Moonlight Sonata' as often as I like."

"Firstly, I absolutely cannot play 'Moonlight Sonata' in public. If the fact that I know it were to get out, that alone would cause a scandal. I never would have played it for you had I realized you were not planning to be discreet."

He gave an aggrieved sigh. "*Fine.* I will keep it to myself."

"Secondly, as much as I appreciate the implied compliment, my rendition of 'Moonlight Sonata' is not, and never will be, perfect."

He leaned back, one eyebrow lifting into a derisive arc. "Really, Miss Chenoweth. Is it possible that you think me an admirer of false modesty?"

"Gracious, no. I am astonished you even know the meaning of the word."

This earned her a single chuckle. Had she not seen the creases at the corners of his eyes, she would have assumed he had merely hmphed, but it was, without question, a chuckle.

"I am not dangling for a compliment," she continued. "I

do not need one. I know very well that my interpretation of the piece is outstanding. I have worked hard to make it so."

He hmphed again, but now the corner of his mouth was turning up, and Ceci felt sure that it was an admiring *hmph.*

"But alas, I will never be able to play the piece as the composer intended. I can prove it to you." She began to play a section from near the end of the piece. "It's this chord, right here." She paused, placing her thumb on the middle C-sharp, then stretching for the D above it with her small finger. "On paper, it doesn't look like such a great reach. Just a half-step above an octave. But my hands are too small."

A shadow fell upon the keyboard. The duke had abandoned the chaise and now stood behind her, peering over her shoulder. "Show me again?"

"See?" she said, repeating the section. "It's the angle. It's exceptionally"—she tried and again failed to reach the D —"awkward."

Much to Ceci's astonishment, he sat beside her on the piano bench. For a split second, her body was pressed against his from shoulder to thigh before she recovered her senses sufficiently to scoot over.

She was enveloped in his cologne. Good lord—he even *smelled* expensive. She'd caught a whiff of it before, but having never been this close to him, she had never appreciated its full impact. It was spicy and sophisticated, all ambergris and vetiver, balanced by the perfect notes of saffron, blackcurrant, and... liquified diamonds and unicorn tears, most probably. Whatever it was, it smelled delicious, and she had to physically restrain herself from leaning forward to sniff his neck.

He reached across her body, placing his own thumb on the C-sharp. The angle was such that the back of his elbow brushed against her left breast. Her nipple turned hard as a pebble and tingles shot through her body. "Which is the top note?" he asked.

"H-here," she said weakly, indicating the D.

He plunked his little finger upon it with ease. The sight of his hands, for once not hidden by gloves, mesmerized her. Each perfectly manicured finger was long. Slim. Even elegant. But although his pale skin was pristine, free of scrapes or, God forbid, callouses, it did not feel accurate to describe his hands as soft, because they had such an obvious sinewy strength to them.

She wondered, for what might be the thousandth time, what it would feel like to have those hands upon her.

She watched him reach for a ninth, then a tenth. It wasn't surprising that he had such a good handspan. He was tall, probably around six feet.

Realizing she had lapsed into silence, she hastily said, "I am envious. I can control how much I practice. But there will always be songs I cannot play because I do not have bigger hands."

His voice in her ear was wicked as he replied, "There are many advantages to them. After all, you know what they say about men with big hands."

She froze, her gaze still fixed upon the piano's keys.

It happened that she did know what they said about "men with big hands." One did not grow up within a half-mile radius of Harrington Astley without overhearing all manner of indecent remarks.

This did not make it any less shocking that he had said such a thing, out loud and directly to her.

She narrowed her eyes and prepared to give him the set-down he so richly deserved.

But wait.

No.

She had a *much* better idea.

CHAPTER 5

*M*arcus waited for Cecilia's response to his ribald remark.

He knew he shouldn't have said it, but really, how could he resist teasing a buttoned-up vicar's daughter? She would chastise him, of course, but that was all right. That would be half the fun.

But when she turned her face up to him, her expression held not a hint of reproach. Her cheeks bore a becoming flush, her dewy lips were slightly parted, and those captivating, wide-set brown eyes were guileless.

"No," she breathed, "what do they say?"

His smirk suddenly felt brittle. *Well, shit.* It honestly hadn't occurred to him that she might not know. But of course, she didn't know—she was a naïve young maiden, the daughter of a *vicar*, for Christ's sake. Not some sensuous widow with whom he was contemplating an affair.

"Oh. Er..." He cleared his throat to stop himself from sputtering like a fool. "Nothing of consequence."

"Oh, dear." Her lips, which were as ripe and full as the rest of her, pursed into a perfect moue. "How embarrassing, not to recognize what I take it is a common turn of phrase. You must think me such a bumpkin." She laid her hand upon his wrist, beseeching, and the thought that sprang into his head was that if her hand was that soft, the skin between her thighs must be absolutely *luscious*.

Her gorgeous brown eyes were entreating as she said, "Won't you tell me, so I'll know next time?"

He felt an unfamiliar tingling sensation sweep across his cheekbones. Good God, was he *blushing*? He did not *blush*. He was a duke, for Christ's sake.

When he managed to speak, his voice was tight and his words came out somewhat rushed. "It's not so common as all that. Forget I said anything about it. Now, what shall you play for me next? Some, er, Mozart. Yes, I should very much like to hear some Mozart."

"Some Mozart? Let's see, there's—"

She gave a little cough and dropped her gaze to the keys so abruptly that Marcus almost didn't catch it.

Almost. But before she was able to duck her head, he saw it.

The corners of her mouth, quirking up.

He felt her shoulder tremble against his.

She was *laughing* at him.

"Miss Chenoweth!" He gave a great exhale, half outrage and half relief. "You have been trifling with me!"

She turned to face him, eyes sparking. "It serves you right! What a wildly inappropriate thing to say!"

"And yet, you seem to have understood my meaning. Who's the unseemly one now?"

She was still struggling to contain her laughter. "Harrington Astley is practically my brother. If I understand your debauched remarks, he is to blame."

"I believe this is the very first time I've been grateful to Astley minor," Marcus said, using the term that denoted a younger brother at Eton. "But how awful of you, Miss Chenoweth, to make me suffer like that."

"Oh, so I'm the awful one?"

"Absolutely atrocious." He studied her for a moment. "Say, you're not nearly as insipid as I thought. There's a favor I'd like you to perform for me."

She pressed the back of her hand to her forehead. "May I? May I truly?"

Her voice was everything that was proper, but her eyes held a trace of waspishness as she delivered this riposte. In a flash, it occurred to him that her expression, delivered by her fine brown eyes, was an exquisite one, so exquisite, in fact, that it would not look at all out of place upon the face of a duchess.

Now where had that thought come from?

"I will permit it," he said, giving an elegant wave to emphasize his largesse. "It is a very particular favor that only you can perform."

"All right. I'll do it."

He tutted at her. "A strategic error, Miss Chenoweth. Are you not going to first ask what the favor is? I might ask you to do all manner of scandalous things, such as playing the 'Moonlight Sonata' in the middle of Hyde Park Corner or dancing naked atop the piano."

She did not rise to his bait, but pursed her lips, looking thoughtful. "The truth is, I owe you a favor. You did not have to ask me to dance last night. Yet you did." She looked up at him, her eyes hesitant. "May I ask why?"

That was when the strangest thing of all happened.

Because, instead of making some flippant remark, Marcus found himself telling her the truth.

"I did it because there is nothing I despise more than a bully. You see, I had to live with one for twenty-eight years."

Her eyes widened with the understanding that the

conversation had somehow strayed into the sincere. "You're referring to your—"

"Marcus, there you are! I looked for you in the library, but —" It wasn't difficult to mark the moment Diana noticed Ceci seated so close to him upon the pianoforte's bench, as she jerked to a stop in the doorway to the music room, her eyes wide.

He rose in one smooth motion. "Diana, may I present Miss Cecilia Chenoweth? Miss Chenoweth is part of the Astley household. Miss Chenoweth, my sister Diana."

Miss Chenoweth's eyes swept over the blue Kashmiri shawl, then paused for a beat on Diana's right arm, but she swiftly raised them to his sister's face. She smiled warmly as she stood and curtseyed. "Lady Diana, it is such a pleasure to meet you."

Diana curtseyed in return. "The pleasure is all mine, Miss Chenoweth." She turned to Marcus. "It's time for us to head to the dressmaker's. We need to stop by the house on the way to collect Aunt Griselda."

"Very well. Miss Chenoweth," he said, giving her a slight bow, "thank you for allowing me to listen to you play."

He offered Diana his arm as they crossed the crimson parlor. "Lady Lucy and Lady Isabella are going to meet us at the dressmaker's," Diana said softly. He could tell she was flustered yet pleased by this news.

Marcus sighed. So, he was to be subjected to an afternoon of gackling. "*Delightful.*"

Once they were ensconced within the carriage, Marcus expected Diana to bombard him with questions about the mysterious Miss Chenoweth, whose company he had chosen over the library.

Instead, she surprised him by bursting into tears.

"Diana! What on earth is wrong?"

"It's L-lady Lucy and Lady Isabella." She accepted the handkerchief he thrust in her face and dabbed at her eyes.

Lucy and Isabella had been the ones to upset her? This was unexpected. Granted, the dark-haired twin was somewhat deranged. But he never would have expected this from the blonde one, who seemed sweet to the point of being saccharine.

"What did they say to you?" he barked. "Tell me what they did!"

"Gracious, Marcus! Nothing like that. It's just"—she paused to blow her nose—"we're going to be friends. I'm sure of it. And I've—I've never had fr-frien—"

She dissolved into another flood of tears. The knowledge that these were happy tears should have come as some comfort.

It did not.

Diana should have been here with him. She should have had dozens—no, hundreds—of friends, and all the finest things London had to offer.

Instead, she had spent the past fifteen years moldering away in an obscure corner of Yorkshire.

One man was to blame.

"I'm sorry," Diana said once she'd regained some semblance of composure. "I didn't expect to react this way. And I shouldn't phrase it like that. I had you, of course. And no one could have been a better friend to me than Aunt Griselda. But…"

"It is not the same thing as having friends your own age," he observed.

"Precisely." Having finished dabbing at her eyes, she glanced up to give him a watery smile, then recoiled. "Marcus! What on earth is the matter?"

"You should have let me kill him!"

It was a mark of how dysfunctional their family was that there was no need for Diana to enquire who it was he regretted not murdering. "No, I shouldn't have."

"I offered. Multiple times."

"The risk was too great. What if you had been caught? You and Aunt Griselda were all I had!"

Marcus glared out the window as the carriage pulled up to Latimer House. "I could have covered it up. Everyone hated him. I daresay the servants would've helped."

"Don't be absurd." Diana allowed him to help her down from the carriage, then looped her right arm through his as they climbed the marble steps. "Someone would have had a pang of conscience."

"You think so, do you? Ellery," Marcus called to the longtime family butler, "I have a question for you."

Ellery's footsteps clicked against the entrance hall's black and white checkerboard marble tiles. "Yes, Your Grace?"

At seventy-three, Ellery was no longer moving as quickly as he once had, and he had shrunk a good two inches so that he now only came up to Marcus's nose. But he was spry for his age, and even if that hadn't been the case, Marcus would never have considered replacing him.

Being in the employ of his father was not for the faint of heart, and most of their servants had lasted less than a year. But Ellery had stayed on as butler for more than thirty years. God only knew what horrors he had witnessed and what unsavory things he'd been forced to do in order to maintain his position for so long.

But the reason Ellery refused to leave was so that there would always be someone to look out for Marcus and Diana. After his mother's death, the old duke had absented himself from the family seat, Hallane Hall, for several years. When he had abruptly returned and recalled that he had a young daughter who could be terrorized, it had been Ellery who notified Marcus. This was not as simple a task as one might think—the old duke monitored the outgoing mail and had even bribed someone in the village post office to serve as his informant. Ellery had therefore been forced to walk five miles through a driving rain in the dead of night to reach the house of a man he trusted to take the letter to the next village. But Ellery had managed to get the letter out, and that was the only reason Marcus had been able to intervene.

The second Ellery wanted to retire, Marcus would arrange for it. He could have a suite of rooms at Hallane Hall, or Marcus would buy him a house of his own and hire servants to wait on him. Anything Ellery wanted, Ellery would have. There was nothing he would not do for this man. Nothing.

For now, Ellery wanted to keep his post as butler, so Marcus had settled for tripling his salary.

"Tell me this, Ellery. Had I murdered my father in cold blood, would you have helped me dispose of the body?"

Placing a hand over his heart, Ellery gave an elegant bow. "It would have been my greatest honor to help you hack the body into pieces and bury them in a shallow grave, Your Grace."

Marcus raised an eyebrow at Diana. But one of the footmen standing by the door shook his head.

"No, sir. Begging your pardon, Mr. Ellery, sir. But that's not right."

It was Diana's turn to give Marcus a triumphant look, but then the footman continued, "If you're wanting to dispose of a body, the thing you need is pigs."

Diana's mouth fell open. Marcus turned to the footman. "Pigs, James?"

"Pigs, Your Grace. Pigs'll eat anything, you see. Even that

no-good rotten son of a..." He cleared his throat. "Begging your pardon, Lady Diana."

"Do you know what I heard?" offered a housemaid who had been polishing the gold gilt staircase. "I heard about this coaching inn with a trap door beneath one of the beds, and underneath the trap door, they kept a huge tub of acid! People would lie down to sleep, and in the middle of the night, they'd spring the trap and dump 'em in that acid. There wouldn't be nothing left of 'em come morning." She pointed emphatically with her rag. "That's as good as he deserved. When I think that they buried him in consecrated ground..." She scowled and began scrubbing at the railings with new vigor.

Marcus smirked at his sister. "You were saying?"

"Fine, brother. You win this time." She rolled her eyes, but she was smiling. "I'll go and fetch Aunt Griselda."

CHAPTER 6

*T*hat evening, Caro and her husband came to dine at Astley House. Caro joined Ceci in her room so they could chat while she dressed for dinner.

Ceci had filled Caro in regarding her strange encounter with the Duke of Trevissick in the music room. Being close friends, Caro knew that Ceci harbored a particular *tendre* for Marcus Latimer.

"It defies comprehension," Ceci said. "You could have married *him*. The most eligible man in all of England. The most handsome man in the *world*. And you chose not to."

Ceci was referring to the fact that Caro had overheard the duke announce his intention to ask for her hand the previous year.

"But I was falling in love with Henry," Caro protested.

Ceci made a sound of incomprehension. She did not wish to insult her friend's husband, who was a fine man and devoted to his wife. But the thought of marrying Henry Greville when you could have had *Marcus Latimer...*

"It was so romantic, the way he came to your rescue,"

Caro sighed. "Especially considering he scarcely dances with anyone."

This was true. This past Season, the duke had danced with precisely two women: Caro, in an apparent attempt to annoy her husband, and Edward Astley's new wife, Elissa.

The latter was a rather obvious attempt to bolster Elissa's reputation. Elissa was the daughter of Edward's former tutor and a confirmed bluestocking who had more important things on her mind than fashion and fripperies. Trevissick had purposefully asked her to dance at her very first ball, then declared in a voice meant to be overheard that the new Viscountess Fauconbridge was "charming."

It did not matter a whit that Elissa had tripped once and stepped on his foot twice. If Marcus Latimer said you were charming, you were charming.

"He even gave Araminta Grenwood the cut direct," Caro breathed.

Ceci felt her cheeks heat. She should probably feel sympathy for Miss Grenwood. It would be the Christian thing to do.

But last night had not been the first time she had found herself the victim of Miss Grenwood's ire. Araminta had been unrelentingly cruel to Ceci ever since the day she learned of her existence, and the duke had truly been her white knight, charging to her rescue…

"Speaking of the duke," Caro said, "something happened at the dressmaker's shop that I have been itching to tell you about."

"Oh?" Ceci reached for a hairpin as she tucked a curl back into place.

"He was quite involved in choosing styles and fabrics for Lady Diana's wardrobe. When offered a choice of two fabrics, he always selected the finer one. No expense was too great."

Ceci felt a pang of envy. She and Lady Diana had both lost their parents. But what a difference, to have such a brother to look after you. "It sounds as if he is devoted to his sister."

"Extremely devoted. I never imagined this side of him! But that is not what I wanted to tell you. When it came time to take Lady Diana's measurements, of course, it was not appropriate for him to remain, so he retreated to the shop's front room with a newspaper. Afterward, he brought an article over to show his sister. Apparently, she reads the papers religiously and has a great interest in politics."

Ceci selected a ribbon to add to her hair, wondering where Caro was going with this story. "What was the article about?"

"La, I've no idea! It was the item immediately next to it that caught my eye." Caro reached into her reticule and pulled out a newspaper clipping. "As soon as I arrived, I asked Yarwood for this morning's edition of the *Times* and saved it for you. Take a look."

Puzzled, Ceci accepted the article. It was extremely short, just one column wide and four inches long. She read aloud, "'The HMS *Lionheart*, which has recently been docked at the Royal Naval dockyard at Deptford for repairs, will make sail at high tide on Thursday the eighth of September, joining Admiral Samuel Hood's squadron in the Leeward Islands. It is commanded by Captain Nathaniel Walker, First Lieutenant James Bilborough, Second Lieutenant George Smith...'" Ceci frowned, trailing off. "I'm sorry, why did you want to show this to me?"

Caro leaned forward and tapped the paper. "Look at the name of the surgeon."

Ceci scanned the paragraph she had indicated until she found it. "'Mister... Mister *Percival Polkinghorne!*'"

The name Percival Polkinghorne probably meant nothing to every other person who had read this article today.

But amongst the boxes of papers her father had left behind delving into her mother's death, there had been a death certificate, stating that her mother had died of a fever. That was suspicious in and of itself, as death certificates were only completed when someone died under mysterious circumstances. Indeed, her father had never accepted the examining physician's conclusion, as his wife had been in perfect health when he left that morning to perform a baptism in the neighboring village.

The name of the surgeon who had assisted with the autopsy was unusual enough that it had stuck in Ceci's mind —Percival Polkinghorne.

Ceci wheeled around to face Caro. "Do you think it could be the same Percival Polkinghorne?"

"La, how many Percival Polkinghornes could there possibly be? And he's even a surgeon. It has to be him!"

"They sail on Thursday the eighth. The day after tomorrow. I wonder what time high tide is?"

"Half six. I sent a footman 'round to the docks to find out."

Ceci rose from the dressing table and began to pace the room. "That means that, if we are to learn anything from him, we must do it tomorrow. Do you think I should write to him, or—"

"No. A letter is too easy to ignore. If your father was right, if he helped to falsify that death certificate, it will take a great act of persuasion to get him to talk. We must tug upon his every heartstring and appeal to his sense of decency. And that can only be done in person."

"But the only address we have for him is the dockyard at Deptford. I can't just go strolling alone onto the docks! To say nothing of the fact that I don't even have the fare for a hackney carriage to get me there."

"Alone? Gracious, no. I would never allow you to go to such a place alone. I will be going with you." Caro paused dramatically. "And I know just whom to bring along to serve as our bodyguard."

Ceci's tense shoulders lowered a fraction. But of course—Caro could ask her husband to accompany them. Lord Thetford would never permit his wife to go to the dockyards alone.

In truth, Ceci was surprised Lord Thetford would allow her to go at all. "Are you sure your bodyguard of choice, as you put it, will agree to accompany us?"

"Completely sure. I will arrange everything. We'll go in the midafternoon, as I am expected at the dressmaker's again tomorrow morning, and you will be accompanying Mama to Latimer House."

Ceci felt warmth flooding her cheeks. "Me? Whatever does she need me for?"

"To play, of course. Lady Diana is to have dancing lessons in the morning, dining practice over luncheon, and she is going to practice for her presentation at Court in the afternoon. La, I'm so jealous that you get to go!"

"Jealous?" That was ironic, as Ceci would have preferred to stay at home. "Why are you jealous?"

"Because no one has been inside of Latimer House in more than twenty years. Not a single entertainment has been held in that great hulking mansion since the last duchess died. And more than that"—she dropped her voice down to a whisper— "the old duke was reportedly so awful, his son wouldn't even bring guests over. Edward is His Grace's dearest friend, and even *he* has never been inside. I will be stuck at the dressmaker's for the next few days, planning Lady Diana's wardrobe. But I will expect a full report."

"And you'll get one. If I make it out alive," Ceci added darkly.

Caro laughed, but Ceci had not been joking. Somehow the prospect of facing the present duke was only a little less terrifying than the thought of encountering his wicked father.

CHAPTER 7

*A*cross town, having just returned from the dressmaker's shop, Marcus was in the study at Latimer House finishing up an odious task, when someone equally odious walked through the door.

"Uncle Eustace." Marcus closed the book he had been reading with a snap. "Who let you in?"

"Come now, Marcus. Is that any way to address your uncle?"

"'Your Grace.'"

His uncle took the chair before the desk, although Marcus had not invited him to sit. "That's not correct, either. Someday, perhaps. I am next in line for the dukedom—"

"*You* will address *me* as 'Your Grace.'" Marcus turned his back on his uncle, sliding the black leather journal onto the shelf behind him and selecting another one of the seventeen identically bound volumes. "If you ever have occasion to address me in the future. It is my hope that our paths shall never cross again."

"Prickly, just like your father."

Marcus refused to rise to his uncle's bait. He opened the

new journal and squinted at the handwritten lines. God, but his father's handwriting had been atrocious. The old duke had been none too organized, either. As best Marcus could tell, at least three volumes were missing from his journals.

Seeing that Uncle Eustace had not taken the hint and left, Marcus said, "Is there a particular reason you're inflicting yourself upon me?"

"There is. My payment didn't come through. No doubt you didn't know, because you inherited so recently, but your father always sent me one hundred pounds a month, deliverable on the first."

Marcus did not deign to glance up. "It happens that I did know."

"Then where is my payment?"

Marcus leveled a hard stare at his uncle, giving him a moment to absorb the truth.

"But... but that is outrageous!" Uncle Eustace surged to his feet. "You can't cut me off."

"And yet, I have, along with your shiftless sons. Be good enough to tell them and spare me from having to repeat this tedious conversation."

"I am your heir! I deserve to live in a style befitting the next in line to a dukedom."

"Then I suggest you find some gainful employment."

"Employment! Employ—" His uncle pulled out his handkerchief and swiped it across his reddening face. "Why are you doing this? We're family, damn it! Nothing is more important than blood."

Although his uncle was now shouting, Marcus's voice was chillingly quiet. "So, you've suddenly decided that family is important? When I was thirteen years old, I wrote to you, begging for your help. It is the only time I ever asked you for anything. Do you remember what you said in reply?"

A fresh sheen of sweat broke out over his uncle's balding

head. "Be reasonable, Marcus. I wanted to help Diana. Really, I did. But your father would have cut me off."

"And that was the only thing you cared about. Not honor, not decency, not giving a safe home to a terrified four-year-old girl." He snapped his father's journal shut. "Well, know this, Uncle. I will be showing you precisely the same amount of consideration you gave to Diana."

Uncle Eustace's face had turned a virulent shade of purple. "Think carefully before you do this. If something were to happen to you, Diana's guardianship would fall to *me*. Is that a chance you're willing to take?"

"It is not, which is why my lawyers are drawing up papers as we speak, naming Lord Fauconbridge as Diana's guardian should anything happen to me. She will inherit an ample fortune, enough to support her in comfort for the rest of her life. You will never be able to touch her. And as to your assertion that you are my heir"—Marcus gave his uncle one last sneer before returning his attention to the journal—"not for long."

"You mean to marry, then."

Spotting an entry that looked promising, Marcus took up a quill and started making some notes. "I do. Before the end of the month."

"It isn't that simple."

He gave his uncle a bland look. "Oh, I daresay I'll be able to find some woman willing to have me."

"There's more to it than that!" Uncle Eustace snapped. "In fifteen years of marriage, your father only managed to sire the two of you. And, as many peccadillos as he had over the years, he never produced a by-blow. You've never sired one, either, and not for want of trying. It would not appear that fecundity runs in your branch of the family."

It happened that the reason Marcus had never sired a by-blow in spite of having an admittedly long list of paramours was because he was meticulous about taking precautions. It also happened that the reason he was so meticulous about taking precautions was because he had witnessed his father suffering from bout after bout of the pox. Which likely also explained why his father had sired so few children.

This was the one and only benefit of having been raised by such a remarkably horrific man. Whenever he was faced with a dilemma, Marcus could ask himself, *what would my father have done?* He would then proceed to do the opposite. Invariably, it proved to be the best course.

His father couldn't be bothered to put on a sheath? Marcus never failed to use one.

So, he had no reason to believe he would share in his father's ailment. Not that there was any reason to explain this to his idiot uncle.

Marcus didn't look up from his notes. "We shall see, shan't we?"

"You're making a mistake. If you should die—"

Marcus was growing tired of his uncle's whining. "You seem rather preoccupied with my death, especially considering I'm not yet thirty and you're almost sixty. I would look to myself." Marcus gave his uncle a hard look. "Especially as I have it on good authority that you're about to be thrown out on your head. James!" he called to the footman stationed outside the library door.

To his annoyance, James did not appear. "James!" he called again. Biting back a curse, he stood and went to the door.

It turned out that James had abandoned his post to use the necessary. As they'd had to fire all of the staff who'd been the old duke's sycophants, they were severely understaffed. Marcus had to go all the way to the entrance hall to find someone.

No matter. His uncle was summarily thrown out,

shouting and snarling about how he would make Marcus pay for cutting off his allowance.

Marcus didn't much care that his uncle hated him. God willing, he'd never see the blasted man again.

Once he was gone, Marcus turned back to his father's journal. With the information he had learned, he could take care of matters tomorrow night. What he was preparing to do would be an odious task, as things involving his father so frequently were.

But he was determined to make things right.

Closing the book, he went to dress for dinner.

CHAPTER 8

*C*eci swallowed thickly as the carriage drove between the pair of carved stone lions that marked the entrance to the grounds of Latimer House. After her unexpectedly intimate conversation with the duke yesterday, she had no idea what to expect.

Edward Astley and his new wife, Elissa, had accompanied Ceci and Lady Cheltenham. This would give Diana the opportunity to dance with someone who was not her brother and would also afford Elissa, who was new to society, some extra dancing practice.

Latimer House was rare for a London mansion in that it was detached. It was huge and had its own grounds. Ceci tried not to gawk as she entered the ballroom, which extended behind the east wing of the house so that it was surrounded by gardens on three sides. It was a sumptuous fantasy in white and gold, with tall French doors lining its walls and frescoes on the ceiling depicting scenes of the Greek gods upon Mount Olympus.

Waiting inside the ballroom was another surprise—Lady Griselda Saxe-Mecklenburg, who was there to observe her great-niece's progress. Lady Griselda cut an imposing figure. She was tall, her height further emphasized by her ramrod-straight posture. She wore her thick grey hair pulled into a severe knot at her neck, and she looked down upon the world over the aristocratic bump on her nose. Around her chair sat three impeccably trained brown and white speckled dogs. The yellow satin gown she wore was the height of Continental fashion. Or at least, it had been thirty years ago. Ceci could not help but feel a pang of jealousy, seeing the previous century's corsetry on display. This dress would have flattered her curvaceous figure, unlike the sky-high waistlines and filmy silhouettes that were popular today. Truly, she had been born in the wrong decade.

Still, were she given the chance to swap figures with one of those stylish girls who were so thin and wan that they could not even achieve a proper fortissimo on the pianoforte, Ceci would choose her own frame without hesitation.

Lady Cheltenham declared that they would start with country dances, which were a bit simpler than the cotillions and reels Lady Diana would also need to learn. Ceci therefore spent most of the morning alternating between "The Hop Ground" and "Bartholomew Fair." It turned out that Aunt Griselda had already taught Diana the basic dance steps, and she therefore progressed quickly. Her movements were naturally graceful, and she picked up the new dances with ease. But more than that, she had that noble air about her that some people could not master with any amount of practice.

After about three hours, Lady Cheltenham clapped her hands. "That was excellent, Lady Diana. I will confess, I had feared that the task before us might prove insurmountable. But your aunt has taught you well, and you are truly a natural dancer."

Lady Griselda rose from her chair. "Well, of course, she

is." Lady Griselda's English was precise, although she spoke with a marked Germanic accent, and her smile as she regarded her great-niece was proud. "She is Lydia's daughter."

"She most certainly is," Lady Cheltenham replied. "We will have her ready by the date of her debut ball. I feel certain of it now." She turned to the duke. "Is everything in readiness for our next lesson?"

"I believe so. Ellery?"

The butler bowed. "Yes, my lady. I have everything laid out per your specifications in the turquoise parlor."

As Ellery led Lady Cheltenham and Lady Diana from the ballroom, the duke turned to the rest of the group. "Lady Cheltenham is going to instruct Diana in serving tea. If it's not too much trouble, I hope you'll all join us so she can practice. I've arranged for some simple fare to be served for luncheon."

Ceci struggled not to gape as they entered the turquoise parlor, a lavish, high-ceilinged room with fine art lining its walls, including one painting that looked suspiciously like a Rembrandt and a sculpture that, if the small plaque affixed at its base was to be believed, was the work of Michelangelo.

It turned out that Marcus Latimer's notion of *simple fare* consisted of veal medallions in a mushroom-cognac sauce, caviar, three different varieties of soup, and a spread of fresh fruit more lavish than what most people served at their wedding feast.

Ceci assumed her chair as unobtrusively as she could. She felt like enough of an imposter surrounded by the finery of Astley House, and the duke's home was ten times as ostentatious. Marcus Latimer blended perfectly with the fine art, between his glossy golden hair, his impeccably fitted dove grey coat and the enormous sapphire stickpin glinting amongst the folds of his cravat.

Meanwhile, she felt sorely out of place and dearly wished she had worn something other than a simple sprigged cotton morning dress from last season.

Lady Cheltenham had already begun instructing Diana. "Of course, you will pour left-handed. It is acceptable to pour with one hand, but if the lid is loose, I find I must sometimes rest my other hand on top of the finial to keep it in place."

"Could I do it like this?" Diana asked, placing the tip of her right arm upon the finial. "My right arm is not merely ornamental. I'm quite accustomed to doing things with it."

"Yes, that will work splendidly," the countess replied. "Imagine that you are dancing, so that you pour with the same graceful quality of movement... Yes, that's it. Straighten out your wrist, dear, and bring your left elbow down... Just so. Now, before you hand the cup to its recipient..."

Once Diana had prepared and distributed seven cups for everyone at the table, they served the luncheon.

"Lady Griselda," Edward Astley said as he handed a bowl of chestnut soup to his wife, "how long have you been in England?"

"For more than forty years now." Lady Griselda nodded her thanks to the duke as he placed some medallions of veal upon her plate.

"What made you decide to settle here?" Edward asked.

"I came to visit my sister, Dorothea—Lydia's mother. She had married the English earl, Lord Dewsbury, a few years before. While I was visiting, I made a good friend, Miss Amelia Marsden. We were both older than thirty—spinsters, as you English say. So, we decided to set up our own house together in the country."

"Did Miss Marsden come to London with you?" Elissa asked brightly.

"Alas, no. She has been gone these seventeen years."

"Oh! I'm so sorry!" Elissa said in a rush.

"Do not fret, dear." Lady Griselda gave a philosophical shrug. "It is what happens when you live to be my age."

"You did not find Yorkshire too remote?" Lady Cheltenham asked.

"Oh, no. Amelia and I preferred the quiet life. And later on, the fact that the house was so remote proved to be a godsend."

"How so?" Elissa asked, spearing a piece of pineapple with her fork.

"It made it harder for the old duke to get to Diana. He was a horrible man, you see."

Trevissick cleared his throat loudly. "Let us speak of something else, Aunt."

"I told my sister not to force Lydia to marry him," Lady Griselda continued, ignoring her great-nephew. "Well, we see how *that* turned out."

"Aunt Griselda!" the duke snapped. "If you would be so kind as to show a modicum of discretion."

Lady Griselda sliced her veal, unbothered. "Do not be so stodgy, Marcus. These are our friends."

Ceci could see a vein pulsing at his temple as he ground out, "There are some topics I do not discuss even amongst friends."

"And that is fine. *You* may choose not to discuss them. But I will say whatever I damn well please." Lady Griselda smiled as she popped a bite of veal into her mouth.

Ceci exchanged an amused look with Elissa across the table. This was the first time she had seen anyone dare to challenge the duke, who was currently glaring daggers at his aunt with ice-cold eyes.

Ceci would have fled the room had he fixed such a look upon her. But Lady Griselda was entirely unperturbed. "Lord Fauconbridge, would you pass the fruit? Thank you." She chose a few slices of orange, then continued, "It was necessary to remove Diana from the old duke's household. He was unfit to be a parent."

"A rather spectacular understatement," Lady Diana muttered.

The duke slouched back in his chair and ran a hand over his face. "Ellery," he called, "would you be so kind as to bring me a glass of the 1792 Calon-Ségur?"

Ellery came striding up to the table, glass already in hand. "I took the liberty of pouring one for Your Grace."

"Bless you," Trevissick muttered, seizing the glass and downing half its contents in one go.

"But," Lady Griselda continued, "once she came to live with me in Yorkshire, Diana never had to see that horrid old man ever again. Well, other than that one time."

"What one time?" the duke snapped, sitting up. "What are you talking about?"

Lady Griselda waved her fork. "We may as well tell him, now that the old duke is dead."

"We may as well," Diana agreed cheerfully.

Trevissick's eyes were slightly wild. "Do you mean to tell me that he came to your house? What was he doing there?"

"Well, he wasn't there to see the heather in bloom," Lady Griselda muttered.

"He was there to take Diana!" The duke's glare swept from Lady Griselda to Lady Diana and back again. "Why did you not tell me at once?"

"Because I handled it, Marcus. You would only have worried." Lady Griselda waved her fork in the duke's direction. "Worry, worry, worry, that is all this one ever does."

Trevissick was not placated. "You handled it, did you? I should like to know how!"

Unperturbed, Lady Griselda spread some caviar on a piece of bread. "If you must know, I shot him."

"You *shot* him?"

At this point, Trevissick began bickering with his great aunt in some variety of German.

Edward Astley looked his friend up and down. "I didn't know you spoke German!"

The duke shrugged but did not pause his argument with his aunt.

"Marcus is fluent in Plattdeutsch, or Low German," Lady Diana supplied. "I speak that as well as Mecklenburgish."

Ceci watched in astonishment as the argument raged on. She didn't understand a word.

Well, hardly a word.

"Donnerbüchse?" the duke asked, frowning. "Wat is en Donnerbüchse?"

"En Blunderbuss," Lady Griselda replied.

"En *Blunderbuss*?" he hissed.

Across the table, Elissa's eyes had gone round as saucers. Lady Cheltenham leaned forward. "Don't worry, dear. If ever there was someone who richly deserved to be shot with a blunderbuss, it was the old duke."

"Oh!" Elissa glanced at her husband, who nodded solemnly. "I'll take your word for it."

Trevissick was still arguing with Lady Griselda, who had apparently had enough. She threw her hands into the air. "You want to know where I shot him?" she said, switching to English. "I shot him in the—"

"Hindquarters," Diana interjected, leaning in front of her aunt. "You might say it was the hindquarters."

"And then I unleashed my hounds upon him." At the word *hounds*, one of the pointers lounging at her feet perked up. She bent down and rubbed the underside of his neck. "*Ja,* Günther. You were there that day, my brave boy." She scratched behind the dog's ears, then straightened. "The horses took off at a run, and he had to go chasing after his own carriage like a pathetic little *Piepenschieter*—"

"Aunt Griselda!" Diana exclaimed.

"—all the while, clutching his *Mors*—"

"Aunt *Griselda*!" Diana said again, but this time, she was laughing.

Lady Griselda drew herself up, chin defiantly in the air. "Yes, well, the point is, that horrible man never dared to show his face at *my* house ever again."

The duke had fallen silent, considering. "When was this?"

"Around six years ago," Lady Griselda said.

"Right around the time he started walking with a limp." The duke steepled his fingers, considering. "All this time I thought it was lumbago."

"No," Diana said, "it was Aunt Griselda."

"I suppose it was." The duke stared unseeingly across the room. "I wish I could have seen that."

"I almost missed it," Diana offered. "You see, as soon as I saw who had climbed out of the carriage, I ran to fetch my sword."

"Good girl," Trevissick muttered in the same breath that Elissa said, "You have a sword?"

"Oh, yes." Lady Griselda smiled fondly at her great-niece. "My Diana is as skilled a fencer as anyone in England. I made sure of it."

"Yes, Diana is outstanding." The duke gave his aunt a pointed look. "Other than a certain disregard for the rules of engagement that she picked up from her instructor."

Lady Diana and Lady Griselda exchanged a baleful look that showed what they thought about the rules of engagement.

Ceci was astonished. She was so used to seeing people fall over themselves in their haste to defer to the duke.

Who would have thought that he had a little sister who

poked fun at him and a great-aunt who lectured him like he was a recalcitrant schoolboy? It made him seem less like an untouchable duke, and almost… human.

Lady Griselda took up her glass. "In any case, that is what I mean when I said that I handled it."

"I suppose you did." The duke stared across the room for a moment, lost in thought, then plucked a cluster of grapes from a nearby platter. "I must own that I could not have done any better. Although I still wish you would have told me."

"How I wish I could tell you such things!" Lady Griselda exclaimed. "But no, you would have spent the next six years breathing down my neck." She gestured to her great-nephew. "He does not trust anyone else to do anything."

"I do trust you," the duke said quietly. "And you proved worthy of my trust on that day. You guarded my most precious treasure."

"But that is just it, Marcus," Lady Griselda protested. "Diana is not a figurine of spun glass that you must place upon a high shelf. You still think she is a girl of four years who requires your protection. You do not see how strong and capable she has become."

"I will never apologize for protecting my sister," the duke snapped. "Perhaps we could save this conversation for a time when we do not have an audience."

"I wish you wouldn't." Edward smiled at Lady Griselda. "You cannot imagine how much I am enjoying this."

The duke snatched up his glass, narrowing his eyes at his friend. "That makes one of us."

The conversation moved on, but Ceci was struck by seeing the duke amongst his family. Perhaps his seemingly perfect life wasn't quite so perfect after all.

CHAPTER 9

*A*fter luncheon, Lady Cheltenham took Diana off for some additional lessons, and Aunt Griselda went upstairs to rest.

Marcus assumed that the rest of his guests probably had other matters to attend to, but Lady Fauconbridge surprised him by saying, "What a beautiful home you have, Your Grace."

"Thank you."

Her eyes were keen. "Am I correct in assuming that such a grand house has an equally impressive library?"

Marcus suspected he knew where this was headed. "The library is commensurate with the rest of the house, yes."

Lady Fauconbridge took her husband's arm, drawing him forward. "If you will forgive me for saying so, it really is shocking that you have never invited your oldest and dearest friend to see your library."

Marcus felt the corner of his mouth twitching. "I take it my oldest and dearest friend's wife would like to see the library?"

"As would your oldest and dearest friend," Fauconbridge said smoothly.

"By all means," Marcus said, leading them up the stairs.

The library was on the first floor and was a mixture of golden walnut wood, crisp white columns, and gold gilt detailing. Lady Fauconbridge actually squealed as she crossed the threshold and padded across the blue and gold Axminster carpet that had been custom-made to fit the room.

Marcus led them up two steps to a raised dais where the shelves were arrayed around an oversized globe. "I believe you will find this area to be of the most interest."

Lady Fauconbridge gasped. "Is that a Gutenberg Bible?"

Her husband turned, holding up a volume he had pulled from the shelf. "Elissa, look! A first edition copy of Newton's *Principia!*"

"It is even inscribed by Newton," Marcus noted. "It belonged to someone named—"

"*Roger Cotes!*" Fauconbridge exclaimed as he lifted the front cover. "Roger Cotes was a brilliant mathematician in his own right. Many think he would have rivaled Newton, had he not died so young. In fact, when he learned of Cotes' passing, Newton said, 'Had Cotes lived, we might have known something.'" He reverently turned a page. "Look, these are his handwritten notations here in the margins. *Roger Cotes...*"

"Edward, look at all of these palimpsests!" Lady Fauconbridge cried, gesturing to a shelf lined with hand bound booklets of ancient parchment. "I'm afraid to even touch them. Why, they must be more than a thousand years old!"

This was surely the only thing that could have torn Fauconbridge away from Roger Cotes' personal notations. He hurried to join his wife. "There are dozens of them," he said, his voice full of awe." He spun to face Marcus. "What works do you have in your collection?"

"I have no idea," Marcus said. "My great-great-grandfather purchased those during a grand tour, one of a number of *objets d'art* he picked up along the way. He plunked them on that shelf, and I believe they've been sitting there ever since."

Fauconbridge's face had taken on a purplish hue as if his head was about to explode. "Am I to understand that no one has opened those palimpsests for more than a hundred years, and you have no idea what they might contain? There could be—"

"Lost manuscripts," Lady Fauconbridge breathed.

"Precisely," Fauconbridge said. He turned back to Marcus. "You need a team of scholars to examine these. They need to be cataloged, and studied, and—"

Marcus gave an elegant sweep of his hand. "I believe I have found my team of scholars." At Lady Fauconbridge's dumbstruck look, he added, "You would be doing me a favor. Who better to undertake such a project than you two?"

Lady Fauconbridge squealed again, bouncing on her toes and clasping her hands in front of her heart. "Thank you, Your Grace! Thank you, thank you, *thank you*!" She spun to face the shelf. "How should we proceed? It feels wrong to just… touch them."

An urgent conversation ensued between the newlyweds. Marcus turned to find Miss Chenoweth standing at the bottom of the dais, struggling to feign a polite interest in the moldering parchments.

Marcus strolled down the steps. In truth, Lord and Lady Fauconbridge's distraction was a welcome development, because he knew how he wanted to spend the rest of his afternoon, and it did not involve palimpsests.

It involved "Moonlight Sonata."

"Come," he whispered, hooking his arm through Miss Chenoweth's.

She kept her feet firmly planted. "Where do you think you're taking me?"

"The music room, naturally."

She shook her head. "Lady Fauconbridge is my chaperone at present. I must stay with her."

"And an effective chaperone she is. Lady Fauconbridge," Marcus called, turning to face the dais, "I am going to take Miss Chenoweth off by herself."

As expected, Lady Fauconbridge gave no sign of having heard. "I fear merely washing our hands will not suffice," she murmured to her husband. "Even the natural oils from our skin could do them damage."

Marcus continued in a loud voice, "Once I get her alone, I intend to debauch her."

"Cotton gloves!" Fauconbridge exclaimed. "What we need are some cotton gloves."

Frankly, Marcus wasn't surprised that Lady Fauconbridge remained oblivious. She was the head-in-the-clouds sort. He would have expected Fauconbridge to notice, however. Then again, he should have known his friend would be distracted by those palimpsests. Beneath his refined exterior, Fauconbridge had always been a hopeless quiz.

"I am speaking about Miss Chenoweth," Marcus said once more for good measure, ignoring the sharp elbow that jabbed him in the ribs. "Miss Cecilia Chenoweth, whom I am about to debauch. Perhaps I will do it on top of the dining room table, for all the servants to see."

"Yes!" Lady Fauconbridge exclaimed. "Cotton gloves would work splendidly. Do you think it would be an imposition to ask one of the duke's footmen if two pairs can be found?"

He turned to gloat. Miss Chenoweth narrowed her eyes at him. "You have made your point."

"The music room is just downstairs, and we will leave the door open. It will be no more improper than what we did yesterday."

"Oh, yes, because that was completely proper," she muttered. But she did accept his proffered arm, which pleased him more than perhaps it should have done.

"Ellery," he said as they came to the library door, "Lord and Lady Fauconbridge are to have full run of the library for the foreseeable future, regardless of whether I am at home. Please have a footman attend them and fetch anything they should require, starting with two pairs of cotton gloves."

Ellery bowed. "At once, Your Grace."

Marcus escorted Miss Chenoweth down the stairs. Today she wore a long-sleeved dress of mauve sprigged cotton with a fichu that covered all of her chest and half of her neck. The dull dress was a tragedy on the woman who had the most luscious figure in all of London.

They came to the music room, with its mint green walls and crisp white plasterwork, and he deposited Miss Chenoweth upon the piano bench. "I wish to hear the same pieces you performed yesterday, in the same order."

She arched a sardonic eyebrow at his high-handed request, but Marcus didn't care. In truth, he had been looking forward to this, his one moment of respite, to a degree that surprised him. His father's death had been a relief, but it had ushered in a host of worries in its wake. He had to ensure that Diana's debut was perfect. Her lack of training in the ways of polite society wasn't even the foremost obstacle. Thanks to his father's sadistic streak, they'd never been able to retain a full complement of household staff. Then he'd had to dismiss the fraction of the servants that had been attracted to the old duke's repugnant behavior, knowing that their own misdeeds would be overlooked. So, here he was, trying to plan the ball of the century for his sister, dealing with his avaricious relatives and the general bother of transferring an enormous estate from one owner to the next, all while worrying that no matter how hard he tried, his beloved sister might be mocked and rejected by society for factors entirely beyond her control.

And that impressive list didn't even include the unsavory task that awaited him tonight.

In short, Marcus had a crush of worries, but for the next hour, he was going to sit back and let Miss Chenoweth's music wash over him. He would emerge refreshed, having achieved the same state of catharsis he did yesterday.

He lay down upon the plush silk settee along the wall and waved a negligent hand. "You may proceed."

He heard her snort, but he also heard her shifting around to face the keys. She drew in a breath, then struck the first chord.

And it was all wrong.

Ceci was only three bars into Beethoven's "Eighth Piano Sonata" when the duke stopped her.

"Why are you playing it that way?" he demanded.

Startled, she glanced over to the settee. He had pushed himself up onto his elbows. His nose was wrinkled in a scowl, and, to her amusement, his usually meticulous hair was sticking up in the back.

"What way?" she asked. "What are you talking about?"

"I want," he said, enunciating each word crisply, as if she were so simple she might not understand, "for you to play it the same way you played it *yesterday*."

Ceci rolled her eyes. As if that was not precisely what she had been doing. But she turned back to the keys and started again.

"No, no, no!" This time, he surged to his feet and crossed the room in three strides. "You're doing it all wrong."

She gave him her most condescending glower. "I am, am I? Pray tell me which note I missed."

"It wasn't a note." He raked a frustrated hand through his hair, which had the effect of settling it perfectly into place.

"But you are not playing with the same depth of feeling as you did yesterday."

"Ah. I think I know what the problem is." She gestured for him to come around to the side of the instrument. "Look beneath the lid. I am going to play a note. See if you can tell me how many strings the hammer strikes."

It took him a moment to locate the correct hammer. "Two."

"That is correct. And that is why you perceive that I am playing with less depth of feeling. The Astleys' pianoforte is a tri-chord model, where each hammer strikes three strings instead of two. Naturally, such an instrument produces a fuller sound and enables a greater dynamic range."

"So, the problem is that I own an inferior pianoforte?"

Ceci flushed. "I would not say it is *inferior*, but—what are you doing?"

He had seized her hand—her *bare* hand, as she had been playing—and was towing her across the music room. He wasn't wearing gloves, either, and the brush of his warm, smooth skin against hers felt startlingly intimate. "I am going to buy a new pianoforte, of course. What about the instrument in the ballroom? Is it a—what's the term, again?"

Face flushed, she had to jog to keep up with his long-legged stride. "That one is also a bi-chord."

"I will need two of them, then. Ellery," he called as they came into the entrance hall, "summon the carriage."

"The carriage?" She yanked her hand from his grasp. "You cannot mean to go right now. A pianoforte is a significant purchase. You need to do careful research before you even contemplate—"

"And that is why *I* am not going to buy a pianoforte. *We* are going to buy a pianoforte. Two of them, rather." He glanced down at her as she sputtered her befuddlement, and his mouth twisted into a grin. This did nothing to restore

Ceci's composure. Having this absurdly handsome man who so rarely smiled looking at her with such an expression... it was almost blinding.

"But you don't even know which model you want!" she protested.

"I know precisely which model I want. I want the one that makes Beethoven's 'Eighth Piano Sonata' sound the way it did yesterday. You will tell me which instrument accomplishes that goal, and I will purchase it. It's that simple."

"But... but..." She shook her head in an ineffective effort to clear it. "I cannot accompany you. I—"

It was on the tip of her tongue to say *I have to head down to the docks by three.* But of course, she couldn't tell him that, so she feebly muttered, "I, er, don't have my gloves."

"Fetch Miss Chenoweth's gloves," the duke ordered one of the half-dozen footmen standing at attention.

A better excuse occurred to her. "Moreover, I cannot ride with you alone in a closed carriage. I would be ruined!"

He snapped his fingers. "Right you are. Ellery, cancel the carriage. We'll take one of the phaetons instead."

"O-one of the phaetons?" she sputtered. "How many do you own?"

"Three," he said, his voice nonchalant.

Ellery bowed. "I pray you will forgive me, Your Grace, but, having anticipated Miss Chenoweth's concern, I took the liberty of requesting one of the phaetons in the first place."

"Outstanding." The duke turned to Ceci. "Ellery really is the best butler. He thinks of everything."

He looped his arm through hers and drew her out onto the portico.

"I cannot possibly ride with you in your phaeton," Ceci

grumbled, nodding as a footman presented her gloves, along with her bonnet and shawl.

The duke was pulling on his own pair of black leather driving gloves. "Of course, you can. It's completely open. The whole world will be able to witness what we are doing, or, more importantly, what we are not doing. It is entirely proper."

"You never take young ladies out for a drive. *Never*. It will cause a storm of gossip if I am seen riding with you in your phaeton."

"Yes, just think what they will say—that you are *well-liked*. That your company is *highly sought after*." He gave a mocking shudder. "How will you endure it?"

She felt her face heating. "I know this is a lark to you, but I have to be very careful with my reputation. Why are we even doing this? It is not an emergency that you do not have the latest, fanciest model of everything, especially an instrument no one in your household even knows how to play."

He tilted his head to the side, studying her, and Ceci repressed the urge to squirm. "Is that what you truly believe? That I am some petulant child who cannot abide the notion that someone owns a better pianoforte than me?"

She felt a twinge of discomfort, to hear it expressed so baldly. But the truth was... "You do own *three* phaetons."

"Ah. And why would any man need three phaetons, when he can only drive one at a time?"

She could not believe she was having this conversation, that she was challenging him in this manner, but she found herself lifting her chin. "Precisely."

"Power, Miss Chenoweth. There is a certain cachet that comes from not merely being rich, or a duke, but from maintaining a certain image. Many people would argue that it is absurd that I am granted influence by virtue of something so frivolous as my, shall we say, celebrity. But those people are asking the wrong question. The question is not whether I deserve this power. I have it, whether I deserve it or not. The question is what I do with it."

This was by far the longest string of sentences she had ever heard Marcus Latimer utter that did not include a sardonic remark. Was it possible he was being sincere?

"And just what do you do with it?" she asked.

"When I attend a charity luncheon for the Ladies' Society, attendance doubles, as do donations. Now that my father is dead, I have a seat in the House of Lords. When I stand up and speak, in favor of the Chimney Sweepers Act Lady Morsley has asked me to re-introduce, or the Slave Trade Act Wilberforce has been trying to pass for years, the papers will report with bated breath every word that I say. Some people's minds will be changed not because of my arguments but because of the way I look while I am making them." He gave a dramatic sigh. "We cannot all be geniuses, like Lord and Lady Fauconbridge, or like you."

Ceci started. "I'm not a genius."

"Certainly, you are. You are the finest musician I have ever heard. But those of us who lack your prodigious talents must work with what we have."

He accompanied this statement with an elegant gesture toward his handsome face. Ceci snorted, and one corner of his mouth twitched up.

He continued, "Although I will privately own that it has a degree of absurdity, I find I prefer for people to take the right side, even if they do so for the wrong reasons. If my flashy image has such tangible benefits, then it is not a mere extravagance. It is something worth cultivating. And I have not even come to Diana."

Ceci swallowed. "What about Lady Diana?"

"You are not a fool. You know that many people would

ostracize her because of her arm. For something over which she has absolutely no control."

His voice tightened over the last sentence, and he paused, clearing his throat. "But the reason she *will* be accepted is because of my reputation. Because no one will dare to cross *me*." He made a bleak sound. "At least, that is what I hope. The truth is, I stay up half the night, wracked with worry about how she will be received." He looked down at her, and his pale blue eyes were uncertain. Which was well within the range of normal human emotions, but unheard of for Marcus Latimer.

He continued, "I would rather someone stab me with a sword than say a single cross word to her. There is this horrible image I can't seem to purge from my mind, that on the night of her debut, someone will make a cutting remark, and she will spend the evening not skipping around the ballroom but sobbing on her bed, and nothing, *nothing* I can say to her will be of any comfort."

Ceci was startled to find that she had taken his hand. For a moment, his blue eyes were earnest, and then regret began to creep in, as if he realized how much he had revealed.

She cleared her throat. "That was a much better argument than I thought you would make in defense of owning three phaetons."

This startled a laugh out of him, and for an instant, he flashed that smile, the one that was rarer than diamonds, at her. He quickly schooled his features.

"And yet," she continued, "it does not explain why you need to purchase a new pianoforte right this instant."

He groaned, tipping his head back. When he looked at her, his eyes were rueful. "Do you have any idea how much I have been looking forward to hearing you play again?"

"Y-you have?" she sputtered. Her heartbeat ratcheted up

as he turned his wrist so that *he* was now the one holding *her* hand.

"I have." He ran his free hand over his face. "Listening to you yesterday… that was the only hour I've spent in weeks in which I wasn't in a state of anxiety over Diana's debut." He shook his head. "You do not understand how talented you are. You transported me away from all of this mess."

Ceci's cheeks were aflame, and she was not capable of speech. This was fortunate because, had she been capable of forming words, she was convinced something mortifying such as *I love you* would be what burst from her mouth.

He looked down at her, and with the sun behind his golden head, he almost seemed to glow. "I just thought that, as you'll be coming here every day for Diana's dancing practice, I might be able to persuade you to play for me before you leave. And then maybe, just maybe, I can make it through Diana's debut."

She felt his gloved thumb circling over the back of her hand not just where his fingers brushed, but also in the pit of her stomach. She took a great gasping breath, realizing she had forgotten to breathe.

"But in order for that to happen," he continued, "I must have the right pianoforte. Which is why I need you to come with me now."

"All right," she gasped. "I'll do it. Although—wait, what time is it?"

He had to pause, as he had already started turning toward the phaeton, which had just appeared at the end of the drive. "What time is it? Why does it matter?"

It mattered because Ceci needed to be back at Astley House so she and Caro could go to Deptford in search of Percival Polkinghorne.

Not that she could say as much.

"I am expecting a student for a piano lesson. At three o'clock," she added hastily.

"I see." He pulled out a glimmering gold pocket watch. "It is just after one. I'm sure we can return you to Astley House in time."

Ceci swallowed. Of course, the errand she must attend to this afternoon was far more important than any music student. It was her one and only chance to find out what had truly happened to her mother. "It is absolutely imperative that I not be late."

He waved this off. "You won't be."

"Oh, really?" Ceci crossed her arms. "I should like to know how you think you'll be able to buy two pianofortes in less than two hours?"

He smirked at her as his phaeton, a glossy burgundy high-flyer picked out in gold, pulled by a pair of gorgeous grey horses, drew up to the portico. "You'll see."

CHAPTER 11

Five minutes later, Marcus was driving his favorite team, his greys, who had turned out to be worth every penny of the five thousand pounds he'd paid Lord Thetford for them, toward Bond Street. "So, where am I headed?"

"Soho," Miss Chenoweth choked out.

He glanced to his left and found her gripping the side of the phaeton with white knuckles. Her face looked slightly green. "Do you get ill in carriages? You look ghastly."

She cut him a sideways glare. "Thank you ever so much."

"Are you in danger of casting your accounts?"

"You need have no concerns in that regard. But are you not going a bit fast?"

"Not at all. The horses are barely trotting." He took a corner, and she squealed. "If I didn't know better, I would think you'd never ridden in a highflyer before."

"I haven't ever ridden in a highflyer," she gasped.

He felt the corners of his mouth pulling up. "You cannot mean it. Surely Nettlethorpe-Ogilvy has taken you for a drive."

"I do not believe he owns a phaeton." The wheel hit a rut, and she gasped. "He p-prefers to... to walk."

To walk. A gentleman did not *walk*. Marcus shook his head. "We need to find you some better suitors."

She cut her eyes to him. "Mr. Nettlethorpe-Ogilvy's character is unimpeachable."

"He dresses like the hurdy-gurdy man."

"He does not!"

"The one with the trained monkey, who performs over by Charing Cross."

"He..." He watched her face fall as she realized that he was right. She drew herself up. "Well, that is no mark against his character."

Marcus snorted. "His character may be flawless, but that doesn't change the fact that he's about as stimulating as three-day-old porridge."

She managed to glower at him even as she clung to the side of the carriage in terror. "He has been a true friend to me, and I will not hear you say a word against him!"

Marcus rolled his eyes. "Fine." But in that moment, he resolved that he was going to send his valet, Sebastian, around to the Nettlethorpe-Ogilvy mansion. Marcus had sent Nettlethorpe-Ogilvy to his own tailor, so the problem wasn't that he lacked decent clothing.

But Nettlethorpe-Ogilvy's valet seemed to possess a preternatural talent for taking perfectly good pieces and assembling them in a manner that made his master look like an itinerant dockworker.

Marcus, on the other hand, employed the finest valet in all of Europe. If there was anyone who could sort Nettlethorpe-Ogilvy out, it was Bastian.

"So," Marcus said, grinning evilly as he took a corner just a hair faster than he normally would have done, "whereabouts in Soho can one purchase a superior pianoforte?"

"John Broadwood and Sons," she choked out. "Their showroom is on Great Pulteney Street."

"Very good."

They drove in silence for a moment. Suddenly Miss Chenoweth shrank down in her seat.

"Come, Miss Chenoweth. We're on a straightaway. Must I slow the horses to a walk?"

"It's not that," she hissed, turning her head sharply to the left. "Lady Melville just stepped out of that milliner's shop. Not only is she a notorious gossip, but she's hoping to ensnare you for one of her three daughters." She chanced a peek over her shoulder and groaned. "Oh, drat! I'm almost certain she spotted me."

Marcus peered down at her, amused by the consternation coloring her cheeks. "Are you really that horrified to be seen with me? You'd think I was a traitor, or perhaps a cannibal. It seems that being a duke is worse."

"It's almost as bad. You already asked me to dance. If I am seen in your carriage, everyone will assume you're courting me. Even though the notion that *you* would be interested in the likes of *me* is utterly preposterous."

Marcus could see her point. He knew enough about the *ton* to know that its members had nothing better to do with their time than speculate about his marital prospects. And it was true that he wasn't courting her.

But as far as being interested in her went... Marcus sneaked a glance down, taking in her exceptionally fine bosom, encased in that mauve monstrosity of a dress, then sweeping up to her wide, dark eyes...

One of the greys tugged at the bit, and he hastily returned his attention to the horses. The truly alarming thing was that Miss Chenoweth's physical charms, which were substantial, were no longer her primary appeal. Nor were her most attractive attributes her colossal talent on the pianoforte or her surprisingly quick wit, although these made her a thousand times more interesting than Marcus had originally thought.

No, the remarkable thing was that Cecilia Chenoweth, the mousiest of all mousy rector's daughters, had a passionate side. And this passionate side was of such depth that Marcus actually thought that it might—*might*—be a match for his own.

She was also dangerous. Marcus preferred to keep his cards close to his chest. Being his father's son, he was in possession of a frightful amount of dirty laundry, which he chose to air precisely never. Hell, Edward Astley was his closest friend, and even he hadn't known half the things Aunt Griselda had revealed during luncheon.

And yet, just that afternoon, he had inexplicably started blathering to Cecilia Chenoweth about how worried he was that Diana's debut would be a disaster. He had opened his mouth, and the next thing he knew, all of his deepest fears and doubts had come spilling out. Which was entirely unlike him. And yesterday, he had been on the cusp of telling her what a horrible bully his father was! God only knew what sort of drivel would have come spewing forth had Diana not interrupted them.

He rather thought the problem was all of that Beethoven. Her unfettered passion had loosened something in him, something he was usually careful to keep tightly screwed down.

Which made it alarming how desperate he was to hear her play again, so desperate that he was, in fact, on the way to spend several hundred pounds on a new pianoforte or two, just so he could achieve that cathartic release.

But never mind. He would just have to figure out how to

enjoy Miss Chenoweth's performance without blathering like an idiot afterward.

How difficult could it possibly be?

He steered the greys onto Great Pulteney Street. It looked like any other bustling London thoroughfare.

But it sounded like another world.

Gorgeous violin music drifted through an open window. "What is that?" he asked, entranced.

Miss Chenoweth had accustomed herself to the phaeton sufficiently that she was only clinging to the side with one hand. "This is a popular neighborhood for professional musicians."

The violin was already gone, obscured by a trumpet, clear and bold and brassy, which quickly gave way to a haunting melody played by an oboe.

There was another sound, too, one that was less melodic. "What's all that pounding?" he asked.

"That is our destination." Miss Chenoweth gestured toward a handsome red brick building. "Broadwood and Sons has its showroom on the ground floor. Their factory is on the upper floors. Stop anywhere."

"Very good." Marcus drew the greys to a halt. His tiger, Colin, who had been riding in silence on the jump seat behind them, was on the ground in an instant, setting up the ladder, then running around to hold the horses.

Marcus descended in three steps, then turned to check on Miss Chenoweth. She swallowed thickly, contemplating the descent with the same expression most men used when facing the gallows.

He offered his hand, and she accepted it gingerly. That blasted fichu obscured his view of her bosom as she bent forward to mount the ladder, but he managed to see six inches of curvaceous ankle, so it wasn't entirely a loss.

"What time is it?" she asked as they strode up to number thirty-three. "I can't be late for my piano lesson."

He consulted his pocket watch. "It is not yet half one. You'll be fine."

She gestured to the small white stone portico. "Speaking of time, I fear you may be wasting yours today."

Marcus glanced at the words carved above the door. "John Broadwood and Sons. By *appointment*." He smirked at her. "Oh, I think they'll see me."

"I'm certain they will, in spite of your lack of an appointment. You are a duke, after all. That's not what I meant."

"Then what did you mean?"

"Broadwood and Sons' tri-chord models are sufficiently popular that they are usually sold out for months in advance. I am certain that they will be delighted to take your order. But they might not have an instrument available for you to take home today."

Marcus flicked a speck of dust off the cuff of his coat. "Based on all of that pounding, they are building a lot of pianofortes up there. I will simply offer an incentive for them to sell me one that is in a state of completion."

She crossed her arms. "An 'incentive.' You mean a bribe."

He shrugged a negligent shoulder. "As you like."

"And what if they refuse to be bribed?"

He rolled his eyes. "Mark my words, Miss Chenoweth. By the time you return to Latimer House, there will be a new pianoforte."

She peered up at him. He had the uncomfortable sensation that her gaze went deeper than his insouciant smirk and flawless tailoring. "Have you ever considered that, duke or no, you cannot *always* get your way?"

Marcus had to bite back an incredulous laugh. Because, of

course, that was how the world saw him, as the all-powerful duke. He was the one who made certain of it, made sure that there was not a single crack in his meticulously crafted facade.

Little could Cecilia Chenoweth imagine how powerless he had been for most of his life.

To be sure, he had never lacked for material security. He didn't wonder whether he would have a roof over his head at night or where his next meal would be coming from.

But if she had been there that horrible day when he was eleven, could have seen him sprinting down that corridor, sword clutched in his hand, could have felt the panic overwhelm him when he heard his mother's scream, followed by silence... The moment he knew with horrible certainty that he was too late...

She would have understood that he knew as well as anyone what it felt like to be powerless.

He had failed to protect his mother, and then he had spent the next seventeen years in a state of anxiety that he would fail Diana in the same way. It was only with his father's death three weeks ago that the horrible burden had been lifted from his shoulders.

The point was, he knew what it was to be powerless.

And he was *never* going to feel that way again. His father was gone, and good riddance. Now that Marcus was the duke, he had the power to make sure Diana would have everything her heart desired. He would control every single detail of her debut. She would never hear a cross word, would never have cause to shed a single tear. Her life was going to be perfect from now on.

Marcus would make certain of it.

Miss Chenoweth was awaiting his answer. Not that he was about to tell her all of *that*.

So, he simply said, "No," then opened the showroom door and ushered her through.

CHAPTER 12

*A*n hour later, after what Marcus considered to be a highly successful errand, he led Miss Chenoweth back outside and helped her climb into his phaeton. This time around, she did not so much as blink when he urged the horses into a trot, nor did she cling to the door.

He wouldn't call Cecilia Chenoweth chatty. But right now she was being as silent as... well, as silent as she'd been for the vast majority of their acquaintance, right up until yesterday, when she'd mustered up the courage to actually speak to him. She stared at the passing buildings with a blank quality to her expression, as if she were seeing nothing.

She was probably put out that he had been right. Broadwood and Sons would be delivering a new pianoforte to Latimer House that afternoon. He hadn't even had to bribe anyone. It turned out that the Prince of Wales had ordered an exceptionally ornate instrument for the ballroom of one of his palaces, then changed his mind once the instrument was complete and refused payment. It had been sitting forlorn in the showroom, waiting for someone to come along who could actually afford it.

It would look spectacular in Marcus's ballroom. And they had promised to have an instrument custom-made to match the décor in his music room by the start of next Season.

As her silence stretched on, he grew concerned. "Miss Chenoweth? Is everything all right?"

"I should not have done that!" she burst out.

He guided the greys around a corner. "What, exactly, is it that you've done?"

Her eyes flew to his, slightly wild. "I played the Beethoven in public!"

Indeed, she had, after the half-witted clerk had implied that she could not possibly be qualified to serve as Marcus's adviser. She had swept over to the Prince's abandoned instrument, whipped off her gloves, and launched straight into the most technical section of the "Eighth Piano Sonata."

Everyone had turned to gape. She had commanded the room.

"Of course, you should have. You absolutely trounced that cod-headed clerk. You were magnificent."

"That is precisely the problem! I am not supposed to be magnificent," she hissed. "I am not *allowed* to. As the daughter of a country vicar, I am expected to be demure, dull, and, in every way, unexceptional."

Marcus tutted. "What a dismal failure you are at being unexceptional. Although I must say, you are quite good at feigning it. You had me fooled, right up until yesterday, when I discovered how hot-blooded you truly are."

She threw her hands up in despair. "And here I am, riding in your phaeton and playing Beethoven in public. You, Your Grace, are a bad influence."

"I am not merely a bad influence. I am the worst influence, but, paradoxically, I think I am tremendously good for you. The world has quite enough dullards in it without you pretending to be one more."

"I have to keep my head down," she protested. "It is what everyone expects of me."

"Well, I think you should pay less attention to the opinions of people who are in every way your inferiors. Play Beethoven in public. Say every cutting remark that springs into your mind. Quit hiding in the corner and take off that hideous sack you call a dress—"

She snorted, which was not particularly ladylike, but Marcus rather liked it. "It will come as a shock to the man who just spent five hundred pounds on a whim that occurred to you one hour ago, but some of us cannot afford better than a *hideous sack* of a dress."

Seeing that the junction ahead was blocked, Marcus swung the greys down a side street. "Well, once you're married to Nettlethorpe-Ogilvy—"

"I find that I am weary of discussing my impending nuptials," she snapped. "Why do we not instead discuss yours, if only for the sake of a little variety?"

"Why don't we?" he countered. "It happens that I plan to marry in the coming weeks. I'm sure all of London has an opinion regarding whom I should choose as my bride. Let's hear yours."

She was rather obviously taken aback, but she recovered quickly. "I should think the answer is obvious. You should marry Lucy Astley."

He frowned. The saccharinely sweet Lady Lucy was about the last woman he could picture himself marrying. "Lady Lucy? Why her?"

She shrugged a negligent shoulder. "You were planning to propose to Caro. Caro and Lucy favor one another."

Marcus rolled his eyes. "I ask someone to dance three times, and every gossip in the *ton* assumes I'm going to propose."

She narrowed her eyes. "You were going to propose! Don't bother to deny it. You said as much to Lord Thetford."

Marcus stiffened, but he was used to holding his composure in far more difficult situations than this. "So I did," he acknowledged, inclining his head. "I wouldn't have thought Thetford would go repeating something like that to his wife."

"He didn't have to repeat it," she said crisply. "Caro was hiding beneath the desk when you made the remark. She heard your every word."

"She was *what?*" He started in surprise, and the greys laid their ears back. He immediately steadied his hands on the reins. "So, she was kneeling at his feet. I had no idea Thetford was such a lucky man... Quit poking me, Miss Chenoweth. Do you want me to overturn the carriage?"

"It was nothing like that!" she snapped. "At that point, she had not so much as kissed her future husband. I'll not have you impugning my friend's honor! But my point is, if that is the type of woman you favor—all golden hair and blue eyes —Lucy and Caro could not look more alike. Your dilemma is solved."

"I would not say that is the type of woman I favor." Miss Chenoweth shot him a skeptical look, and he had to suppress a snort. If she had any idea about the type of woman he truly favored and how closely she resembled his *beau idéal*...

Ceci arched a brow. "You expect me to believe that?"

"I do because it is the truth. You know of my longstanding friendship with Fauconbridge. You will not be surprised to learn that I wanted him to marry Diana."

Ceci frowned. "You were convinced the two of them would suit?"

"I didn't give it the slightest thought," Marcus admitted. "Believe me, had you grown up with my parents as your model, it would not have occurred to you that marriage could serve as a source of personal happiness."

The corners of her mouth twitched. "I suppose not."

"More importantly, had Diana married Fauconbridge, I would never have had to worry, not for a single second, that she was being mistreated." And, although he could not begrudge his friend the happiness he had found, could not wish he had never crossed paths with Elissa St. Cyr, how Marcus yearned for the comforting certainty of knowing that his little sister would always, *always*, be afforded the respect and kindness she deserved.

Marcus caught Miss Chenoweth studying him as the greys trotted along, and it occurred to him that he had revealed more than he had intended.

He cleared his throat. "Any man would want that for his sister."

"An important consideration, to be sure," she finally said. "But that doesn't explain why you planned to marry Caro."

"It's simple," Marcus said, nodding as they passed Lord Abbot, who was on horseback. "I wanted him to marry my sister. The least I could do was return the favor. And although I do not pretend to be suffering from the same midsummer madness that overcame her eventual husband, I think the two of us would have done well enough. Caro, as you call her, is very beautiful, and she has a fine wit. I actually like her, a statement I can make about vanishingly few people. I daresay we would have had a better marriage than nineteen couples out of twenty."

She was still watching him rather too closely. "But you admit you did not love her."

"Not in the slightest. Just a few months ago, I would have sneered at such an absurd remark."

She fixed him with a pointed look. "And now?"

What was it about this woman that tempted him to

answer these impertinent questions? Well, he was already in for a penny, so he might as well make it the full pound. "There is no one I hold in higher regard than Fauconbridge. I have known him for decades, and I can honestly say, I have never seen him a tenth so happy as he has been since marrying the former Miss St. Cyr. It makes me wonder…"

"Yes?" she pressed.

He shook his head. "It makes me wonder if I should perhaps set my sights higher than 'tolerable' for my own marriage."

He glanced at her out of the corner of his eye. It was time for him to regain the upper hand, to put her back on her heels. "And that, Miss Chenoweth, is where you come in."

*C*eci had forgotten how to breathe.

He had not meant that how it sounded. It was ridiculous that the thought had even occurred to her!

Although adding the words *that is where you come in* after *set my sights higher than tolerable for my own marriage* would normally imply *something*, Ceci reminded herself for the millionth time that there was no hope, not even the faintest sliver, that *Marcus Latimer* would ever propose to *her*.

He was still speaking. "Yesterday, I asked you for a favor."

It was on the tip of her tongue to shout, "I volunteer!" Even though she knew the favor to which he referred could not possibly involve holy matrimony.

"And," he continued, "as I said, it is my wish to marry in the coming weeks."

Now Ceci's heart was thundering like a herd of stampeding elephants.

He turned his head to glance at her and frowned. "Are you well?"

"I'm fine," she managed to choke out.

He curled up his nostrils. "You look positively dyspeptic."

"Thank you ever so much," she muttered.

"I say," he said, giving her a sharp look, "you didn't think that I was proposing, did you?"

"Of course not!" Her voice sounded suspiciously over-vehement to her own ears, the classic denial that instead served as a confirmation.

"Because I'm not," he continued, ruthlessly pouring salt into the bleeding wound where her heart had been just moments ago.

She attempted a breezy laugh. It came out sounding more like a squirrel being strangled, but it was the best she could do. "Believe me, Your Grace, never would I imagine that I, a lowly rector's daughter in a *hideous sack* of a dress, would ever be within a thousand leagues of your list of candidates."

She chanced a glance at him and found him frowning as if torn between the harsh fact that it was true and a genuine dislike of hearing her disparage herself. "I apologize for my earlier remark about your dress, Miss Chenoweth. I meant only that such a homely garment does not do justice to your manifold charms."

Now she was positive her cheeks would burst into flame. She waved this off. "Think nothing of it. I assure you, I did not." Which, of course, was a lie, but surely the good Lord would forgive her for trying to cling to a single shred of dignity.

He cleared his throat. "The favor to which I referred was your assistance in evaluating potential candidates. I would like to have your unvarnished opinion about them."

She peered up at him, confused. "I am not unwilling to advise you. But surely there are better people to serve as your guide. This is my first full Season in London. I do not count nearly as many people amongst my acquaintances as, say, Lady Cheltenham. Why do you not ask her?"

"Although I admire Lady Cheltenham's judgment more

than almost anyone's, she is ill-suited to this particular task. As one of the leading tastemakers of the *ton*, people take pains to pander to her."

"Whereas no one cares a farthing about impressing the penniless daughter of a country vicar," Ceci said, unable to keep a hint of waspishness from creeping into her voice. Dear Lord, could this afternoon possibly get any more humiliating?

He frowned again and started to speak. She held up a hand to stop him. "No, no, it's all right. We both know it's true." She began smoothing a non-existent wrinkle in her skirts in order to avoid his eye. "It happens that I have already stated my opinion on the subject. It seems you wish to marry the sort of person who would bother to be kind even to someone as lowly as myself. Well, no one could be kinder than Lucy. And, like Caro, she is extremely beautiful." She clasped her hands and lifted her chin. "You could not do better."

His expression looked… pained. "I would never say anything against someone who has welcomed my sister so warmly. But I fear we would not suit. Lady Lucy is very *sweet*"—he said the last word in the same tone most people would reserve for the word *putrid*—"and my sense of humor is, how you say…"

"Appalling?" Ceci supplied. "Degenerate? Repugnant? Inexpressible? Unamusing?"

"*Unamusing?*" He cut his eyes away from the horses to cast her an aggrieved look. "The point is, I need someone who will not shrivel in the face of a withering riposte. And I am fairly certain that is not Lady Lucy."

"Well, if you're looking for someone as acerbic as you, you should choose Isabella."

"I can assure you that Lady Isabella would reject such a match. She is the rare, *exceedingly* rare woman who has no interest in me." Ceci glowered up at him to find his expression all smugness. "No, really. Observe the way she looks at me: as if I were a particularly foul-smelling form of pond scum."

She studied him a beat. "And yet, you do not seem to mind her disdain."

"Indeed, I do not. Anyone who shows kindness to my sister is automatically in my good graces. But more than that..." He paused, considering his words. "She troubled to make up her own mind about me, rather than following the herd. Paradoxically, I admire her for it, even though she concluded that I am revolting. Whoa, now—what's this?"

A crush of carriages had formed ahead, forcing Marcus to bring his team to a halt. Ceci craned her neck to see what was going on. It appeared that a wagon with a broken wheel was blocking the junction.

"Oh, dear. What time is it?" She had to make it over to Deptford today. If she missed this chance to speak with Percival Polkinghorne, she might never discover what had truly happened to her mother!

Marcus consulted his pocket watch. "It's a quarter to three."

A quarter to three! That was far too close for comfort. What if Caro didn't wait for her? Although... that was ridiculous. Of course, Caro would wait for her. But what if she was delayed by an hour or more? Did they lock everything up in the evening? What if they couldn't get in?

She wrung her hands. "I'm just worried about my—"

"Piano lesson, I know. Do not distress yourself. Should you be late, I will compensate you for your usual fee. How much do you charge?"

"A shilling." Of course, it wasn't the shilling she was fretting over. "But I can't miss it. I *must* be back at three."

"I will give you ten shillings," he said, not troubling to conceal his exasperation.

"That... that won't suffice," she sputtered. "The, er, damage to my reputation could cause me to lose multiple students. No one wants an unreliable instructor."

"*Fine*," he said, turning the carriage. "I will take my brand-new phaeton down this sad excuse for an alley, just for you. Let's hope it fits."

It was so narrow, Ceci could have reached out and touched the brick wall of the building next to her. But Marcus managed to guide his team through without scraping his carriage.

When they emerged on the other side, Ceci sighed with relief, because now she recognized where they were, and they weren't all that far from Astley House. No wonder he thought her so ridiculous—she could have climbed down and walked if need be, and she would've made it on time. "Thank you for doing that."

He responded with a grunt. She cast about for a change of subject. What had they been discussing? Oh, yes—his marital prospects. "Well, if neither Lucy nor Izzie meet your requirements, then you are fresh out of Astley sisters."

"Therein lies my problem," he said as they pulled into Cavendish Square. "But I am confident you can help me identify someone suitable."

"Who are you considering?" Ceci asked.

They were coming up to Astley House. He drew the horses to a halt, then glanced over at her, his ice-blue eyes inscrutable. "I... I'm not sure," he said stiffly.

"You must have someone in mind," she pressed.

"I..." He was staring at her with a slightly faraway expression. Was it her imagination, or did his gaze stray to her lips?

Suddenly he shook himself, then descended the ladder his

tiger had set up in three quick steps and hurried around the carriage. "I have been so busy with Diana's debut, I honestly haven't given it much thought. I suppose I should endeavor to do so."

Just like that, he was back to his normal, aloof self. Ceci sought to restore her own composure. "I believe that will be more productive than my grasping at straws. Clearly you did not think much of my first two suggestions. And, with your permission, I will mention it to Caro and see if I can pry a few names out of her." Seeing his expression close off, she held up a hand. "I will be discreet. I can say I heard a rumor that you might wed this Season and frame the conversation as idle speculation, nothing more."

He reached up to help her down. "That will be acceptable. And appreciated."

Ceci felt her cheeks heat as she accepted his hand. She managed to get down the ladder in a fashion that wasn't entirely ungainly.

He did not immediately release her hand. He was peering at her with that enigmatic expression again, the one she didn't quite know what to make of.

Ceci cleared her throat. "I'd best head inside. I must prepare for my—"

"Piano lesson," he finished for her. Abruptly, he was all motion, waving an elegant hand and leading her up the front steps. "Thank you for your assistance today, both with the pianofortes and the more personal matter." He bent over her hand, the gesture practiced and smooth.

But instead of stopping the requisite two inches above her knuckles, he surprised Ceci by pressing his lips against them. To be sure, they were both wearing gloves, but Ceci couldn't contain a gasp as goosebumps shot up her arm.

He froze, his head still hovering above her hand. After a moment, he slowly straightened. Ceci fancied from his dazed expression that he was no less discomfited by his own actions than she.

He gathered himself. "Good afternoon, Miss Chenoweth," he said with a bow.

And then he was gone, hurrying atop his phaeton and sending the greys along.

Ceci rubbed her temple and nodded to Yarwood, who stood at attention, holding the front door. It had been a strange afternoon, one of the strangest of her life.

But she needed to put all of that out of her head for the moment. The errand she was about to undertake was of far higher importance.

She was heading to Deptford. To the docks.

And if, through some miracle, they could make it to the HMS *Lionheart* and find this Percival Polkinghorne, she would finally learn what had happened to her mother.

CHAPTER 14

*T*en minutes later, the Greville carriage pulled up to the curb in front of Astley House. Ceci scrambled inside and blinked at its two occupants: Caro, and her lady's maid, Fanny.

"Where is Lord Thetford?" Ceci asked as the carriage started forward.

"Henry?" Caro chuckled. "La! Surely you weren't expecting him."

"But... but..." Ceci shook her head to clear it. "You said you would bring the perfect bodyguard."

"And I did." Caro gestured to Fanny with a theatrical flourish while Fanny preened.

Ceci peered at Fanny in the dim light of the carriage. To be sure, Fanny was a plucky sort, accustomed to rough neighborhoods, and daunted by next to nothing. But they were going to *the docks*, for goodness sake!

She turned to Caro. "I must confess, when you said you would bring a bodyguard, I assumed it would be your husband."

Caro tutted. "Henry is the dearest man. But, like all men,

he has certain preconceived notions about what places are and are not appropriate for a woman to go. There was too great a risk that, even if I were to employ my *considerable* powers of persuasion, he would have tried to bar us from going entirely. He would've insisted upon going down there with Harrington, and let's be honest—they do not paint nearly as sympathetic a picture as a beautiful young lady, orphaned and alone. No, if we are to have any prayer of getting this information out of Mr. Polkinghorne, you must be the one to do the wheedling."

"I suppose that makes sense," Ceci said. "And you think that Fanny will provide us with sufficient protection?"

"She will," Caro insisted.

"Does she have a gun?" Ceci asked.

"No," Caro said brightly, "but she does have her parasol!"

Ceci stared at her best friend, wondering if she had taken leave of her senses. A *parasol*? They were going down to the Deptford docks, crawling with sailors and smugglers and God only knew what kinds of criminal miscreants, with naught but a lady's maid bearing a *parasol* for protection?

Ceci rubbed her forehead as she gazed out the window. This was a disaster. They weren't going to get within a hundred yards of the *Lionheart*, and this was her one and only chance to find out what had really happened to her mother. She felt tears welling.

A familiar carved lion flashed by the window. Ceci gasped and pounded on the roof. "Stop! Stop—pull in here!"

Caro and Fanny peered at her curiously as the carriage drew to a halt. "I will be back," Ceci said, opening the door, "in five minutes."

≈

Five minutes later, Ceci climbed back into the carriage, followed by the new addition to their party. "Caro, I believe you have already met Lady Griselda Saxe-Mecklenburg."

Caro smiled brightly. "Yes, I have had the pleasure. Good afternoon, Lady Griselda."

Ceci quickly introduced Fanny and Lady Griselda. As she took her seat, Lady Griselda deposited a leather pouch on the plush velvet squabs between herself and Ceci. It settled heavily into the cushion with a loud metallic clank.

Everyone's eyes flew to the pouch. Caro gave a startled laugh. "Goodness, Lady Griselda, whatever do you have in there?"

"Oh, that?" Lady Griselda waved a hand. "That is nothing. That is just in case!"

As the carriage crossed London, they filled Lady Griselda in on Ceci's debacle. When they explained how Caro had stumbled upon Mr. Polkinghorne's name in the newspaper, Lady Griselda nodded firmly. "But of course, you must speak to this man! It is only natural that you should want to know what happened to your mother."

Ceci quietly marveled at having found the only matron in London who thought going down to the docks in order to interrogate the man suspected of falsifying her mother's death certificate was a perfectly reasonable course of action.

"Now, Ceci," Caro said, "when you speak to him, you must look both very beautiful and very pathetic. Like this." She made her eyes large and sad, moulding her lips into a tremulous pout.

"So, I need to look like a spaniel begging for table scraps," Ceci muttered.

"And ya should thrust out your bosom," Fanny added, demonstrating.

"Fanny!" Ceci cried.

Fanny continued, undeterred. "The timing is important.

You want to do it right when you sense he's about to refuse you. Right when you need for him to reconsider, ya see?"

"Good gracious," Ceci muttered. "Lady Griselda, would you please talk some sense into these two?"

But Lady Griselda shook her head. "You must listen to your friends. Men are very stupid when it comes to a fine pair of eyes and a healthy bosom. And you want him to talk, do you not?"

"I suppose I do," Ceci admitted.

"Clever girl," Lady Griselda said. "Ah, here we are. This is it, yes?"

They piled out of the carriage. The docks were gated off, in an occasionally successful effort to prevent goods from being pilfered. Caro strode right up to the worker manning the gates and gave him a brilliant smile. "Good afternoon, my good sir. We're looking for the HMS *Lionheart*. Would you be so kind as to direct us?"

"I…" The poor man gaped at Caroline, mouth hanging open. Which was perhaps unsurprising. Caro was regarded as the most beautiful woman in all of England, and when she was pouring on the charm, as she was now, fluttering her fan and batting her eyes, Fanny had seen her make a man walk straight into a wall.

The man shook himself. "I can't let anyone pass who's not on the list."

"The list?" Caro asked with fake innocence. "What is the purpose of this list? That is a very handsome jacket, by the way. It brings out the blue of your eyes." She tapped his elbow playfully with her fan.

The man managed to close his mouth, which had been gaping open. "The list is to make sure nobody's on the docks who shouldn't be. To prevent thieving," he added at Caro's look of practiced confusion.

"Thieves!" she cried, throwing her head back and laughing. "But you could not possibly think *I* am a thief!"

"N-no, m'lady."

"Nor any of my companions."

This was the first moment the man managed to tear his eyes off of Caro in order to see that she had companions. "Of course not."

"Perfect," Caro purred, slipping around him. "Now, which way did you say the *Lionheart* was again?"

"It's… it's over yonder," the man said, pointing to the right. "But—"

"La!" Caro was already lifting the latch on the gate. She smiled up at the gatekeeper, her eyes sparkling. "This shall be our little secret."

"But, my lady—"

Caro gave him an exaggerated wink as Ceci, Fanny, and Lady Griselda scurried through the gate behind her. "I promise, I won't breathe a word to a soul." She pressed his forearm. "Thank you ever so much for your assistance."

Then the four of them were striding down the dock, Caro and Ceci in front and Fanny and Lady Griselda bringing up the rear. "She's good," Lady Griselda said to Fanny.

"That she is," Fanny agreed.

Caro proved it three more times, employing every tactic in the book, from flirtation to fake tears, each time someone stopped to question them.

And then the *Lionheart* was before them. Sailors were carrying casks and crates and even a live pig on board so it would be ready to sail at dawn. This was it, the moment when Ceci would finally learn something about what had happened to her mother. Her throat was as tight as a sailor's knot, and her palms as clammy as the underside of the hull.

She drew up short as a sailor stepped into her path.

"Just what're ye doing here?" the man growled. He looked

to be around forty years of age. He was short and considerably squatter than most of his fellow sailors. His clothes were splattered with what looked to be grease stains.

"Oh, I beg your pardon, sir!" Ceci said. "We have some urgent business with this ship's surgeon, Mr. Polkinghorne."

"The hell you do," the man said, his face set in a scowl.

Caro stepped forward, the familiar, coquettish smile firmly in place. "We just need the quickest word with Mr. Polkinghorne. We would be ever so grateful if you would fetch him for us."

The man snorted, but he did look Caro up and down. "If you're feelin' so grateful, you'll have to prove it."

"Prove it?" Caro gave a sparkling laugh. "However would I prove it?"

"By giving me a peep at those bubbies, for a start," the man said, leering at Caro's chest. "Then we'll go around the corner and you can milk my bull, if you take my meaning."

Caro froze. Ceci knew her friend was a sophisticated married woman and a skilled flirt.

But Caro was deeply in love with her husband, and there was absolutely no possibility she would be willing to *milk* this man's *bull*, whatever that meant. Caro, who was never at a loss for words, was at a loss for words, which was a sure indicator that she was in distress. Ceci reached out and seized her hand, drawing her back away from this horrible man.

Unfortunately, this had the effect of capturing the man's attention. He swept his gaze across their party, and his eyes were appreciative. "Yes. In fact, unless you want me raising a fuss and turning you lot over to the Thames police, I'll be enjoying a little something from all three of ye," he said, indicating Caro, Ceci, and Fanny.

Ceci's heart was in her throat. The man could hardly assault them in broad daylight, but if he summoned the police and word got out that they had been there, it would cause a great scandal. Caro could shake it off, being married and a noblewoman. But Ceci's reputation would be in shreds, and that would be the end of her fourteen piano students.

Ceci and Caro stood clinging to each other, frozen in place.

But not Fanny. Fanny gave a low chuckle and strode forward, swinging her hips. "Why not?" she purred. "But enough of this nonsense about milking yer bull. It's been an age since I've had a decent ride. I'll wager you're just the man who can give it to me." She drew her fichu seductively from her neckline and thrust out her bosom in precisely the way she'd demonstrated in the carriage. As predicted, the man's eyes flew to her impressive cleavage.

His eyes were so fixed that he did not see Fanny's parasol as it swung in a wide arc before connecting with the side of his knee. His leg buckled, and he shouted an oath.

That was all the opening Fanny needed. She grabbed him by the collar and shoved him up against a nearby mooring post. She brought her parasol up and poised its tip right at the hollow of his throat. "Quit your yarping, you revolting old letch!" she shouted. "How dare you speak to my mistress that way!"

His hand was halfway raised, and Ceci could tell he was debating the merits of making a grab for the parasol, trying to determine whether he could push it out of the way before Fanny crushed his windpipe, when the unmistakable metallic clink of a firearm being cocked came from just behind them.

Every eye flew to Lady Griselda, who had an ornately engraved blunderbuss trained at his head. "My apologies," Lady Griselda said. "It took an age to get this unholstered." She kicked her hem out in frustration. "I would've been faster if I didn't have to wear these bloody skirts in Town."

Fanny looked Lady Griselda up and down. "I like you."

Lady Griselda nodded regally. "And I like you."

Fanny returned her attention to the sailor. She put just enough pressure on the handle of her parasol to make him recoil all the way back against the post. "Now I'm going to tell you what's about to happen. You're going to go on that ship, and you're going to fetch Mr. Polkinghorne."

"The hell I am!" he spat. "First of all, if I go in that ship, I'm not coming out. Second, you can't just come where you've got no business being and threaten a man with a gun. I'm in the right here. And I've got a dozen witnesses who'll say as much."

Surely enough, they had drawn the attention of the sailors who had been loading the ship. A cluster stood at the far end of the dock, openly staring.

"That's right," the man said, emboldened. He fixed his gaze on Lady Griselda. "You've kicked the hornet's nest this time, you mad old bitch."

"Oh, my gracious. He doesn't even know!" Caro smirked into the man's face. "According to DeBrett's, that *mad old bitch* is first cousin to the King of Denmark."

Lady Griselda arched an eyebrow. "So I am."

"How I should hate for this to turn into a *diplomatic incident*," Caro said, enunciating her words so crisply they all but crackled in the cool afternoon air.

"*Fine*," the man spat. "I'll go and fetch him."

"Oh, no," Fanny said. "You've not moving a blessed inch." She jerked her head toward the cluster of sailors down the dock. "Have one of your friends fetch him. We'll let you go once he's here."

The man growled his displeasure, but seeing he had no choice, shouted the instruction to his fellows down the dock.

For the next three minutes, they glowered at each other in a stalemate before a man emerged from the ship. He looked to be around sixty years old, with a neatly trimmed

109

grey beard and spectacles. His dark coat and trousers marked him as a gentleman amongst the crowd of sailors. "Jameson?" he called, stopping twenty feet away. "What's going on?"

"These *ladies* say they need to speak with ye," their captive said, his voice dripping with irony.

CHAPTER 15

*P*ercival Polkinghorne managed to hold out for all of five minutes.

Ceci could tell at once that he recognized her. His gaze swept curiously over Mr. Jameson, Caro, Fanny, and Lady Griselda. But when his eyes fell upon her, they widened, and a touch of panic came into them.

Ceci couldn't say she was surprised. She had found a miniature of her mother amongst her father's effects, and the family resemblance was striking.

"I'm afraid I could not say," Mr. Polkinghorne replied after Ceci explained their predicament. "I've performed so many autopsies over the years, it's all but impossible to recall the details of any one, especially one that took place nineteen years ago."

Fanny scowled at him. "You're a terrible liar, is what you are. It's plain as day that you recognize Miss Chenoweth!"

"Well…" Mr. Polkinghorne gave Ceci a cringing sort of look. "I do recall the general case you're describing, only because the circumstances—a girl being left motherless at such a young age—were so tragic. But I fear I have no recollection of the medical details of the case." After three minutes of such remonstrations, Lady Griselda asked laconically, "Shall I shoot him? Perhaps in the foot?"

"No!" Ceci cried, in the same breath that Caro and Fanny said, "*Yes!*"

Having noticed the blunderbuss, Mr. Polkinghorne was now in a bit of a panic, if the whites of his eyes were any indication. Yet he held firm.

Right up until the moment Ceci burst into tears.

"Miss Chenoweth!" he exclaimed, waving his hands as if that would stop her. "You… you mustn't do that, now!"

"She was my mother," Ceci sobbed. "My *mother*! And I-I don't even remember her."

Mr. Polkinghorne was looking everywhere but at Ceci. "It is terribly sad. But… you know, stiff upper lip, and all th—"

"I know she didn't die of a fever," Ceci cried as Caro came over and wrapped an arm around her waist. "My father hired an army of investigators. I've read their reports. She was perfectly fine when he left that morning to perform a baptism in the neighboring village, but by the time he returned, she was dead. And they had taken the body away, and they refused to let him see it."

"I know it must seem irregular to you as a layperson," Mr. Polkinghorne said. "But three physicians and a surgeon concluded it was a fever."

"I'm not angry with you." Ceci accepted a handkerchief from Caro and dabbed at her eyes. "I know that, whatever happened, it must have involved someone very powerful. Or else one of you would have been willing to tell the truth. To cooperate with the investigation. But no one ever was. My father went to his grave without getting justice for his wife. And if you won't help me, I will never learn the truth about what happened to my own m-moth—"

"All right." Mr. Polkinghorne whispered the words, but

they had the impact of a thunderclap. He offered Ceci his arm. "Let us go where we might have a little privacy."

Ceci allowed herself to be led twenty feet down the dock, still within sight of her party but out of earshot in the whistling wind.

Mr. Polkinghorne twisted his hat in his hands. "Firstly, you must allow me to apologize for the role I have played in this fabrication. The only thing I can say in my defense is that you were more right than you could possibly know when you said that a powerful man was involved. I... I didn't have any choice but to say it was a fever. Or at least, that's the way it seemed at the time."

There was a roaring in Ceci's ears. Time seemed to slow. The passing of each second was excruciating as she waited to finally, *finally* learn the truth about her mother's fate. "How did my mother really die?" she whispered.

Mr. Polkinghorne stared down at the boards beneath their feet as he said, "Without question, it was by strangulation."

"Strangulation." Ceci had suspected, based on her father's obsessive research, that it would be something along those lines.

But she found there was a difference between *suspecting* your mother's last moments had been filled with violence and terror and knowing it of a certainty.

Mr. Polkinghorne bowed his head. "I am so sorry, Miss Chenoweth."

He started to turn away. Her head was swimming, but she managed to grab his arm. "Wait, Mr. Polkinghorne. Do you know who did this?"

His face was stony. "I do not."

She wrung her hands. "But you were there. You were there on the day after my mother died. You must have some idea—"

He shook his head. "Anything I say would be no more than speculation."

"I understand that," Ceci said hastily. "I would not consider it to be carved in stone. But anything you might have heard, any rumors, might serve to point me in the right direction for further inquiry."

He made a slashing motion with his hand. "I will say no more. Indeed, I fear I have said too much already."

He started to turn. "Wait, Mr. Polkinghorne. One last thing." She swallowed, gathering up her courage. "You said a powerful man was involved. Would you at least tell me whom I am up against?"

He gave a humorless laugh and again shook his head. "You ask dangerous questions, Miss Chenoweth."

Then he strode down the dock back toward his ship, leaving Ceci standing alone with tears streaming down her face.

CHAPTER 16

*M*arcus alighted from the carriage, his boots clicking against the cobblestones of the dark, dirty street. The streets here were narrow enough that this was as far as he could go by carriage. He would have to make the rest of tonight's journey on foot.

Two men accompanied him as he entered the rookery of Whitechapel: his burliest footman, Mick, and his not-so-burly valet, Sebastian.

Bastian was chattering about the visit he had paid to Archibald Nettlethorpe-Ogilvy's valet that afternoon. "His name is Jack Rattigan, and he used to be a forgemaster at Nettlethorpe Iron."

A sudden movement from a nearby alleyway made Marcus's hand fly to the sword at his hip, but he relaxed as he saw it was only a cat. The heavy pouch he wore tied on his other side made a slight clink as it settled against his hip. "From forgemaster to valet—a curious trajectory."

"Isn't it?" Bastian's eyes were bright with excitement, and, unlike Mick, who was busy scanning their unsavory environs, he seemed unperturbed to be strolling through one of London's worst neighborhoods. "He injured his shoulder —quite badly, from what I gather. He can't raise his arm higher than his heart. And so he could no longer perform heavy work at the forge. It happened that Mr. Nettlethorpe-Ogilvy was in need of a new valet, so he offered the position to Jack so he would have some way to support himself."

"Ah," Marcus said. "That explains why he is so spectacularly bad at his job."

"He truly is atrocious," Bastian agreed. "He had no idea how to put together an outfit, or which pieces were for day or evening. He didn't even know the names of most of the fabrics. I took the liberty of laying out a few ensembles for Mr. Nettlethorpe-Ogilvy, including one for Lady Diana's ball. And just as I was getting ready to leave, who should appear but Mr. Nettlethorpe-Ogilvy himself! That is why I was a few minutes late this afternoon. I hope Your Grace will pardon me, but I simply had to give him a more flattering hairstyle."

"I'm not certain that what Mr. Nettlethorpe-Ogilvy was previously sporting could be described as a *style*. But I'm sure whatever you did for him was an improvement."

"It certainly was." Bastian gestured to his own golden locks. "I cut it *a la Brutus*—short all over, but with a little movement toward the top. It turned out far better than I could have hoped. Mr. Nettlethorpe-Ogilvy has a strong jaw and surprisingly good cheekbones. I doubt anyone will start calling him a beau, but his features have a certain rugged appeal, and I fancy I was able to flatter them."

Marcus found he was not unreservedly enthusiastic about the man who was courting Cecilia Chenoweth suddenly having a *rugged appeal*. He'd wanted the man to stop being an eyesore. For her to find him handsome would be entirely excessive. But he kept his tone neutral as he replied, "If he will not show up at Diana's ball looking like a scarecrow, then I am grateful. How did this former forgemaster take your advice?"

"With ill grace, I'm afraid. He spent most of my visit glaring at me from the corner with his arms crossed. At one point, he even snarled at me!"

Marcus tutted sympathetically and was about to offer a kind word, but when he glanced at Bastian, he found that his valet did not precisely look upset about this turn of events. His eyes were bright, and he had high color in his cheeks. If anything, he looked... excited.

With his blond hair and boyish good looks, Marcus was under the impression that Bastian had more than half of the housemaids sighing after him. But come to think of it, he couldn't recall any whispers of him having a sweetheart or about an affair gone wrong.

Was it possible that this was because his romantic interests lay in another direction entirely?

He found he didn't really care if his valet was a molly. If that was indeed Bastian's preference, it was one of the few sexual acts Marcus hadn't personally tried, so he wasn't exactly in the position to cast the first stone.

Besides, he rather suspected that Aunt Griselda was of a similar persuasion and that her *dear friend* Miss Marsden had, in truth, been something more. As the person who offered Diana succor when everyone else refused, Marcus's good opinion of Aunt Griselda was unassailable. He supposed that had helped to broaden his thinking.

"He did surprise me, though," Bastian continued. "Just as I was getting ready to depart, he asked if I would come back tomorrow and show him how to press clothing. So, perhaps he was not entirely ungrateful for my efforts."

"You're doing the Lord's work, Bastian," Marcus said solemnly.

Bastian kept up the conversation—about Nettlethorpe-

Ogilvy's fearsome valet, Diana's debut ball and what Marcus would wear for the occasion, and a dozen other topics—but Marcus found his attention drifting.

Lord knew he had enough worries on his mind, from the unpleasant task he would perform in a few short minutes to Diana's debut ball.

But he found his thoughts returning, time and again, to Cecilia Chenoweth.

It had come as a shock, the degree to which he had become disconcerted when he realized that his quip about her dress had hurt her feelings. Marcus liked to think he was a nice person—

Well. In the interest of honesty, that was not true. *At all.* He could be the biggest arse in all of London when he put his mind to it.

But, although he could at times be brutal, he had a personal code, which could be best summarized that he did not punch down. It was one thing to tell Nettlethorpe-Ogilvy, one of the richest and most influential men in Europe, who had princes and kings call upon him at his forge to beg for an order of the superior cannons that only his factory could make, that he dressed like an itinerant circus performer. Nor did he feel the slightest pang of guilt for telling his horrible uncle that he could go fuck himself right up the arse and do it with a bayonet.

No doubt that was the reason he found Cecilia Chenoweth's wounded dignity so disquieting—because she was a penniless orphan.

Oh, yes, keep telling yourself that. It hasn't a thing to do with her big, brown eyes. And what's the reason you can't stop thinking about her, Marcus?

He pushed that question aside as he flipped up the collar on his cape. Although Marcus generally preferred his greatcoat, Bastian had insisted that nothing was more *apropos* for an evening of clandestine midnight assignations than a cape, a point Marcus had found difficult to refute.

But he would have words with Miss Chenoweth tomorrow. Not about her dress, or Marcus's poorly-thought-out commentary thereupon.

But about the words he had overheard Aunt Griselda muttering to herself in Mecklenburgish when she had returned to Latimer House late that afternoon. If his great-aunt was to be believed, Marcus wasn't the only one who'd made a clandestine journey to unsavory parts of town after the two of them had parted ways.

"This is it, Your Grace," Bastian said, gesturing to an alley so narrow Marcus would have to turn sideways to enter. "George Street."

One could be forgiven for assuming a roadway named after the monarch would be a bit grander, but George Street consisted of one drab tenement house after another. Marcus did not complain. He held his nose—spiritually, if not physically—and slipped inside the narrow passage.

The way soon opened, albeit slightly. Bastian nodded to a house toward the left. "That's it there. Number seventeen. The Kimbrells live on the second floor."

"Excellent. You've done an outstanding job tracking them down, Bastian. Thank you."

It was true. The fact that no one tied a finer cravat was the primary reason Marcus kept Bastian around.

But Bastian had uses beyond keeping Marcus in the first state of men's fashion. Everyone liked him. His affable mien caused people to tell him things, to give him information they would normally keep close to their chests. With Bastian, one minute you were discussing the weather, and the next thing you knew, you had told him where your great-grandmother kept the key to her jewelry box.

It was a talent Marcus would need in the coming weeks, in which he would be paying more visits like this one.

Bastian bowed gracefully. "You know I would do anything for Your Grace."

Marcus started forward, but Mick stepped into his path and jerked his chin toward the building. "Why don't I go in first and see what's what?"

Marcus waved this off. "That won't be necessary."

"But Yer Grace—"

"I appreciate the offer, Mick. But I must be the one to do this. You and Bastian will be on the landing should I need you."

Mick frowned but didn't argue.

Marcus hadn't been sure whether the occupants of the room would open the door to his knock, especially at this late hour. But they did, and Marcus used their momentary confusion to sweep into the room before they had the chance to ask who he was and what the hell he was doing there.

Marcus took in the plain wooden furnishings, the laundry hanging from the ceiling, and the chipped teapot. He noted the flinty look in the man's eyes, and the lock of grey-streaked hair that peeked out from beneath the woman's dingy white cap.

They were both gaping at him incredulously. Marcus gave them a regal nod. "You are wondering who I am and why I am here. I will not beat around the bush. I am the Duke of Trevissick."

Marcus had wondered if the Kimbrells would question his identity and whether he was really a duke. They did not. To be fair, he was wearing silk evening clothes, a ruby-and-gold stickpin that had been in his family for three hundred years, and a mink-lined cape. It was one of his more ducal ensembles.

And it appeared to have convinced them that he was, in

fact, the Duke of Trevissick, because the woman gasped and the man stepped in front of his wife, fists raised.

Marcus held out his hands placatingly. "Not *that* Duke of Trevissick, Mr. Kimbrell. My father is dead."

"And may his black soul rot in hell for all eternity!" Mr. Kimbrell spat.

"Rhys!" Mrs. Kimbrell hissed. "You mustn't say such things. This is the man's son!"

"I beg you, Mrs. Kimbrell, not to distress yourself. I know it will be difficult for you, in particular, to believe, but no one is celebrating my father's death more assiduously than I. How I wish I had thought to bring a bottle of brandy. We could have raised a toast to his black soul rotting in hell for all eternity, as Mr. Kimbrell so eloquently put it. I agree wholeheartedly, that is where it belongs."

This stunned the Kimbrells momentarily into silence. Mr. Kimbrell was the first to recover. "Why have you come?"

"As I mentioned, my father is dead. The responsibility of the dukedom has passed to me." He gave Mrs. Kimbrell a steady look. "And I take my responsibilities seriously."

Her eyes were wary. "What do you mean by that?"

"Let us not mince words. My father was a monster. He left in his wake a slew of amends that must be made." Marcus inclined his head toward Mrs. Kimbrell. "And that includes to you."

She clutched a fistful of her dress just over her heart, and when she spoke, her words were high-pitched and frantic. "How—how do you know about that?"

"My father kept a journal." Marcus tried to make his voice gentle. "That is how I know that, on the fourteenth of August, 1782, he forced himself upon you."

Mrs. Kimbrell used her apron to scrub at the tears that were suddenly streaking down her face. Her husband rushed to her side, wrapping an arm around her shoulders, then turned to glower at Marcus. "Why in bloody hell did you come?"

"Perhaps I should not have," Marcus acknowledged. "I see now that my desire to make amends in person was selfish, as it has brought back distressing memories for Mrs. Kimbrell. Please accept my apologies. It probably would have been better to send my recompense anonymously."

"Recompense?" Mr. Kimbrell looked him up and down. "What recompense?"

Marcus unhooked the leather pouch he had concealed beneath his cloak. He set it on the scarred wood of their table, where it made a heavy metallic clink. "Five hundred pounds."

"*Five hundred—*" Mr. Kimbrell's expression turned from astonishment to scorn in a second. "There's no way there's five hundred pounds in that little sack."

"Well, of course not," Marcus said, sifting around in his pocket for the other item he had brought for Mrs. Kimbrell. "What sort of half-wit brings five hundred pounds sterling into Whitechapel in the middle of the night? That is twenty pounds of it. The rest"—he handed a folded sheet of paper to Mrs. Kimbrell—"has been deposited in an account in your name at the institution of Cuthbertson and Baker."

The Kimbrells were stunned into silence, their heads bent over the paper. Marcus continued, "At present, the rest of the money is invested in a variety of dividend-paying stocks. I would suggest you leave it there, as it will generate an income of around fifty pounds a year. But, should you prefer to cash it out, I will not attempt to stop you. It is yours, Mrs. Kimbrell, to do with as you please."

She looked up at him then, her eyes filled with misery. "Why are you doing this?"

It took an effort to hold himself still, but a duke did not squirm. He met Mrs. Kimbrell's gaze, thinking he owed her that much. "Nothing can ever make things right or undo the injury you were subjected to by my father. This is what I am able to do. And, as insufficient as it is, I would prefer to do this much than to do nothing."

Mrs. Kimbrell nodded sadly, returning her gaze to the documents.

"I would like to add that I am profoundly sorry for what my father did. However," Marcus continued, his voice taking on a note of steel, "allow me to make one thing clear. My little sister, Diana, will be making her debut in a few short days. Given who her father is, it will come as no surprise that her life up until this point has been a misery. I am determined that she will have her every heart's desire from now on."

Marcus's voice shook as he added, "If you do anything to cause a scandal that mars Diana's debut, then I will *ruin* you. If your actions cause my sister to be sad, then mark my words—by the time I am finished, they will clean up what's left of you with a *rag*!"

The Kimbrells exchanged an astonished look. Marcus drew himself up. "I bid you good night," he said, spinning on his heel and sweeping out of their rooms with a swirl of his cape.

CHAPTER 17

The following day, Miss Chenoweth accompanied the Astleys to Latimer House to provide the music during Diana's dancing lessons.

Marcus had once again arranged for a luncheon to be served. As soon as it concluded, Lord and Lady Fauconbridge scurried off to the library to bury their noses in his palimpsests, and Diana repaired with Lady Cheltenham to the parlor to continue their lessons.

Finally, it was here—the moment in which he would get to hear Cecilia play, really play, and his cares would be eased, if only for an hour. Trying not to look overeager, Marcus came and stood beside her chair and offered her his arm.

They walked in silence toward the music room. He had asked Ellery to have the new pianoforte wheeled in there as soon as Diana's dancing lesson concluded, and he found it ready and waiting.

"I suppose you'll be wanting to hear the Beethoven," Miss Chenoweth said, peeling off her gloves as she settled on the bench. She could not suppress a little hum of pleasure as she played a few notes, and Marcus had to bite back a smile at her obvious enthusiasm for the new instrument.

He did want to hear the Beethoven.

But there was one thing he wanted to do first.

Marcus made sure his expression was all innocence as he strolled across the room. "Yes, indeed. But I also wanted to ask—did you make it back in time for your music lesson?"

Her head snapped up. Her voice had a breathless quality as she asked, "My... my music lesson?"

You know, the one you lied about. The one you didn't teach.

Marcus took his time arranging himself on the sofa. "Yes, the one you were so concerned about missing yesterday afternoon. How was it?"

"Oh, erm." Her cheeks were flushed. Marcus was enjoying this a little too much.

She shrugged negligently, but she was a terrible liar. "It was... you know. A fairly typical music lesson."

Marcus stroked his chin. "Typical. An interesting choice of words. Do you typically conduct your music lessons at a dockyard?"

All color drained from her face. "How do you know about that?"

He couldn't hold in a wry smile. "I happened to be coming down the stairs just as Aunt Griselda arrived back at the house. I overheard her muttering the most fascinating things about you, the Deptford docks, and how London wasn't nearly as dull as she had anticipated."

That put some color back in her cheeks. "I had hoped she would be more discreet."

"Now, you mustn't be mad at Aunt Griselda. She did not see me at first, and even after she did, she did not realize she had given anything away, as she was speaking in Mecklenburgish. While Diana is fluent in several of the Germanic dialects, the only one I can converse in is Low

German. But even though I cannot speak it, I understand Mecklenburgish better than she realized." Marcus leaned back, smiling smugly. "So, Miss Chenoweth, I already know you have been up to something. There is no use denying it. You may as well go ahead and tell me what you were doing at the Deptford dockyard yesterday."

"I... I..." She swallowed thickly.

And then she surprised him by bursting into tears.

CHAPTER 18

*W*as there anything more humiliating than crying before the object of one's affection?

If there was, Ceci could not think of it. In particular, when one was doing the messy, uncontrollable hiccoughing, running-at-the-nose sort of crying in which she was presently engaged.

What a sight she must look, and in front of the most immaculate man in London! She turned toward the far wall and began sifting around her pocket for a handkerchief.

One was pressed into her hand before she could locate her own. It was immaculately white and the Trevissick crest was so impeccably executed in gold thread that she instinctively balked at the notion of using it to staunch the assorted fluids flowing from her facial orifices.

Seeing her hesitation, Marcus solved this problem for her by proactively dabbing at her cheeks. His thumb grazed her temple, and she shivered. "It's all right. Take it."

She did so, hesitantly. She was still refusing to look at him, and so it came as a surprise when he took her hand and drew her from the piano bench, leading her to the striped sofa he had been occupying moments before.

He settled her on the sofa, then sat beside her, wrapping an arm around her shoulders. Ceci could not decide whether this was the best or the worst thing that had ever happened to her. Marcus Latimer touching her in any capacity was the primary fodder of her daydreams, and here he was, all but taking her into his... well, perhaps not his *arms*. Strictly speaking, it was only the one arm. But still!

Yet, when she had imagined a moment such as this, never had she pictured herself with red eyes, blotchy cheeks, and mucous streaming from her nose.

She tried to scoot away, but he held her firmly in place. "I'm sorry," she gasped, giving her nose a hasty blow. "I know nothing repulses a man more than a crying woman."

"Ah, but that is most men. You have forgotten that I am a brother. I can therefore confirm through years of experience that a crying spell is neither contagious nor fatal. I even know what to do in this situation."

It was good that one of them did. "And what, pray tell, is that?"

"The important thing is to repress one's instinct to lecture the crying party on how best to go about solving their problems. I am given to understand this is not what most women want. What one should do, in addition to providing the proverbial shoulder to cry on, is listen. Well, that isn't quite true. I have been known to occasionally utter a soothing platitude such as, *There, there,* or *Everything will be all right.* Still, the process is much less daunting than most men would have you believe."

"Oh, dear!" Ceci started, seeing a wet spot on the sleeve of his bottle-green jacket. "I'm so sorry, Your Grace. I seem to have... er... dampened... your jacket."

"Think nothing of it." Marcus waved this off, fishing

another handkerchief from his coat pocket. He did not use it to blot the wet spot on his sleeve but pressed it directly into her hands. "Bastian—my valet—will take care of it. Besides, I have forty-seven other jackets."

Ceci sat up, blowing her nose. "Do you truly?"

"Probably. I have no idea. But who cares? Whatever happened down at Deptford yesterday, it has upset you profoundly. Why don't you tell me about it so you can feel better?"

"Oh, you don't want to hear about it." At his skeptical look, she added, "It's just some messy family history."

He raised a single eyebrow. "You've met my family. I believe the words that come to mind are stark, raving, and mad. And believe me, those are *by far* the best family members I possess. Truly, Miss Chenoweth, you had better tell me. Who else are you going to commiserate with regarding your messy family history? The Astleys?" He snorted. "Do not mistake me, there is no one I hold in higher regard. But they do not know the meaning of the words family dysfunction. You might as well be speaking Mecklenburgish. Meanwhile, when some of us say we have skeletons in our closets, we mean it literally."

Ceci had to wonder if he had a point. Although she had spent the better part of yesterday afternoon crying on Caro's shoulder, she still felt adrift. It wasn't that her friend didn't care. But Ceci's problems were alien to the wealthy daughter of an earl who had been declared the toast of London the moment she made her debut, then managed to ensnare the man she'd always wanted to marry within two weeks of making her bow. When Caro murmured *Everything will be all right*, it did sound like a platitude, not because she did not care, but because she had never experienced troubles of this magnitude.

But Marcus... Marcus had sailed through these waters before.

Ceci suspected he might actually know how to maneuver around the rocks.

"It all started," she began slowly, unable to believe she was speaking these things out loud, "on the night my father died."

Marcus found it hard to countenance, but Cecilia Chenoweth's family was every bit as maladjusted as his own.

To be sure, her father was not so bad as his. Which was not to suggest she had no reason to be upset; being better than the old duke was a spectacularly low bar. And yet, there was a certain security in having always known the unvarnished truth about his father.

He could appreciate that, while Cecilia's father had many admirable qualities, they would only have served to make it more jarring when all of his secrets came spilling out into the open.

And the fact that he had left her destitute was absolutely inexcusable. Marcus had inherited the dukedom a mere three weeks ago, and he was already moving assets around and setting up trusts to make sure that would *never* happen to Diana.

Beside him, Cecilia dabbed at her eyes. "I've suspected for months that her death involved foul play. I had thought I would be well prepared, that I could face yesterday's conversation stoically. But learning that she had been *strangled*..." She trailed off, her voice ragged with emotion.

"That's probably the worst part," Marcus agreed. "Knowing that her last moments were filled with terror."

Cecilia looked up at him, and he could read the question in his eyes—was he speaking from experience?

He surprised himself by telling her. "My mother died by my father's hand. I know it is typically annoying rather than helpful when someone says they understand. But, to a certain extent, I do."

"I'm so sorry," she said swiftly. She bit her lip, and he could tell she was torn between wanting to know more and not wishing to pry.

"It's all right if you want to ask questions. I know this is the type of thing you can't discuss with many people."

Her body sagged with relief, and the brush of her soft, full breast against his chest drew his gaze to her decolletage.

Not the time, Marcus. The girl was distressed. He could keep his cock in check for once in his life.

"Did your mother die the same way?" she asked. "By strangulation?"

"No." It felt strange to be speaking the words aloud, to be discussing the incident he never discussed with anyone. Not even Diana, whom he had been careful to always shield from this horrifying truth. "My father pushed her down the stairs. I am given to understand that she broke her neck in the fall."

Sympathy flooded her brown eyes. "Oh, my gracious! I am so terribly sorry." She bit her lip, considering her next question. "You said you were given to understand. You did not see her, then?"

"No. I heard her scream, though, and believe me, that was bad enough." He cleared his throat, which had gone rusty. "I was eleven years old. I usually kept my sword with me at all times." He gave her a sad smile. "That was the reason I took up fencing and practiced it so obsessively—thinking that, if I could become good enough, I would be able to protect my mother from him, even though I was small. But that morning, I forgot it in my room."

She was rubbing his back, which was nice. Soothing. He continued, "As soon as I realized my father had gone into one of his rages, I ran to my room to get it. I had it in my hand, and I was sprinting back to the foyer. But I heard her scream before I could get there. I would have seen her, too, had it not been for Ellery. He came charging up the stairs and caught me in a bear hug on the landing. I remember beating at his shoulders, demanding that he let me go. But he just kept saying, *No, my lord. She would not want you to see that. She would not want you to remember her this way.*" His voice was gruff as he added, "He was right."

Her brown eyes were so beautiful, glistening with fresh tears. "I see now why you hold Ellery in such high esteem."

At some point during the conversation, she had laid her head upon his shoulder, and Marcus marveled at how natural it felt, sitting on a sofa, his arm draped around Cecilia Chenoweth, discussing all his deepest, darkest secrets.

He... he liked this. Being open with her. *Intimate*, and not merely in the physical sense.

What an alarming thought.

He cleared his throat. "Yes. That, and a thousand other similar acts. It may sound strange, considering I am a duke and he is my butler. But he was more a father to me than the old duke ever was."

Her face fell at the mention of fathers. "That has been the other thing I've had trouble reconciling. It was always me and my father. We were a duo. I thought I knew him as well as I know my own reflection." She bowed her head. "It turns out I didn't know him at all. And not only that, as I've been going through his papers, I've been discovering things I didn't even know about myself! I had always believed that I was born and raised near Cheltenham, but that isn't true. It turns out I'm from Cornwall!"

Marcus shrugged a negligent shoulder. "That doesn't come as much of a surprise."

Her voice rose in pitch. "I assure you, it came as a surprise to me!"

He held up a placating hand. "I meant only that your surname, Chenoweth, is native to Cornwall. The reason I know is because I was born there myself."

"Oh. I didn't know even that much." She rubbed at her temple. "I feel like I don't even know who *I* am anymore."

He didn't want to mumble some meaningless platitude, so he said only, "I'm sure it must be terribly disconcerting."

They sat in silence for a moment, then she asked in a small voice, "Does it ever get better?"

He considered his words carefully. "Yes and no. It doesn't ever stop being awful that your mother is gone, nor that she died in such a horrible way. I have thought of my mother, have felt her loss, every day since her passing. But it will not always feel as raw as it does today. You will become practiced at dealing with those thoughts, in the same way you become practiced in playing a difficult passage on the pianoforte. You will learn to feel them without letting them overwhelm you." He paused. "I hesitate to offer you advice, mere minutes after vowing not to lecture you—"

"Please do." She swiped her thumbs beneath her eyes. "At this point, I'm desperate to try something, anything, that might lessen the pain."

"The thing that has helped me more than anything is taking action. Doing something that honors your mother, that would have made her proud. For me, it has always been looking after Diana. Protecting her, making sure she would not share the same fate as my mother, has provided my sense of purpose in the years that followed. Even on my worst days, it gave me a reason to keep going."

Despair registered on her face. "I have no family left. There is no one for me to look after, and nothing for me to do."

He shook his head. "Don't you see? You're already doing it." She gave him a skeptical look, but he ploughed on. "For almost twenty years, your mother has been denied justice. But in just a few months, you have made more progress toward uncovering the truth than your father was ever able to do."

She shrugged, looking uncomfortable. "That was more luck than anything."

"Not luck so much as pluck. Not one woman out of a hundred would have gone down to those docks. But that is not all you've been doing."

She frowned. "I'm fairly certain that it is."

"Remind me who organized a charity auction that raised more than three thousand pounds for the Ladies' Society last Monday."

She attempted to wave this off. "The Ladies' Society is already a popular charity. With the foundation Anne has laid, anyone could have organized the auction and achieved the same result."

He wasn't about to let her off the hook so easily. "How many hours did you spend planning the auction? Soliciting donations? Writing out invitations?"

"I... I don't know."

"A great many, I'll warrant. And while it's true that many people *could* have done it, you were the one who actually did. How many women fleeing their abusive husbands will that three thousand pounds support? Thirty? Fifty? Because of *you*."

She shook her head, but he could tell his words were starting to seep in. Although her eyes were still sad, they no longer looked defeated. "I'm not sure how much credit I can take. Almost a third of the money we raised was donated by... by you."

She sat up perfectly straight, rounding on him. "That's why you did it!"

"That's why I did what?"

"That's why you joined the Board of the Ladies' Society! Because it helps women in the same situation as your mother."

He gave an elegant wave of his hand. "Very good, Miss Chenoweth. You have solved the riddle of why the most depraved man in all of England was inspired to take such a charitable turn. I make light of it, but truly, I hope you will continue your work with the Ladies' Society. You will see how much it helps. Never do I feel closer to my mother than when I am doing something on its behalf. I can't believe I'm about to say something so trite, but there are times when I can feel her smiling down on me."

"If that is trite," she said, dabbing at her eyes, "then I am determined to be the tritest woman in the British Isles. That sounds wonderful, compared to what I have been feeling these past twenty-four hours."

He rubbed her shoulder, which made her magnificent breasts tremble. He forced himself to avert his eyes, as he was trying not to be depraved for the first time in his life. "I know it's awful now. But you're doing all the right things. Keep going. Your mother would be so proud of you."

She huffed. "Now that's laying it on a bit thick. I'm not sure she would be proud that her daughter is a penniless wallflower imposing herself upon the Astleys."

He gaped at her. Was this how she saw herself? Did she truly have no idea? "You are the most accomplished woman of my acquaintance. Your talent on the pianoforte is extraordinary. That is no accident of birth. You earned that skill through hours of practice. And you are a genuinely good person. Do you know how few of those there are in

London? I could probably count them on one hand. Why, you won't even let me make sport of Nettlethorpe-Ogilvy—"

She poked him in the arm. "No, I will not."

He shook his head. "My point is, of course your mother would be proud to have such a daughter, who is every bit as kind and talented as she is beautiful."

"B-beautiful?" She blinked up at him, startled. Time seemed to slow down. For the past half hour, he'd been struggling to ignore the fact that he was touching her. Now, all the places her body pressed against his came roaring to the forefront of his consciousness—the side of her soft, luscious breast, pressing against his chest. The curve of her neck, fitted so perfectly against his shoulder they could have been puzzle pieces. The petal-soft skin of her inner arm beneath his fingers.

The air felt charged with electrical current as if lightning was about to strike. "You don't think I'm beautiful," she whispered, then licked her lips, trapping his gaze.

"Do I not?" he asked, his voice guttural.

He could feel her heartbeat fluttering in her throat and realized that his hand had moved of its own accord and was stroking up the elegant column of her neck, past her jawline, and into her hair. He was drowning in her eyes, those simmering pools of caramel. Then they abruptly disappeared as her eyes closed and her mouth opened and his lips yearned toward hers—

"Your Grace."

His lips had brushed hers more fleetingly than a butterfly's wing, so lightly he couldn't be entirely sure he hadn't imagined it. He glanced up to find James the footman standing framed in the doorway, his face beet red.

"Beg pardon, Your Grace, but the confectioner is here. They've sent over some samples for your approval."

Marcus bit back a curse. Not yet having acquired a

duchess to plan Diana's ball for him, such tasks were falling to him. He turned to see that Cecilia had managed to extricate herself from his embrace and was now seated on the far end of the sofa. "Miss Chenoweth, would you join me in sampling a few sweetmeats?"

Her cheeks were redder than James's. "I thank you, Your Grace, but I had best be going. I need to return to Astley House to prepare for a—"

"Piano lesson," he said along with her. She hadn't mentioned expecting a student that afternoon, and Marcus suspected her "lesson" was about as real as the one she'd taught yesterday afternoon.

Still, it was hard to blame her for rushing off after having been caught in such a compromising position. The consequences of the most innocent of kisses could be severe for a woman, even if they were non-existent for him. "Of course. Allow me to see you out."

She was through the door before he could offer her his arm. As he exited the music room, he paused before James. "I am counting on your absolute discretion, James."

The footman visibly gulped. "You will have it, Your Grace."

"Do not breathe a single word. Not even to the other servants."

James nodded vigorously. "No one will hear of it from me."

"Good man," Marcus said, pressing a guinea into his hand.

He trailed Miss Chenoweth to the entryway, but by the time he reached the front doors, she was already gone.

CHAPTER 19

*D*uring the next three days, Marcus was so busy with preparations for his sister's debut ball that he didn't have time to corner Ceci and force her to play Beethoven for him.

Ceci told herself this was for the best. Sometimes she thought the moment he had almost kissed her had been a figment of her imagination. Other times she wondered if it had been real, but only because she had taken a leave of her senses and thrown herself at him. Both possibilities sounded ludicrous, and yet, each seemed more likely than the notion that *Marcus Latimer* had meant to kiss *her*.

He tried to foist some of the planning off on Lady Griselda, but she proved indifferent to the task. "Yes, yes," Ceci overheard her saying after Marcus asked her to meet with the florist on his behalf, "bring whatever flowers you think. What does it matter? They all look the same."

Marcus, who had taken two determined strides toward Ceci, stopped short, his nostrils flaring with annoyance. Casting her what her obviously deluded brain concluded was a sultry look, he turned on his heel and went to deal with the florist himself.

Meanwhile, Ceci made her escape.

The worst thing, aside from the mortification, was not being sure if he actually *had* kissed her. She thought his lips had touched hers, but the moment had been so brief, so fleeting, she couldn't be entirely sure.

At least it wasn't her first kiss. It would be incredibly awkward to be unsure if one had or had not been kissed. But Mr. Nettlethorpe-Ogilvy had kissed her at a ball last month, a stiff, closed mouth pressing together of the lips, after which he had stepped back, cleared his throat, and said, "Well, then."

The fact that kissing Marcus for one-thousandth of a second had been a million times more stimulating than a proper kiss with her likely future husband did not bear thinking about.

At least the Season was entering its last gasp. Soon Marcus would take Diana back to Cornwall, and Ceci would return to Gloucestershire with the Astleys where she could be alone with her humiliation. If Marcus meant to marry as quickly as he said, he would certainly have a bride by next Season. Six months from now, he would no doubt have forgotten that she even existed.

Three days later, Marcus stalked across the ballroom. On the raised platform at the far end, the twenty-piece orchestra he had hired was tuning up. Marcus had purchased the contents of every hothouse around London so that, in spite of the crisp autumn weather, every pedestal was adorned with urns of white roses accented with blue delphinium. The refreshment table sagged under the weight of the spread Messrs. Grange had provided, and so many beeswax candles illuminated the space it was brighter than daytime—at least, the version of daytime one experienced in London during the month of September.

He had done absolutely everything to ensure that his sister's debut ball would be a magnificent success, an event that would be talked about for years to come. Diana had been presented at Court that afternoon. It had gone splendidly.

But tonight would be the real test.

The ball would not start for another half hour, but Marcus had asked a select group to gather in his study for a preparatory meeting.

As he strode in, he was pleased to see that the dozen men had arrived on time.

Well, Marcus reflected, counting. All save one.

Just then, Harrington Astley strode into the room. This was the first time Marcus had seen him wearing the uniform of the riflemen's regiment in which he had recently purchased a commission.

"Well, well, well—look what we have here," Lord Thetford said, slapping his friend on the shoulder. "*Lieutenant* Astley. You look damn good in that green coat, if I—"

Marcus cleared his throat. "If you would be so kind, Thetford, as to save your congratulations for a more opportune moment, there is important business at hand." He took up a stack of papers, copied out by his secretary, and passed them around the room.

"What's this?" Michael Cranfield, the Earl of Morsley, asked, squinting at his sheet.

"This," Marcus said, starting to pace the room, "is a copy of Diana's dance card. As you can see, you have each been assigned a particular dance."

"Assigned?" Harrington gave him a strange look. "Don't you think your sister might like to choose her own partners?"

"Not tonight," Marcus said firmly. "Nothing can be left to chance. Tonight will set the tone for every event in the future. I intend to make it clear that she will only be dancing with the finest gentlemen of the *ton*. Rakehells and fortune hunters need not bother."

"The finest gentlemen of the *ton*?" Archibald Nettlethorpe-Ogilvy, who, to Marcus's infinite annoyance, did indeed look a thousand times better in the outfit and haircut Bastian had selected for him, scratched his head. "I don't understand why I'm on this list. You don't even like me."

"That's not true. I tolerate you," Marcus hastened to reassure him.

Nettlethorpe-Ogilvy didn't seem to appreciate what a significant compliment this was, as he cast Samuel Branton, a barrister who also served on the board of the Ladies' Society, a beleaguered look.

"Well, that doesn't explain what I'm doing here," Harrington Astley noted. "You definitely don't like me."

"Indeed, I do not," Marcus confirmed, pinching the bridge of his nose as he regarded the man who had once started a strangely persistent rumor that Marcus had brought the silver-plated chamber pot of King Henry IV with him to Eton because he was too pompous to shit in anything else. "And yet, I had no choice but to put you down for the supper dance. You see, I am worried that Diana might be tongue-tied with nerves tonight, and you have a singular ability to carry on talking, no matter how much your conversational partner might wish you would shut the hell up."

Harrington grinned. "I really do," he said to Thetford, who murmured in agreement.

"And so," Marcus concluded, "you have your assignments. Do not be late. Do not leave my sister standing in the corner, not for one second. And the moment your dance concludes, you will return her to my Aunt Griselda. If Diana wishes to have some lemonade, you may bring it to her there. There will be no repairing to the balcony and absolutely no interludes in the garden. Have I made myself clear?"

There was a murmuring of agreement, and the men began filing out of the room. All save Edward Astley, who had stolen over to the sideboard and poured a couple of brandies.

He handed one to Marcus, then clinked glasses with him.

After they had both taken a sip, Edward said, "Everything is going to be all right."

"It is," Marcus agreed.

He would make sure of it. *Had* made sure of it.

And if it wasn't, he would rain down retribution on whoever dared to ruin Diana's night.

CHAPTER 20

*M*arcus found his sister at the top of the stairs. Diana was peering over the railing from the far corner, out of sight of the milling throng below. Absolutely everyone who had been invited had turned up, and they had turned up early, not wanting to miss even a second of the first event held at Latimer House in more than twenty years.

"How are you holding up?" Marcus asked as he approached. He was inordinately pleased to see how well Diana looked in the ensemble selected by Lady Thetford. The mazarine blue gown was simple but perfectly cut, everything about it flattering Diana's figure and complexion. Marcus's first instinct had been to send her out wearing half her weight in diamonds, a not-so-subtle declaration of the regard in which he held his sister. But Lady Thetford had prevailed upon him to take a slightly less ostentatious approach. Diana therefore wore gleaming, white pearls, both draped around her neck and woven into her hair. The effect was elegant but more appropriate for a young girl making her debut.

Diana rubbed her arm with her hand, which was one of her tells; she was nervous. She noticed the direction of his gaze and stopped herself, clenching her fingers into a fist and burying it in her skirts. "I am nervous," she admitted, "but I daresay no more than any girl making her debut."

Marcus nodded. "You are ready for this. You will do extremely well. I am sure of it." He reached into his pocket and withdrew a small object. "This is for you. A memento, to remember tonight."

It was a fan, finely wrought in silver, set with seed pearls, and with a wrist loop made of silk in the precise shade of her dress. "Oh, Marcus! It's lovely," she exclaimed, flipping it open. "Wait." Diana frowned, peering at the fan's leaves. "What's this?"

"It is designed to serve as both fan and dance card," he explained, gesturing to the name written on each leaf. "Those will be your partners."

She glowered up at him. "Marcus! You didn't really arrange every single one of my dances without consulting me, did you?"

"Of course, I did. I want tonight to be perfect. You don't want to be led out by a rakehell, or a fortune-hunter, or a *Tory*." Marcus wrinkled his nose in distaste.

She sighed as she slipped the loop around her wrist. "It's not so much that you chose my partners. I know hardly anyone, so I could use some guidance in that regard. But I would have liked to have at least a dance or two free so I can spend time with Lucy and Izzie."

Marcus was pleased to see that Diana's friendship with the twins had progressed to the point that they had dispensed with their titles. "You will be able to spend time with them. Between dances."

"For all of two minutes," Diana grumbled.

Marcus was unrepentant. "Trust me. It's better this way."

Diana crossed her arms. "It's my debut. Shouldn't I have some input?"

"I will let you know just as soon as your input is required." He took her arm and led her toward the stairs. "Come. It's time to make your entrance."

She cast him a sideways glare, but by the time they rounded the bend in the stairs, she had settled her features into the characteristic Latimer expression of slightly aloof elegance. The crowd fell silent, parting before them like the Red Sea as Marcus led Diana toward the ballroom.

Marcus didn't know how Diana was doing, but his heart was thundering. He was more nervous than he'd ever been in his life as he stepped through the ballroom doors. Tonight had to go perfectly for Diana. It just had to, and he hated the fact that the outcome was beyond his control with the intensity of a thousand blazing suns.

He would not have credited that a ballroom full of people could be so completely silent, but other than the whisper of silk as those in the back craned their necks to get a look at the mysterious, reclusive Lady Diana, there was not a breath of sound.

Unfortunately, this rendered the whispered remark uttered by Lady Pritchard audible not only to her daughter, for whom it had been intended but to everyone in a twenty-foot radius, including Marcus and Diana.

"It's true, the rumors are true!" Lady Pritchard hissed, screwing up her nose. "Look at her arm! Not a sight one expects to see in a ballroom."

He and Diana halted in unison. Marcus, smoldering with white-hot rage, was opening his mouth to burn Lady Pritchard to the ground when Diana lifted her chin. In an icy voice that carried across the silent ballroom, she said, "I see that you are admiring the lace on my sleeve, Mrs...."

She turned her head and regarded Lady Pritchard down

the length of her nose, scorn and confidence radiating from her ice-blue eyes in equal measure.

It was an expression of absolute superiority that was her birthright as a Latimer. It communicated her message, *because there is nothing else worth remarking upon in the vicinity of my right arm… now is there?* every bit as effectively as words could have done.

Marcus, who was matching Diana's expression with an extra dose of condescension mixed in for good measure, wasn't about to throw Lady Pritchard a lifeline by making introductions, so she was forced to sputter, "I-I am Lady Pritchard."

"Lady Pritchard." Diana's eyes now took on a slightly perplexed quality, as if she could not quite countenance that someone so obviously lacking in the social graces had managed to marry into the nobility. She shook her head slightly as if to clear it. "It is Honiton lace. The finest in England. Absolutely everyone remarks upon it."

"It is lovely." Lady Pritchard gave a nervous laugh. "You certainly carry yourself with a great deal of confidence for so young a girl."

Pity seeped into Diana's eyes. "How, exactly, did you expect the sister of a duke to carry herself?"

She did not wait for an answer, and indeed, it seemed that Lady Pritchard did not have one. "Come, brother. I am needed to open the dancing."

Now the ballroom was full of frenzied whispers. Marcus could have burst with pride. "Well done, Diana!" he murmured. "I must say, I was expecting you to be petrified before such a large crowd. How did you do that?"

She gave him a satisfied smirk. "I practiced, is what I did. I came up with that one myself. I rehearsed it, and a dozen other similar remarks, over and over with Lady Cheltenham, so I would have something withering to say for every occasion." She laughed. "Lady Cheltenham came up with some very good retorts. Lucy's were not so useful. She asked why I did not simply say, *You know, that really hurts my feelings.*"

Marcus rolled his eyes to show what he thought of that. It might work for Lady Lucy, but not for a Latimer. A Latimer did not have feelings that could be hurt, as far as the world needed to know.

"And," Diana continued, "I fear Izzie's suggestions will be of little use, either, as they are *far* too scathing—"

Marcus drew his sister to a halt and turned to face her. "Should the situation warrant it, you will use Lady Isabella's most caustic suggestions without hesitation and know that you will have my full support."

Diana's smile reached her eyes. "Thank you, Marcus."

There was a clip of shoes on the parquet floor as Diana's first partner approached. Fauconbridge bowed. "Lady Diana, I believe that the honor of the first dance is mine. Shall we?"

Marcus nodded to his friend as he surrendered his sister. He didn't like sending her out to face the wolves alone.

But, as Diana had reminded him, she was not some meek little lamb. She was a Latimer and had teeth and claws as sharp as anyone in that ballroom.

From this moment forward, she would need them.

He struggled to keep his features aloof as the orchestra struck the opening notes and his little sister made her bow.

CHAPTER 21

When a handsome man approached Ceci to claim the first dance, she started to decline on the basis that she had already promised it to Archibald Nettlethorpe-Ogilvy.

Then she realized with a start that the handsome man *was* Archibald Nettlethorpe-Ogilvy!

Now, standing across from him in the set, she couldn't quite believe her eyes. His new haircut gave shape to his face instead of swallowing it whole. And his properly fitted evening clothes made it clear that he was broad of chest, not broad of gut, and that the only things making his sleeves bulge were the impressive muscles of his arms.

The more waspish members of the *ton* liked to whisper that he looked like a blacksmith, and tonight he did, in the best possible way. As he led her out, Ceci saw several women, both debutantes and the not-so-happily married, directing admiring looks his way.

Ceci agreed that Archibald looked miles better than before. But when she looked at him, she did not feel particularly affected. He inspired no feelings of giddiness, nervousness, or the like.

Out of the corner of her eye, she caught sight of Marcus. He was stalking the edge of the ballroom like a panther, ignoring his guests in favor of watching his sister's every move. Just with that brief glimpse, Ceci felt her pulse trip and color rise to her cheeks.

She sighed. She was starting to accept that she would never see Archibald as more than a friend. But the fact was, she would probably have to marry him nonetheless.

With all of society being in attendance tonight and neither of them possessing titles, they were far enough down in the set that the dancing would not reach them for another few minutes. Ceci leaned forward. "You cut your hair."

"Yes," Archibald said, self-consciously brushing a stray lock off his forehead. "It was our host's doing. Trevissick sent his valet, Sebastian, 'round to offer my own valet a few pointers. I made the mistake of walking into the room. That was when he cornered me."

Ceci bit back a smile, and not just at the notion that a mere valet could corner the hulking man who stood before her. Marcus always acted so mortally offended by Archibald's lack of effort regarding his turn-out. Why wasn't she surprised that he had been the architect behind this transformation? "It looks very well on you."

"Thank you. I actually like it." Ceci tried to hide her astonishment that Archibald had even noticed what his hair looked like. "I could never be bothered to get it cut, but when it's this short, it takes no time at all to make myself presentable. I see now that, paradoxically, taking the time to get it cut will *save* me time in the long run."

There was no repressing her smile now. How like her friend to only care how efficiently he could move through his day, squirreling away extra minutes to be spent in his machine shop.

Archibald leaned forward. "Do you know much about our guest of honor tonight?"

"You mean Lady Diana?" At his nod, she added, "I do, a little. Lady Cheltenham has been helping her prepare to make her bow. She brought me along to play during her dancing practice."

"I am to dance with her later. The way her brother described her, I assumed she must be a helpless, doe-eyed sort of girl." He frowned. "Suffice to say, she was, er, not what I was expecting."

Ceci laughed, recalling the way Lady Diana had summarily skewered Lady Pritchard. "I believe the reason for the discrepancy lies with the duke. You won't believe it, but he is the world's most overprotective big brother."

"Ah." Archibald considered a moment. "That's consistent with what he said earlier."

"Rest assured, Lady Diana can hold her own." Ceci gestured down the line of dancers. "Just look at her—she's doing marvelously."

She truly was. Watching Diana make her way down the line of couples with Edward Astley, no one would ever guess that this was her first ball. Her steps were light and graceful, and she held her head with the confidence of a queen.

The lead couple had just reached Isabella Astley and her partner. As Lady Diana circled her friend, she whispered something in Izzie's ear that caused her to burst out laughing. An instant later, the dance carried Diana down the line, a jubilant expression on her face.

Ceci couldn't help but smile herself, to see the shy girl who had so recently been languishing in the wilds of Yorkshire enjoying her debut so thoroughly. She glanced at

Archibald in order to give him a commiserating look, but he was still staring down the line of dancers.

But it was not Lady Diana who had captured his eye. Ceci couldn't help but notice that his gaze was riveted upon Isabella, who was still smiling at her friend's jest.

Seeming to realize he had been staring, Archibald cleared his throat and turned guiltily to face front. Was it her imagination, or had his ears gone slightly pink?

That was... interesting. Ceci suddenly wondered why he was courting her and not Izzie.

The dancing reached them at last. Ceci hooked her arm through Archibald's as they began their promenade. "Will you be dancing with Lady Isabella tonight?" she asked, trying to make her voice sound natural.

He was not the most accomplished dancer, but Ceci thought it was not a coincidence that Archibald chose this moment to trip over his own foot. "L-lady Isabella? Ah, no."

The steps took them apart. When they came together again, Ceci said, "If you like, I could speak to her. See which dances she has free."

Again, they parted. If Archibald found it odd that the woman he was ostensibly courting was trying to arrange for him to dance with someone else, he gave no sign of it, for when they were reunited, he merely said, "That is very kind of you, but I have never danced with Lady Isabella before."

When the steps brought them together once more, Ceci observed, "Surely there is a first time for everything."

The next time they met, Archibald's voice held a note of melancholy. "I feel quite certain she would not want to dance with the likes of me."

Ceci let it go but felt a sudden determination to prove him wrong.

CHAPTER 22

*T*wo hours later, Marcus re-entered the ballroom. It was midway through the ball, and the supper break had just concluded. People were starting to trickle in for the resumption of the dancing.

Lady Cheltenham materialized bearing two glasses of champagne. She handed one to him. "Have you heard the latest gossip, Your Grace?"

"Most probably not," he said, clinking his glass against hers and taking a sip. He had, after all, conversed with almost no one, keeping the entirety of his attention fixed upon Diana as she made her way through the dances.

Lady Cheltenham leaned in. "Caro encountered Lady Pritchard across the punch bowl. Everyone is saying Caro cut her so hard that you could hear her neck crack."

Marcus had to tamp down a grin. "Did she truly? I am sorry to have missed that."

Lady Cheltenham sighed theatrically. "*I* wanted to be the first one to give her the cut."

"Surely that right should have gone to me. As it stands, I will probably have to call upon her one week hence to make sure her fall from grace does not become irrevocable."

The countess clucked sympathetically. "It will be an odious task, but I agree. Assuming she behaves herself, she should be offered an olive branch." She took a sip from her champagne. "In a strange sense, we should be grateful to Lady Pritchard. She gave Diana the perfect opportunity to demonstrate, publicly and inescapably, that she is not to be trifled with."

It was true. Diana's very fine riposte had set the tone for the evening. After watching Lady Pritchard go down in flames, no one was about to commit social suicide by making a snide remark about her missing hand.

Not only that, but the dancing had been going beautifully. He hadn't seen Diana miss a single step. One would have thought she had taken lessons from the finest dance masters, rather than learning the steps from Aunt Griselda on the edge of a moor.

Speaking of Aunt Griselda, she was standing in a cluster with Cecilia Chenoweth, Lady Thetford, and Lady Morsley. As Lucy Astley had borrowed her mother for a quick word, Marcus drifted over to eavesdrop.

Lady Morsley shook her head. "I still cannot believe you didn't ask me to come!"

"Anne," Lady Thetford said, "be reasonable. Your husband would have throttled us for the mere suggestion that you go to Deptford."

Lady Morsley was not placated. "I can handle my husband. And I would have been a valuable addition to your party. Out of the three of us, I'm the only one who has ever shot someone!"

The countess was referring to a bit of heroics she'd performed on behalf of the Ladies' Society, in which she had burst into a criminal lair and rescued her husband, who was being held at knifepoint. She had also rescued a dozen chimneysweep boys for good measure.

Aunt Griselda exclaimed, "You have shot someone? Very good, you must tell me the story." She hooked her arm through Lady Morsley's and towed the bewildered countess toward a pair of chairs along the wall. "Finally, there is someone interesting to talk to!"

Cecilia caught his gaze, her eyes brimming with mischief. Marcus mouthed the words *stark, raving, and mad,* and a giggle burst from her lips.

Dear God—he had just made a *joke.* Not a scathing retort or a withering set-down, but an actual joke.

What on earth had got into him?

Still, her reaction made Marcus feel a fraction better. His focus tonight had obviously been on Diana.

But he was also aware that she had danced with the newly handsome Archibald Nettlethorpe-Ogilvy.

Twice.

He was about to whisper something else to see if he could earn another one of her smiles when a sound from the far side of the ballroom made every hair on the back of his neck stand on end.

He would recognize that sound anywhere.

Diana's laugh.

He whirled around. Sure enough, Diana had just entered the room on the arm of Harrington Astley, to whom Marcus had assigned the supper dance. His curly brown head was bent down toward her golden one, and whatever she said caused him to bark out a laugh of his own. He whispered something in return which caused Diana to clutch his arm as she chortled.

It swept over him in an instant.

He had spent the last week in a state of constant anxiety

that something would go wrong and his sister would wind up crying on the night of her debut.

But that hadn't come to pass. Diana was a success—a magnificent success. Everything was going *perfectly*.

And just look—she was *happy*.

Marcus couldn't help it. He did something he absolutely never did in public.

He smiled.

The sound of shattering crystal recalled him to the ballroom. Refocusing his gaze, he saw that no fewer than four women had swooned, apparently overwhelmed by the sight of his smiling visage.

Footmen were already rushing over to clean up the mess. Marcus repressed the urge to roll his eyes as he turned his back on the recumbent women, three of whom had fainted into suspiciously flattering poses.

The orchestra was starting to tune up. Beside him, Lady Cheltenham was studying him assessingly. "You know, it's terribly bad luck for the host not to dance at least once at his own ball."

"Is that so?" Marcus had never heard of this superstition before. He was fairly certain the countess had just made it up.

But now that the suggestion was made, he found it tremendously appealing. "Miss Chenoweth," he said, setting his champagne flute on a passing footman's tray and extending a hand, "would you do me the honor?"

She accepted his hand, and he led her across the ballroom to join the set. Marcus knew people were staring at him, knew that the fact that he was dancing with Cecilia again would be remarked upon. But he was in such a jubilant mood that he didn't care. He *wanted* to dance, wanted to bask in Diana's triumph.

And there was only one person he wanted to share this moment with.

The sea of heads turned as he led her toward the top of the set, and several feminine faces settled into scowls. He hoped he wasn't effectively painting a target on her back.

They took their place at the top of the set, and the dance began. Marcus felt weightless as he skipped down the column of dancers, Cecilia on his arm. Unlike the first time they had danced, she was actually looking at him tonight, the coy expression in her gorgeous brown eyes just for him.

The feeling that swept over him was strange. Unfamiliar. He was fairly certain it was euphoria.

Was this the happiest moment of his life? He rather suspected so.

Halfway down, Marcus danced a turn with... Aunt Griselda?

"I told you I've still got it!" Aunt Griselda called to her partner, Harrington Astley.

Astley took her hand as they performed a complex series of kicks. "I didn't doubt you for a second."

Marcus caught Cecilia's eye, and did the unthinkable—he smiled, for the second time in one night.

Now the gossips' tongues would really be wagging, but Marcus didn't care. When the dance concluded, he placed Cecilia's hand upon his arm, leaned down, and whispered, "Come with me."

CHAPTER 23

*C*eci was amazed by Marcus's ability to cut through the crowded ballroom like a knife through butter.

To be sure, dozens of people came up and tried to waylay him, but he simply kept going, nodding and telling everyone he would speak to them later.

Ceci, who always seemed to get cornered by the most boring person in the room, wondered if a similar technique might work for her.

Somehow, she doubted it.

He led her up a flight of stairs to a hallway lined with portraits of his ancestors. Given that there were probably a thousand guests in attendance tonight, it wasn't deserted, but it was a far cry from the crush of the ballroom.

"So," Ceci began, straightening the skirts of her mint-green muslin gown, "which of your noble forebearers did you want to show me?"

Marcus did not appear to be attending, for he was staring down the length of the hall. Suddenly he grabbed her by the arm and hauled her... straight into the wall?

She had clearly failed to notice a door because the only

thing she smacked into was Marcus's shoulder when he stopped short in front of her. The space she found herself in was not quite pitch-black but close. A gloved finger came up and pressed her lips. Only then did Ceci realize she had yelped in surprise. "Quiet, Miss Chenoweth," came a familiar, sardonic voice. "Do you want everyone to hear you?"

"Where are we?" she hissed.

"In the secret passage, of course." She couldn't make out his face in the darkness, but she could hear the smug smile in his voice. "Come."

He threaded his fingers through hers and led her through a long, skinny corridor.

Now that she wasn't entirely discombobulated, the ramifications of being alone with one of London's most notorious rakehells in a shadowy corridor crashed over her. "What if someone saw us leave together?"

"Watch the stairs," he instructed, not slowing his pace. "They didn't. I waited for a moment when no one was looking."

Ceci struggled not to trip over her skirts as they ascended a spiral staircase with only a trace of light. "Still, someone is bound to have noticed us come in together! Do you think they will not also notice that we suddenly disappeared?"

They must be nearing a window, because there was now enough light that she could make out his eye-roll. "There are a dozen public rooms along that corridor. They'll think we went into one of them but not be sure which one."

She wrung a handful of her skirts. "But if they did see us—"

"They didn't."

"But—"

"Live a little, Miss Chenoweth."

They had reached the top of the staircase. Enough moonlight poured through a glass-paned door that Ceci could finally see properly. Marcus opened the door and gestured for her to go through, and—*oh!*

It was a little stone balcony, perhaps ten feet across, with a balustrade of sculpted marble and a little stone bench just big enough for two. There were no blossoms on the rose bushes sprouting from the two stone urns positioned at either end, and the plants had been pruned back in anticipation of the autumn chill. But they were at the very top of Latimer House on a cloudless night, and the balcony needed no other adornment than the brilliant, starry sky above them.

"Oh, M—" She bit her lip, realizing she had almost called him Marcus. "It's beautiful," she added hastily.

He smirked as he led her over to the railing. "I suspected you would like it."

She tipped her head back to look at the stars. The orchestra was playing a cotillion, the music light and beautiful, just close enough to hear but far enough away to feel like they were in their own little world.

Ceci rubbed her bare arm with a gloved hand. How she wished she had her shawl. Were it not for the distinct possibility of freezing to death, she would stay out here all night.

Marcus suddenly came up behind her, pressing his chest against her back and wrapping his arms around her. Ceci yelped in surprise, then laughed nervously. "Wh-what are you doing?"

"You're cold," he said, and he was standing so close, she could feel his vocal cords vibrating against her temple.

Ceci shuddered as if to prove his point, but this time for an entirely different reason. "A proper gentleman would offer me his coat."

"What a shame there isn't a proper gentleman here." He squeezed her tight. "I prefer this. I suspect you do, too."

It was a good thing it was dark out because Ceci was blushing so hard she had a horrible suspicion her face had gone blotchy. "This is… nice," she admitted.

"Thank God you think so because most of my coats fit tightly enough that I can't get into them without help from my valet. I'd return to the party looking a rumpled mess, and then everyone would know you'd had your wicked way with me."

Ceci snorted. "Oh, yes. Seductive temptress that I am."

He trailed a hand up her arm, his gloved fingers leaving gooseflesh in their wake, then stroked across her collarbone. His voice was dark as he murmured, "You won't hear any argument from me."

She stepped hastily to the side. This moment was so unexpected, she hadn't had a blessed minute to decide what she wanted. On the one hand, being on a starlight-drenched balcony with Marcus Latimer was the stuff of her daydreams.

But, no matter what they did tonight, he wasn't going to marry her. He had told her so directly. *Inescapably*. He had, in fact, asked for her help in finding someone else to marry!

Although a part of her didn't care. She had never expected that Marcus would want to marry the likes of her. And, if someone had noticed their disappearance, she would be ruined regardless of whether she allowed herself to enjoy the kiss she'd been dreaming about for years.

Maybe it wouldn't hurt to indulge her fantasy. Not enough to truly ruin her.

But surely one memory wasn't too much to ask.

She was a little nervous about looking at Marcus, as she had pushed him off, and she had enough experience to know that most men did not take rejection well. But when she finally summoned the courage to raise her eyes, she found him looking at her with patient amusement.

That amusement turned to smug satisfaction as she edged back toward him along the railing. Still, he didn't make things easy for her. "So," she said awkwardly, once her shoulder was pressing against his.

"So," he returned. She could hear the laughter in his voice.

"I, um…" She cast about for something to say. "You mentioned your valet earlier. Mr. Nettlethorpe-Ogilvy said you were the one who sent him to his house, and he was the architect behind his remarkable transformation."

Oh, dear—*that* had not been the correct thing to say if the scowl that descended over his features was any indication.

"You find his transformation remarkable, do you?"

She gave a nervous laugh. "He certainly looks different."

His cold eyes bored into hers. "Do you find him handsome?"

"Many women do, I think. I saw him receiving a number of admiring looks as we crossed the ballroom."

He spun away from the balustrade, placing a hand on either side of her, trapping her against the marble railing. His voice when he whispered in her ear was as black as midnight. "I did not ask about *many women*, Miss Chenoweth. I asked about *you*."

She was breathing hard as if she had been running. "He is certainly not the most handsome man of my acquaintance."

She felt the whisper of his breath on her throat. "And who would that be?"

She swallowed. "I think you know."

He gave a satisfied purr, and she felt the rumble deep in the pit of her stomach. "But he's such a good man, Nettlethorpe-Ogilvy. *He* would never whisk you off to a deserted balcony."

Ceci froze. It happened that the one and only time Archibald had kissed her, he had done precisely that.

She turned her head a fraction and found Marcus's gaze

fixed on her. "He has, hasn't he? Did he kiss you?" He read the answer in her eyes, and his scowl deepened. "Was it tonight? Under my own roof?" he growled.

"N-no!" she gasped. "It was weeks ago."

"Weeks ago?" Now his frown was one of confusion. "And he hasn't tried to do it again? Just how bad was this kiss?"

"It wasn't bad! It was..."—Ceci combed through her brain for a word that wouldn't be an outright lie—"entirely tolerable."

"*Tolerable?* A kiss should not be *tolerable.*"

"Oh, it should be intolerable, then?"

Now she was really in trouble because he had released the balustrade. He peeled off his gloves and threw them to the tiles at their feet. Just as his fingertips found the delicate skin of her upper arms, his rich, dark voice returned to her ear. "If a man knows the first thing about kissing, then the thing that will be intolerable is every minute that comes afterward, when his lips are not on yours. A real kiss will haunt your dreams. You will *ache* for it."

"I already ache for it," Ceci blurted, then froze, realizing what she had said.

"Ah, my sweet, innocent Cecilia." He brought his hands up and framed her face, his fingertips a warm contrast to the cool night air. "I will *always* relieve that ache."

Had she been capable of speech, she would have said something like *Yes* or *Please* or *For the love of God, hurry*. But the best she could do was to close her eyes and tip her head up toward his.

She was therefore surprised when his lips descended not upon hers, but on her neck. Who knew a neck could be so sensitive? She hadn't, but she certainly did now. She gasped. She shuddered. Her trembling hands grasped at his shoulders, frantically searching for anything resembling a bearing as she was roiled by wave after wave of sensation.

Marcus growled his approval and pulled her body flush against his. And Ceci might have been an innocent, but her best friend was married—*very* happily married—and Caro had told her enough about what went on between a man and a woman that she knew exactly what the steely bulge pressing into the softness of her stomach meant. Marcus might not be undone, as she was.

But make no mistake—he wanted her with an equal ferocity.

He was kissing his way up her neck, across her jaw, and then on her earlobe, which made her sink her nails into his shoulder. He did not seem to mind, for his growl was one of approval.

And then he started inching closer to her lips. First, he kissed her temple. Then, it was her cheekbone. He pressed another kiss just a fraction of an inch closer. And it all felt wonderful but also dreadful, because she needed his lips upon hers, needed them *now*, and when he feathered another butterfly kiss across her jaw, she turned her head and claimed his lips with her own.

She could tell she had caught him off guard, but he recovered immediately. And oh! If this was what kissing was, it was a wonder people ever did anything else! Marcus kissed the way a virtuoso violinist performed a concerto: with absolute confidence, precision, and passion. His lips were soft as satin and their every brush caused new nerves to spark to life. Ceci could feel a crescendo carrying her higher and higher, and she wondered how high she was capable of going.

Marcus answered that question, at least in part—*higher than this*—by sweeping his tongue across the seam of her lips. She opened for him without thinking, trusting implicitly that, whatever he wanted to do to her, she would enjoy it.

That was when the trembling began in earnest. Whether

his tongue was sweeping across her lips, teasing the roof of her mouth, or tangling with hers, the effect was the same: pleasure, of such a blinding intensity that she felt it not just where their lips met, but in other places as well. Her nipples, which were hard as stones, and not just due to the chill night air. Her skin, which craved his hands. And the juncture between her thighs, which had begun to throb like a heartbeat.

She couldn't get enough. Had she not been so overwhelmed by the sensations he was invoking in her, she would have been mortified by the way she was rubbing herself against him, like a cat begging to be petted, and by the tremulous whimpers that kept rising in her throat. But she was too far gone to feel embarrassed. She felt nothing but pleasure tangled up with desperation.

Marcus slid his lips off hers and began kissing his way down her neck. She responded with a moan of protest and felt his lips curve into a smile against her throat.

"What?" she gasped.

"I knew it would be like this with you," he said, nuzzling the point where her pulse thundered. "I knew it from the first time I heard you play."

"And how exactly am I?" she asked, heart pounding.

"*Perfect.*" His eyes locked upon her heaving bosom. He tore his gaze up to hers. "If you don't want me to touch you here, tell me so at once."

"No, I…" He looked up sharply, no doubt thinking she was refusing him, when that had been the opposite of her intention. "I do want it," she admitted.

He was cupping her breasts before she had even closed her mouth. His hands, as he had bragged before, were big, but her breasts were bigger and overflowed his grasp. He groaned, his expression one of savoring as he tested the weight of her.

Ceci bit her lip. Her nipples, she was discovering, were exquisitely sensitive, and she wanted so much more than this tentative touch.

Abruptly, his hands disappeared. She yelped in protest, then noticed that they were skimming over the front of her bodice. "I must see you," he said, undoing pins with a suspicious level of efficiency. Within seconds, he had her gown gaping open. He reached inside her stays and chemise and lifted her breasts out, exposing them to the cool night air.

Abruptly self-conscious, Ceci had to tamp down the impulse to cover herself with her hands. While she tried not to spend too much time worrying about such things, she knew that her figure was more curvaceous than what was considered fashionable. Meanwhile, Marcus had probably never taken a lover whose body was less than perfect.

"My *God*, Cecilia."

Cringing, she squeezed her eyes open, unsure if his response was one of approval or revulsion.

His nostrils were flared, his face curled into a snarl. Ceci fumbled to pull up the bib closure of her dress with trembling fingers. "I'm sorry."

"Sorry?" He tore his eyes from her chest, his expression offended. He snatched her hands up in his and pulled them away from her dress. "Don't you dare think there's anything wrong with you. There's not. You are *magnificent*." He reached out and filled his hands with her breasts, and a groan rose from deep in his throat. "You cannot imagine how I have dreamed of this moment."

"You... you have?" she gasped.

"*Yes*."

Ceci wasn't able to formulate a reply, because that was the moment he started circling his thumbs over her nipples. And *oh*—that felt almost *too* good! The wicked sensations drove away any trace of self-consciousness. In the face of this onslaught of pleasure, there was no room to worry about anything else.

With a snarl, Marcus knelt before her on the smooth grey pavement stones and sank his lips into the lower swell of her right breast. Ceci began making a blubbering sound, which was embarrassing, but she couldn't seem to stop herself. She felt his tongue upon her skin, and then his teeth, and cried out in frustration. Without meaning to do it, she dug her hands into his hair, her fingernails scouring his scalp, and guided his mouth up to her nipple where she needed it.

He growled his approval before giving her the long, deep pull she craved. Now they were both making animal sounds. He was suckling her so hard, she would probably have bruises come the morning, but the sensations he was evoking were so delicious she didn't care.

He removed his lips from her nipple, and she clawed desperately at his shoulders, trying to hold him in place. When it turned out he was only switching to the other side, she forgave him in an instant.

Another minute of his ministrations and her whole body was bucking and shaking. She felt pleasure, so much pleasure, from what he was doing. But a different sensation, one of unmet need, centered at the meeting of her thighs, had been building with each passing moment, and now it reached the point in which her agony exceeded her elation.

Ceci cried out in frustration. Marcus rose smoothly.

"No, Marcus! Please! I—I need..."

"Hush," he soothed. "I will take care of you."

He led her to the bench and positioned her so that she was lying on her back. She was so far gone that she made no protest as he bent her knees and then drew her skirts up to her waist, exposing her most intimate parts to the moonlight. He slipped down to kneel between her trembling thighs. "Ah,

Cecilia." He pressed a kiss to the delicate skin between her legs. "You are so beautiful here as well."

Without further preamble, he spread her legs wider and pressed a kiss to that special pearl hidden within her folds. Innocent though she might be, Ceci knew about this spot. Although she had never been daring enough to touch herself there, Caro had told her that this was the place from which a woman derived the most exquisite pleasure.

But nothing Caro had described could have possibly prepared her for the sensations Marcus was evoking. He made a lazy swirl around her center with his tongue, and her entire body jolted. It wasn't merely that she had never experienced so much pleasure before. Ceci had never imagined that this level of bliss could exist.

She dimly realized that her fingers were digging into his scalp as if she were afraid he would try to escape. If Marcus was contemplating such a move, he gave no sign of it. His eyes were fierce as he looked up at her, reveling in her enjoyment of his ministrations. When he adjusted himself slightly, stroking a fresh batch of nerves, Ceci cried out and arched her back. She could feel him groan against her core, could see his excitement at her obvious pleasure in his eyes.

She was growing more desperate. He switched from the light, flicking motion he had been using to laving her with the flat of his tongue. She sat halfway up, a string of babble spewing from her mouth. Encouraged, he increased his pace, and although she had never experienced it before, Ceci knew she was about to crest. The pleasure was unimaginable, almost unbearable.

He held her there on the precipice for an eternity that was probably no more than three seconds, and then she tumbled over. Wave after wave of pleasure assaulted her. Her legs were shaking wildly, and she threw her head back like a pagan sacrifice to the moon and stars overhead.

Some time must have passed before she next became aware of anything, because Marcus had risen from the ground and was now seated on the bench, her head in his lap. His smile was the very definition of smug male satisfaction.

Ceci tried to sit up but immediately swayed. Marcus smirked as he pulled her to him, cradling her head against his shoulder.

From this angle, she was staring down at the still-prominent bulge straining the front of his breeches. She looked up at him guiltily. "Do you want me to, um… do something? For you?"

He tucked one of her curls back in place. "As much as I do want that, I fear I have kept you away from the party for too long as it is. We'd best make our way back before our absence is noticed."

"I'm sorry," she said in a rush. "I don't know what came over me. I should have—"

"Hush. You were overwhelmed at your first experience of pleasure."

It was a statement, not a question, but he happened to be correct. Flushing, Ceci nodded.

He looked even more smug than usual, which was really saying something. "I cannot tell you how pleased I am to have been the one who got to show you that."

He drew her to her feet, and the look he gave her made her toes curl in her slippers. His whisper was husky in her ear. "My turn will come soon, I hope."

She nodded jerkily.

"Come. We must restore you to rights."

Ceci's hands shook as she tried to re-pin her bodice. Marcus brushed her off and set about doing it himself, proving to be as competent as any lady's maid. Ceci shuddered to think how many women he had performed a similar service for, to be so adept at it.

"Almost done," he said, but he was struggling with the final pin. "Ah, I see the problem. Your necklace is tangled up in the fabric."

He pulled it out and started to unsnarl the chain, but suddenly froze. The self-satisfied expression was gone in an instant, his face falling curiously blank as he held the black metal key up to examine it in the moonlight.

"Where on earth," he said slowly, "did you get *this*?"

*C*eci gave a nervous chuckle. She tried to take the key from him, but he was peering intently at the twisted snake in the moonlight.

She cleared her throat. "Never mind that. I know it looks macabre. It's something my father gave me, just before he died."

Marcus's eyes flew to hers. "Do you mean to tell me that your father, the *vicar*, had a key to Paradisium?"

Ceci gasped. "You know what it is?" At his nod, her hand flew up, covering his where it still grasped the key. "What did you say it was called? Para…"

"*Paradisium Voluptatis* is its full name. It's Latin, meaning "paradise of pleasure," one of the names used in the Bible to refer to the Garden of Eden. Better known as Paradisium for short."

Ceci stroked her thumb along the shaft of the black key. "Hence the snake." She shook her head, unable to quite believe she was finally learning the identity of the key, and so unexpectedly. "I never would have guessed something so sinister was a biblical reference. Is it some sort of religious society, then?"

He snorted. "Not in the slightest. Paradisium is what's known as a hellfire club." She stared at him blankly, and he added, "A hellfire club is a place where men go to get up to the most shocking, most depraved behavior."

Ceci frowned, looking at the key. "So, it's a gentlemen's club but more scandalous than White's. More like Boodle's?" she asked, referring to the establishment men went to when they really wanted to play deep.

He laughed. "No, my innocent Cecilia. Nothing like Boodle's. How can I phrase this... The reason you have never heard of Paradisium is that nothing that is done there is suitable for a young lady's ears. At Boodle's, the behavior might be ill-advised. Drinking too much, playing too deep. But a man goes to Paradisium to do things from which his reputation would never recover. Things, in some cases, for which he might hang."

Ceci glanced up at him, alarmed. How did Marcus know all of this? Surely he wasn't a member of such a place? She knew he had a terrible reputation but hadn't thought it was quite *that* terrible. "You seem to know a lot about it."

One corner of his mouth twitched. "Only a bit. My father was one of the founding members, and he secured a membership for me when I came of age. I went exactly once, to see what the fuss was about. I made Fauconbridge go with me—that will give you an idea of how much trouble I got up to. We wandered around for an hour, then left."

Ceci's shoulders sagged with relief. "Well, if Edward was there, I know you didn't commit any hanging offenses. Frankly, I'm surprised he agreed to go."

"I'm not. Fauconbridge might be a bit of a square, but he's loyal. He could see I was curious enough that I was going to visit, with or without him. He wasn't about to let me go in there alone."

She bit her lip. "Why did you never go back?"

"Do not mistake me—I'm no choirboy. I earned every stain on my reputation. But wandering around Paradisium"—he stared out into the night as if trying to find the right words—"there honestly wasn't that much to see. Lots of empty hallways lined with closed doors. There were horrible sounds coming from behind some of those doors— screams and the like. A few men were in the public rooms, passed out with drink or insensible with opium." He shrugged. "It did not strike me that anyone there was enjoying themselves all that much, nor did it seem like a path I wanted to be on. I decided I preferred my more pedestrian vices."

She gave a nervous laugh. At his curious look, she said, "It's just that I'm sure your vices, as you put them, would not seem at all pedestrian to me. But, of course, men are allowed to do such things. Before marriage. And after it."

She could feel her cheeks burning. Why had she added that last bit? Whatever Marcus planned to get up to after he married, it was absolutely no business of hers.

He was studying her. She tried to turn away, but he caught her beneath the chin and forced her to look at him. "It is true that society looks the other way when men fail to keep their wedding vows. But you should know, Cecilia, that I am going to be faithful to my wife."

She laughed, incredulous.

"No, really," he continued. "It has always been my intention. It is why I have sown my wild oats so thoroughly. But I am not two and twenty anymore. I can honestly say that I am ready to settle down."

His eyes were sincere, an unfamiliar look for Marcus Latimer, but a terribly appealing one. It was so easy to imagine that this message was for her, that it was important to him that she believe his words.

But, of course, that was ridiculous. She wasn't going to be his bride. He had made that inescapably clear.

"I can see your skepticism," he continued. "But it's true. You see, my father was unfaithful to my mother…"

He trailed off, staring out into the night. Ceci's heart suddenly ached for him.

She squeezed his arm. "You're nothing like your father, Marcus. You know that, don't you?"

"I do. I have made certain of it. But what I'm trying to say is that his unfaithfulness hurt her. It was one hurt among a great many, but I know that it did. And"—he made a slashing motion with his hand—"I will never hurt my wife that way."

"I know you won't," Ceci whispered. "You would never do that."

The strangest thing was, she really did believe him.

She had seen the absolute respect in which he held his aunt and sister, and the reverence with which he spoke about his mother.

She was probably an idiot for believing that one of the most notorious rakes in London, a man who had probably taken dozens of lovers, was really going to be faithful to one woman for the rest of his life.

But believe him she did.

It was probably her imagination, but she fancied she saw relief in his eyes. "Good," he said gruffly. He cleared his throat. "So, regarding your key. Do you have any idea how it came into your father's possession?"

"I don't. He pressed it into my hands with his last few breaths." She squeezed her eyes shut, remembering. "By that point, he couldn't speak very fluidly, but he gave me to understand that it was, well, the key to unlocking the secret of my mother's death." She frowned. "I don't see how, though. Even if it will unlock the front door, the secret could be anywhere inside. It could take a lifetime to find it."

"Ah. It would be a problem, were it a key to the front door."

She glanced up at him, startled. "Is it not?"

"No. You don't need a key to get into Paradisium. Were it that simple, your father could have marched through the door as soon as this came into his possession. The door is guarded, and only members, and their guests, are admitted."

"But you're a member," Ceci breathed.

"I am, and I will gladly go and see what's inside the locker that opens to this key."

"Thank you." Tears pricked at the back of Ceci's eyes. Was it possible? Was she truly going to learn what had happened to her mother?

She accepted Marcus's proffered handkerchief and dabbed at her eyes. "You said it opened a locker. What kind of locker?"

"They were intended to be wine lockers so members could bring in their preferred libations. But, as I said, the doormen are very strict about only admitting members. I'm given to understand that the wine lockers therefore became a convenient place to store all manner of contraband. More secure than even a safe deposit box."

Ceci rubbed her thumb along the shaft of the key. "I wonder what we'll find inside."

"It could be anything. But I do find it intriguing that you have key number four. There were seven founding members who presumably received the first seven keys. So, it is likely that this once belonged to one of them."

Biting her lip, Ceci drew the chain up over her head. She had worn it everywhere with her for the past year, scarcely taking it off. It felt strange not to have the familiar weight against her heart, and she felt a pang as she handed it over to Marcus.

He was studying her face. "What is it?"

"Oh, nothing. It's just that I've spent the last year guarding that key, taking it everywhere with me. It's not that I don't trust you," she hastened to reassure him. "But I do wish I could be there in the moment you open the locker."

One corner of his mouth turned up. "What impeccable timing you have."

She blinked at him, not following. "Whatever do you mean?"

"Once a year, Paradisium hosts a masquerade ball. It is a recruitment event of sorts for prospective members and the most inconspicuous occasion for me to show up with a guest. It happens that this year's ball will take place the day after tomorrow. If you like, I could bring you."

"Oh!" Ceci froze. She did want to be there when the locker opened.

But she wasn't so naive as to imagine it was a good idea for a virginal young woman to attend a masquerade ball at such a place.

Marcus seemed to be thinking along the same lines. "Just to be clear, if you are spotted, if someone realizes who you are, you will be ruined. Completely, irrevocably ruined. But, as it is a masquerade ball, there is some chance of concealment." His face split into a lazy grin. "I wouldn't have even mentioned it to most young ladies. But you're not most young ladies. You're the girl who went to Deptford."

Ceci nodded tightly. "I know you need an answer. But may I think about it overnight?"

"Of course." He draped the chain around her neck again, his lips twisting wryly as he tucked the key securely into her bosom. "Come, we need to return you to the party."

They slipped back into the hall of portraits and made

their way back to the ballroom. If anyone had spotted them, there was no indication of it.

Just after four in the morning, the ball ended and Ceci piled into the Astley carriage to make her way home.

She should have fallen asleep the moment her head hit the pillow after such a long night.

Instead, she lay awake, staring at the shifting shadows on the ceiling, thinking not about her interlude with Marcus on the balcony, but what on earth she was going to do next.

CHAPTER 25

*A*s much as he would've liked to sleep until midday, Marcus dragged himself from his bed at ten o'clock sharp the next morning. The errand he had to perform was that important.

It turned out that he wasn't the only one. Diana and Aunt Griselda were also waiting under the front portico as the carriage pulled 'round to take Ellery to the posting inn from which he would depart to pay a much overdue visit to his family.

He and Ellery took the rear-facing seat, leaving the forward-facing one to the ladies. "Too much fuss," Ellery clucked, although Marcus suspected he was secretly pleased. "I could've just walked."

"And I could have insisted upon sending you the entire way to Holywell in the ducal carriage," Marcus countered, "with a full complement of outriders and footmen. In fact, I would still like to do just that."

"Absolutely not," Ellery said, looking scandalized. "I would rather not go than put Your Grace to such trouble."

That was the only reason Marcus had finally yielded—because Ellery had threatened to cancel his trip entirely.

"I still say you should have departed the moment the old duke dropped dead," Marcus said. "It is a travesty that you haven't visited your family in more than twenty years."

Ellery drew himself up with wounded dignity. "And missed Lady Diana's debut? Out of the question."

"She was a sight to behold," Aunt Griselda said. "Diana did splendidly. As I knew she would."

Marcus joined in the collective murmurs of agreement. Of course, he would never forget his sister's triumph.

But the real revelation last night had been Cecilia Chenoweth. If he lived to be as old as Noah, he would never forget the sight of her, undone by her innate passion, lost to everything but the pleasure he was giving her. He still could not believe she had trusted him like that, that she had offered herself to him so sweetly in the moonlight.

A thought had been rattling around his head ever since. He knew he had told her that he intended to marry someone else.

But really, there was no reason he couldn't marry Cecilia Chenoweth. He didn't need an heiress. He was already obscenely rich. And, although there would be gossip were he to marry so far beneath his station, when had he ever given a damn what people were saying behind his back?

He had always known that he would have to marry one day and had assumed that, when the time came, he would do so with a sense of resignation.

But the notion of marrying Cecilia was... surprisingly appealing...

"Marcus. Marcus!"

He blinked to attention and found his three companions staring at him expectantly. "Yes?"

"Is it all right?" Diana asked.

It appeared his thoughts had wandered for longer than he had realized. "Is what all right?"

"The horse, and the house party," Diana said, a trace of exasperation in her voice.

"Tell me again?"

Diana rolled her eyes. "I spoke with Lord Thetford while we were dancing. He has offered to train a saddle horse just for me. It will be accustomed to one-handed reining, and he said he could train it to be ridden sidesaddle without a crop."

This was one of the challenges Diana faced—although any horse that was cavalry-trained could be steered with one hand, those animals relied heavily on signals being conveyed through the legs. Diana solved this problem by riding astride in Yorkshire where there was no one around to see, but in Town, she would be expected to ride sidesaddle. Complicating things further, horses trained for sidesaddle relied upon a riding crop to signal the horse in the place of the rider's leg on its far side. Managing both reins and a crop with one hand was challenging under ideal circumstances, and Marcus worried what might happen if the horse were to spook.

Diana continued, "He says he has some experience training horses for former soldiers who have returned from the war missing an arm or a leg. There is a particular filly he has in mind for me who is highly intelligent. If we're interested, he will train her over the winter, and she'll be ready for me next Season. What do you think?"

Thetford would probably charge him a small fortune. But the viscount really did train the best horseflesh, and in truth, Marcus wouldn't want his sister riding anything else. "I think it a splendid suggestion. If it is something you desire, then by all means, tell him to proceed."

"Very good. I will." Diana looked pleased and relieved. It

struck Marcus that it was no trifle for her to be able to go for a ride in the park like every other girl of her station.

She leaned forward. "And what about the house party?"

Marcus tilted his head. "Which house party was this?"

"Gracious, Marcus! Were you even attending? I was just saying that the Astleys are going to the Cadogans' estate for a few days. It is in Broxbourne, just a couple of hours outside of London. They invited me to join them."

Marcus knew the Cadogans. Mrs. Cadogan was first cousin to Lady Cheltenham. He had even paid a visit to their estate in Broxbourne. "Do you wish to attend?"

"I do," Diana said. "Lucy and Izzie will be there. And Aunt Griselda has offered to come as my chaperone."

"That's fine, then." Marcus leaned back against the squabs, his thoughts again drifting to Cecilia.

"You seem distracted, nephew," Aunt Griselda observed. "Reminiscing about your dance?"

Marcus narrowed his eyes at Aunt Griselda. She'd made a few pointed remarks about Cecilia this morning, suggesting that their absence from the ballroom had been noticed. He sought to change the subject. "I wasn't the only one. I saw you dancing as well, Aunt."

"If one is to be seen dancing, one always prefers it to be on the arm of a handsome young officer." Aunt Griselda nudged Diana with her elbow. "Isn't that right, Diana?"

Marcus repressed the urge to snort. Aunt Griselda clearly did not realize that the officer in question was the insufferable Harrington Astley, the man who had once stolen all of Marcus's trousers and hung them from the top of Eton's Lupton Tower, forcing him to scurry bare-arsed across the schoolyard to retrieve them.

Marcus glanced at Diana and found that her cheeks had turned scarlet. Frowning, he reached for the latch on the carriage window.

"What are you doing?" Diana asked.

"Opening the window," he said crisply.

She gave him a strange look. "I can see that. What I meant was, why are you opening the window on such a cool autumn morning?"

"Because you are overheated."

Diana pulled her blue Kashmiri shawl more closely around her shoulders as the glass pane slid open. "I'm not. In fact, I wish you would shut that."

"Your cheeks are flushed," he countered, reaching for the latch on the other window.

Diana slumped down in her seat, glowering at the buildings streaking by outside the carriage. "Why listen to me? What would I know about whether I'm overheated?"

Marcus ignored her sarcasm and was just propping the second pane open when he heard his sister gasp.

He turned to peer through the window on Diana's side of the carriage to see what had shocked his sister.

What he saw shocked Marcus, too.

He pounded his fist on the roof. "Stop the carriage!"

A crowd had gathered around the man and the two children, blocking one section of the junction. Marcus shouldered his way through, ignoring the yelps of protest he left in his wake.

The man swayed on his feet. Dirt streaked his face, and he smelled like the only bath he'd had in months had been in a vat of blue ruin.

Barely half ten and drunk as a wheelbarrow.

"A bob," he slurred. "I told you, don't show yer face unless you've got a bob each for me. And what's this?" He held up a few coins, his expression derisive. "Just four pence between the two of you! And what do I see but breadcrumbs on yer dress." He grabbed the girl, who Marcus knew from his work with the Ladies' Society was probably around eight, even though she was closer in size to a five-year-old.

"You bought rolls!" the man thundered while the girl shrank backward. "I didn't give you leave to buy no rolls!"

Marcus had almost reached the front of the scrum of onlookers. The boy, who couldn't be older than ten, clenched his scrawny hands into fists. "Leave her be! It was just the one roll, for Molly. We didn't have nothin' to eat yesterday, and she was hungry!"

"You'll eat after you've brought me my two shillings!" the man shouted. "Worthless brat!"

Several things happened in rapid succession.

First, the man raised his fist, no doubt to backhand the little girl again. That was what Marcus and Diana had seen him do through the carriage window.

But her brother shoved her out of the way, stepping into the path of the drunkard's arcing fist. "*Neil!*" Molly screamed.

Marcus decided he liked Neil. Quite a lot, in spite of the fact that he was a barefoot street urchin who was literally crawling with lice.

Fortunately, this was the moment Marcus finally pushed to the front of the crowd. He pulled his sword free of its sheath with a metallic hiss and stepped in front of Neil and Molly, pointing the blade at their worthless father. "Touch them and I'll gut you like a fish."

The drunkard recoiled, swaying off balance in a way that would've been comical under different circumstances. He recovered and came blustering forward. "You've got some nerve! You might be some rich toff, but you ain't got no say here. These two are mine, and a father has the right—no, the duty—to flog his children when they step out of line."

This happened to be true in a legal sense. A man was the head of his family and could beat his wife and children as much as he pleased. This was the reason no one in the crowd had lifted a finger to help. However much they might disapprove, the man was within his legal rights.

It happened that Marcus didn't give a toss about this piece of shit's legal rights. "This is my authority," he snapped, slashing his sword so that it hissed through the cool autumn air. "You'll have a hard time filing a complaint when you're lying dead in the street."

The man's face had turned ruddy with rage. "You'll hang for murder!"

Marcus gave the man a contemptuous look. "As a duke, I can only be tried before the House of Lords. Do you really imagine they would convict me for ridding London of such worthless filth?"

Not that the members of the peerage who would serve as his jurors, should it come to that, cared about children like Neil and Molly. But the prevailing evidence suggested that the father was forcing his children to support his drinking habit through petty theft and pickpocketry. And if there was one thing the members of the peerage hated, it was having their precious baubles stolen.

Marcus therefore spoke sincerely when he added, "They'd probably petition the king to grant me another title."

The man's hands clenched into fists. Marcus watched his face turn from red to burgundy and felt sure he was about to explode.

"Fine!" he snapped, rounding on his children. "But that's it! You two are dead to me now. Don't come around begging when ye need my support!" He spat upon the cobblestone street. "I'm well rid of ye both."

He spun on his heel, pushing and shoving his way through the crowd until he disappeared from sight.

Marcus slid his sword back into its scabbard. That had gone more easily than he had thought. "James," he called to one of his footmen, "take Neil and Molly to the Ladies' Society. Mrs. Godfrey will know what to do."

James strode over and gestured for the children to follow him. There was a smattering of applause from what was left of the crowd as Marcus turned on his heel and climbed back into his carriage. He did not acknowledge it. He hadn't done it for an ovation.

He had done it because, even though the gulf of position and fortune that lay between them was as vast as the North Sea, he had once been that little boy.

Nobody said anything as he resumed his seat in the carriage. None of his companions' faces bore a trace of surprise.

This was his family, after all. They knew who he was.

Marcus rapped upon the ceiling of the carriage. "Drive on."

CHAPTER 26

*T*hat afternoon, Caro came over to take tea with Ceci. They huddled together in Ceci's room so they would not be overheard.

Ceci had just finished telling her friend about everything that had happened on the balcony... and she did mean everything. Caro had always been open with her, and prior to last night, everything Ceci knew about what went on between a man and a woman had come courtesy of her friend. She trusted Caro's discretion implicitly.

"So now," Ceci concluded, "I don't know what I should do."

"La! You should marry him, of course!"

"Marry him?" Ceci hissed. She had thought it obvious that this was *not* the question she was asking, seeing as this option was *not* on the table.

Her, a duchess? Had her friend taken leave of her senses?

Caro leaned forward, dropping her voice low. "It came as a surprise to me, as I've never so much as kissed anyone but Henry, who is a very generous lover. But I'm given to understand that most husbands do not perform the *particular service* you received from the duke. That he was willing to put aside his own pleasure to take care of you is an excellent sign. And you've always pined for him. I know you have. Now that you've established that the two of you are compatible, there is no reason to hesitate."

"No reason, other than the fact that he has not asked me," Ceci muttered.

"He will." Caro reached for a biscuit. "Mark my words, he will."

"He won't!" Ceci set her cup aside. Why was her friend unable to grasp this simple truth?

Caro took a prim bite of her biscuit. "Have you seen the way he looks at you? The same way the lion in the Tower menagerie looks at a beefsteak."

Ceci cast her eyes heavenwards. "He specifically told me he won't marry me!"

Caro shrugged a negligent shoulder. "Henry said the same thing about me, if you recall. Look how that turned out."

"That was entirely different. Henry made that remark when he was one and twenty. It was less an indictment of you so much as an expression of not wishing to marry anyone so young. Marcus, on the other hand—"

"Oh," Caro trilled, "it's *Marcus* now, is it?"

"—declared he wouldn't marry me less than a week ago, while emphasizing that he is looking for a bride and hopes to marry in the coming weeks." She gave a miserable laugh. "It just won't be to me."

Caro smiled as if she had not heard her. "You cannot imagine how insufferable I'm going to be once you're a duchess."

"Caro!"

Caro poured herself another cup of tea. "So, if you're calling him Marcus, is he calling you Ceci?"

"Yes. Well… no. He seems to have settled upon 'Cecilia.'"

"Have you told him you usually go by Ceci?"

"No. Mostly because… there's something about the way he says it. *Cecilia.*" A shiver coursed down her spine even at her pale imitation of the duke's deep voice. "It… does things to me."

Caro took another biscuit. "Good things, from the sound of it."

"Yes. But we've wandered off track. The question I am contemplating is whether I should attend this masquerade ball at Paradisium, or whether I should stay home and let Marcus retrieve whatever's in that locker."

Caro didn't even hesitate. "You should go, of course."

Ceci rubbed her temple. "If I'm recognized, I would be irreparably ruined."

"So, don't get recognized. It's a masquerade ball. All you need is the right costume."

"Which I do not have, nor do I have time to pop into one of the costume shops to find something suitable."

Caro waved her teaspoon. "Leave that to me. I've the perfect solution. Henry and I will accompany you and act as your chaperones."

Ceci shook her head. "That won't help. This isn't riding with a man in a closed carriage, where the presence of my married friend can save me from ruination. This is an entirely different level of scandal."

"It is, but I daresay you'll feel more comfortable with Henry and me there, regardless. And I will take care of renting you a costume. La, I have to go 'round and choose something for us to wear anyway. It will be no trouble to get something for you at the same time." Caro leaned forward and squeezed Ceci's hand. "There are costumes in which no one will recognize you, Ceci. You must trust me on this."

Ceci sat back, considering. People wore all sorts of

bizarre costumes to these things, some of which concealed the wearer from head to toe.

"You promise you'll get me something where no one will recognize me?" Ceci asked. "Like the bear or the coffin with feet?"

"Precisely! Just leave it all to me. By the time I'm through with you, no one will ever guess that a modest vicar's daughter is the woman beneath the mask."

Ceci bit her lip. The truth was, she did want to go. Partially because she wanted to be there to see her father's mission at last come to fruition.

But if she was being honest, she also wanted another evening, and another adventure, with Marcus.

"All right, then," Ceci said grudgingly. "Thank you."

Caro squealed. "You won't be sorry. You know how much I enjoy planning the perfect ensemble. Now, what do you think Henry and I should go as? Romeo and Juliet? Too trite?" She frowned, noticing Ceci's drawn expression. "What's wrong? You're not having second thoughts already, are you?"

"It's not that." Ceci felt heat flood her cheeks. "It's just... I also need to decide what to do about Marcus."

"We've already discussed this. You should marry—"

"Can we please stop talking in circles?" Ceci interjected. "He is not going to ask me to marry him. It is settled. Final. Irrefutable."

Caro eyed her knowingly. "And yet, even given your assumption—your *erroneous* assumption, I should say—that a proposal will not be forthcoming, you want to continue your affair."

Ceci wrung her hands. "I feel like the most terrible person in the world. Because I know I'm probably going to wind up marrying Archibald before the year is out. But the truth is..." She closed her eyes, swallowing. "I do want to have another rendezvous with Marcus. Even knowing nothing will come of it. I just want to know how it can be with someone I'm completely enamored with." She looked at her friend, her eyes beseeching. "Do you think I'm horrible?"

"Not in the slightest. Although,"—Caro leaned forward and squeezed Ceci's hand—"I do not think you should marry Archibald if you have so little enthusiasm for the match."

"What choice do I have? And don't say that I should marry Marcus. That is not a realistic option."

"Surely you know that you will always have a place with my family. You have friends, Ceci. Friends who care about you."

Ceci shook her head. "I'm imposing."

"You're not. I know my mother is happy to have you. Why, look what a tremendous help you were with Diana's dancing lessons! You're a part of the family."

Ceci sighed. "Your mother has told me as much a hundred times. But almost a year has passed, and still, I *feel* as if I am imposing. It seems that no amount of kindness or reassurance can banish that particular conviction. No, if Archibald proposes, I have to accept, as there is no guarantee that I would ever receive another offer. And that is why I feel so wretched for even considering an affair with Marcus. How could I do that to Archibald? He deserves a bride who will come to him a maiden, not one who might be carrying another man's child."

A gleam came into Caro's eyes. "There are things you could do, ways to give and receive pleasure, that would leave your maidenhood intact. Similar to what you did with the duke on the balcony."

Ceci took up her teacup but only to wring the handle. "It's one thing to be on the receiving end of such an act. But I have absolutely no idea how to go about performing one."

Caro's smile was smug. "And that is why you have me."

She set her teacup down and leaned forward. "I'm going to tell you *exactly* what to do…"

CHAPTER 27

"*I hate* you."

"La! Of course you don't!"

"I do." For the seventeenth time, Ceci reached beneath her cloak and attempted to tug the bodice of her Cleopatra costume up so it concealed some fraction of her decolletage. For the seventeenth time, she failed. In addition to the fact that the costume was intended to be daring, it had been cut for someone with a far less substantial bosom.

On Ceci, it left almost nothing to the imagination.

She glared at Caro, seated across from her in the hackney carriage that was conveying them to Paradisium. Caro wore a frilly pink shepherdess costume. She looked beautiful in it, naturally, as fresh as a spring morning and the perfect blend of innocent and alluring.

Her husband, who was dressed as a wolf, appeared to agree. He had been grinning at his wife for the entirety of the carriage ride in a manner that was entirely apropos for his costume.

"I told you to get me the bear or the coffin with feet! Something that would conceal me entirely!"

Caro tutted. "Ceci, you are meant to be on the duke's arm tonight, playing the role of his paramour. Do you honestly expect people to believe that the duke's lover would come dressed as a coffin?"

Ceci groaned. She hadn't thought of that, but of course, Caro was right. Everyone would expect Marcus to have the most gorgeous woman in the room on his arm. "Still, you could have chosen me something a bit more modest."

Caro shook her head, causing the blonde ringlets Fanny had carefully sculpted to bounce. "You're supposed to match with your escort, the way Henry and I do. Wait until you see what His Grace is coming as. Then you'll understand why your costume is so perfect."

"Perfect?" Ceci glared at her friend in disbelief.

"Perfect," Caro insisted. "Also, between the mask and wig, it offers excellent concealment. Only a tiny bit of your face is showing."

Ceci had to own that this was true. The costume came with its own mask painted to look like her eyes were rimmed with kohl. Combined with the black wig, which had a fringe concealing her entire forehead, the only parts of her face that were visible were her lips and chin.

Caro laughed. "And trust me, no one is going to suspect it's you. Everything about that costume screams *Goddess of the Nile*, not *shrinking vicar's daughter*."

Ceci reached into her reticule for the item she had grabbed as she left, just in case she lost her nerve. "That's it. I'm putting on my fichu."

"Don't you dare!" Caro hissed, grabbing for the filmy white cloth. "You'll ruin the line of the dress!"

A brief struggle ensued, complicated by Caro's shepherdess crook, which had been laid diagonally across the carriage's interior with one end sticking out a window. "Let... it... go!" Ceci grunted, pulling on the length of cloth.

"Cleopatra did *not* wear a fichu!" Caro gave a cry of triumph as the filmy cloth slipped from Ceci's grasp.

"Do you know what I think?" Henry asked. "I think you should turn this into a show. People would pay a lot of money to watch the two of you wrestle over that fichu, especially if you do it in those costumes."

Caro rapped her husband's knuckles with her fan, but she was smiling. "Henry, you are absolutely atrocious. Ah, here we are."

"Give me back my fichu," Ceci hissed as the carriage drew to a halt around the corner from the club's entrance.

Caro opened the door and scurried onto the pavement, smiling triumphantly. "Oh, what a shame! I seem to have dropped your fichu in this great, muddy puddle. Don't fret, I'll get you another one." Her eyes held an evil gleam as she added, "*Tomorrow*." She raised a hand and waved. "Your Grace! Your Grace, over here!"

Ceci stumbled out of the carriage just in time to see Marcus striding toward them. She froze, jaw agape, because he was wearing a *skirt*, and a short one at that. He had paired it with sandals that, in spite of his leather shin guards, left most of his legs exposed to both Ceci's gaze and the cool night air. The skirt was made of brown leather strips and fell a few inches above his knees. He had completed his costume with a matching leather breastplate, a plumed helmet which he carried under his arm, and a red cloak draped jauntily over one shoulder.

Her frazzled brain finally pieced together that he was dressed as a Roman centurion. On ninety-nine men out of a hundred, the costume would have looked absurd.

But—she could not believe she was having occasion to think this—Marcus Latimer had *gorgeous* legs, the perfect combination of lithe and muscled, and dusted with golden hair.

She dropped her gaze to the pavement and swallowed thickly as her eyes fell upon his toes. Dear God, even his feet were beautiful.

"Here, Ceci. Let me help you with your cloak."

Ceci was so disconcerted that she only realized Caro's intentions after her plain brown woolen cloak was being whisked away from her shoulders. She made a futile grab for it, but her friend was too quick.

Swallowing, she turned to face Marcus, forcing herself to lift her chin.

He did not do anything so graceless as to stumble or stagger. But she saw a flare of heat flash through his eyes as his gaze swept up and down her body. His pace slowed, taking on a leonine quality, as if he were stalking his prey—which, of course, was her.

"Miss Chenoweth," he said darkly, taking her hand and maintaining eye contact as he pressed a kiss not to her knuckles but to the inside of her wrist.

The moment was broken by Lord Thetford, who suddenly loomed between them. "You can't call her that. She's supposed to be in disguise."

Marcus's eyes did not leave hers. "Right you are. We shall have to go by our characters' names for the evening."

Ceci cleared her throat nervously. "I'm not sure I'll remember to answer to Cleopatra."

"Good." The duke ran his thumb across the palm of her hand. "Because I prefer to address you as 'Goddess.' You'll only have to remember to call me Marcus."

She blinked up at him, entirely disoriented. "Marcus?"

He gave an elegant sweep of his hand. "I am Marcus Antonius, of course."

Suddenly she understood the reason Caro had said her costume was perfect.

They were dressed as two of history's most legendary lovers.

"Mark Antony and Cleopatra," she observed. "I'm not sure this was a good idea."

"I can assure you, your costume is the best idea."

"Things didn't end well for Antony and Cleopatra."

His blue eyes, normally as chill as ice, were molten. "No. But I have a feeling we will both be reaching a happy ending tonight."

"Come with me, *Marcus*," Lord Thetford snapped, grabbing the duke by the shoulder. "We need to have a little chat."

The two men removed themselves a few feet and began to argue in hushed whispers. Ceci couldn't hear what was being said, but they were clearly in disagreement.

Marcus eventually said something that gave Lord Thetford pause. He narrowed his eyes, pointing a finger at the duke's chest. Marcus held up his hands placatingly, and whatever he said was apparently good enough to satisfy Caro's husband, because he gave a grudging nod, and the two of them strode back over.

Marcus offered Ceci his arm. "Shall we?"

He led them around the corner to Paradisium's main entrance. A red carpet had been laid over the white marble steps for the occasion of the masquerade.

The plan was for Caro and Henry to watch over her from afar. Caro was far more recognizable than Ceci, and standing next to her good friend would increase the odds that someone might make the connection and guess Ceci's identity. Once they crossed the threshold, Caro therefore mouthed the words, "Good luck," before sweeping across the room on her husband's arm.

Marcus had donned his plumed helmet, which had an

attached mask of burgundy velvet in the same shade as his cape. Even with the mask, he was instantly recognizable. Surely no other man in London could have pulled off that skirt.

They hadn't even made it across the foyer when a man dressed as a satyr waylaid Marcus with a hand upon his arm. It took Ceci a moment to recognize him as Lord Winthrop.

"Bloody hell, Trevissick," Lord Winthrop said, his gaze sweeping up and down Ceci's body before coming to rest upon her chest. "You have all the luck."

Marcus hmphed in agreement as they continued to the ballroom.

It was on the smaller side but otherwise looked much like any other ballroom, and Ceci supposed what was going on could be termed dancing. But only in the loosest sense. Drunken, lascivious lurching would be a more apt description.

The good news was, she was starting to feel less self-conscious about her costume. One woman, dressed as Gaia, was naked from the waist up, her costume consisting only of a few artfully draped vines of silk leaves. Another was clothed from shoulders to feet, but, as the muslin was so thin as to be entirely transparent, she might as well have been nude.

And she knew she was comparing herself with women who were actual courtesans. But suddenly her costume's deep vee neckline felt positively modest.

The tension in her spine eased a fraction.

Marcus leaned down to her ear. "Do you want to dance?"

"Um..."

A man dressed as the devil lurched past them, in pursuit of an equally drunken nun. He caught the nun around the waist, and the two of them went down in a tangle, then began engaging in sloppy, open-mouthed kisses. In the small room, they were taking up a good third of the space that was intended for dancing.

"Perhaps not," Marcus said wryly.

"Maybe some punch?" Ceci suggested, spying a refreshment table in the corner.

Marcus shook his head. "I would advise against the punch. God only knows what it's been adulterated with. *They* probably had the punch," he said, tilting his head toward the couple on the floor, who were now grinding against each other, heedless of the throng that surrounded them.

"I see." Ceci bit her lip as she scanned the room. "I feel as though we should stay at least a short while. It will draw too much attention if we go straight to the locker and then immediately leave."

"I agree."

"Is there a garden, or—"

"I say, Trevissick," a masculine voice said. "Where'd you find this ripe little thing?"

An older man dressed in a garish yellow jester costume materialized before them. Ceci was horrified to see his hand reaching toward her breast.

Marcus slapped it down before he could touch her. "Hands to yourself, Dorrington. She's mine." His gaze swept up and down Ceci's body. "And I am not willing to share."

The man chuckled as he stared at Ceci's breasts. "I daresay I would keep her all to myself, too. Well, there's no need to wish you an enjoyable night. It's clear you're going to have one."

Marcus made a grunt of agreement as he led Ceci away. They'd made it all of four steps when another man stepped into their path. He was dressed as Cupid and looked the part with curling blond ringlets and a jaw so smooth it could only be because his beard was yet to come in. He was staring at Ceci with a hangdog sort of longing.

"Who's your friend, Trevissick?" he asked, gripping his bow with white knuckles.

"None of your concern," Marcus said, leading Ceci around.

The young man stepped defiantly into their path. "Look," he said, eyes entreating. "I know she's yours for tonight—"

Marcus's jaw had tightened to steel. "For more than tonight."

He once again tried to lead Ceci around the young man, but he had the nerve to reach out and grab the duke by the arm. "She's perfect," the young man said, voice tremulous. "Utterly perfect. And we both know you're going to tire of her in a fortnight. She'll be wanting a protector after that. And that could be me." He turned to Ceci, giving her a hopeful smile.

"You're mistaken," Marcus said, shifting his gaze to Ceci's face. He reached up and brushed a strand of her wig off of her face. It was hard to make out his expression due to his mask, but his eyes were tender as he said, "I've decided I'm keeping her."

Ceci reminded her poor, stupid heart, which had begun tripping hopefully, that Marcus was playing a role tonight. That his insistence that he wanted to keep her was merely a gallantry. She mustn't take these words at face value, because that certainly wasn't how he had meant them.

Marcus ignored the young man's sputtered protests as he swept across the ballroom, Ceci in tow.

He bent his head to her ear. "We've got to get you out of here. With you looking so delectable, pretty soon I'm going to have to start beating men back with my sword."

Ceci nodded. She was feeling stunned by the reactions she had elicited thus far. On the one hand, it was overwhelming, coming into this den of excess and sin, and slightly terrifying, having strange men try to grab at her person. Why, if she didn't have Marcus beside her, they would have succeeded!

But being here, on Marcus's arm, was also exciting. And, even if their attentions were executed in such a way as to be an insult rather than a compliment, the fact that so many men were casting lustful looks her way made her realize something. She had always thought of herself as the pudgy rector's daughter who blended into the wallpaper.

But maybe that wasn't right. Maybe she had attractions she had never properly considered.

Maybe when Marcus referred to her as a goddess, he wasn't just making sport.

They had come to a long hallway, richly carpeted in burgundy and gold and lit by glowing sconces on the walls. Marcus turned to the footman standing at attention. "We'd like a room."

"Of course, Your Grace," he said with a bow. "If you'll follow me."

Ceci was so preoccupied by her racing thoughts that she hadn't given any consideration to where Marcus was taking her.

Glancing around, she saw that they had been brought to a small but elegantly appointed bedroom with a gleaming four-poster bed hung with crimson silk curtains and a matching counterpane.

"Will this do, Your Grace?" the footman asked.

"It will," Marcus said, nodding as he handed him a coin.

The footman retreated silently, and then they were alone.

Ceci swallowed. Well, if she was going to take Caro's advice, she would not find a better opportunity than this.

Now it just remained to see if she had the courage to go through with it.

CHAPTER 28

The second Marcus saw Cecilia in her Cleopatra costume, he decided he was going to have one commissioned for her just as soon as they were married.

That they were getting married was now beyond question. If he was only going to fuck one woman for the rest of his life, that woman needed to be Cecilia Chenoweth.

He could already picture the improved costume. It would be made of a finer muslin, one that was slightly transparent. It would be designed to be worn without chemise or corset so he could see both her rosy nipples and the dark triangle at the juncture of her thighs.

He wanted to see her not in that mask, but with real kohl lining her sloe eyes. Bastian could figure out how to apply it. He was going to order her a pair of golden sandals, and he would wager he could find some gold bracelets in the Latimer family vault. Speaking of the family vault, there was an emerald amongst the family jewels the size of a quail's egg. He was going to have it set as a pendant with a golden chain in the shape of a snake. Already he could picture it dangling seductively around her neck, nestled between her breasts.

Yes, he was going to buy her that costume.

And then, they were going to lock themselves in the ducal bedchamber for a week.

She peered around the room, her expression one of wonder and curiosity. One could be forgiven for expecting a virginal miss to fly into hysterics at the prospect of being closeted in a bedroom at a den of iniquity with a known scoundrel.

But, as he had come to discover, Cecilia Chenoweth wasn't your typical virginal young miss.

He cleared his throat. "I thought we might spend an hour or so in here." He crossed the small room in two steps, coming to stand behind her, then trailed his fingertips up her arm. "What could be more natural than that I would desire to be alone with you?"

Marcus knew exactly how he wanted to spend the next hour, but he didn't want her to feel forced. Still, he couldn't resist bending down to press a kiss against her nape.

Abruptly, she spun to face him, sliding her arms up around his neck and pressing her breasts against him. The coquettish gleam in her eyes looked... promising. "How shall we pass the time, Your Grace?" she asked suggestively, trailing a hand across his chest.

He responded with a growl, backing her up against the wall and capturing her lips in a ferocious kiss. While he devoured her mouth, his fingers fumbled with the shoulder buckles holding his breastplate in place. He wanted the damned thing off. He longed to feel those glorious breasts pressing against him.

The breastplate fell to the floor, leaving him in only a short-sleeved, red linen tunic and the leather belt from which the cingulum, the leather strips that formed a skirt of sorts, dangled. He pulled her flush against him. They both groaned at the contact. Marcus was on fire for her, had been for weeks, and that was before he saw her in this glorious excuse for a dress. A little voice in the back of his head—his conscience, perhaps? Who would've imagined that he had such a thing?—reminded him that she was both a virgin and his future duchess, so he couldn't rip the dress from her body with his teeth and fuck her right up against the wall.

But, innocent though Cecilia might have been, timid she was not. Her tongue tangled with his with little art but great enthusiasm, and her hands could not seem to get enough of his chest through the thin linen of his tunic. When Marcus brought his hands up to cup her glorious breasts, she groaned aloud and bit his lip, but he didn't mind. He loved pleasuring her to the point that she lost control.

Her mask and wig were somehow already on the floor. He yanked open the ties at the back of her dress, then slid the sleeves down her shoulders. She helped him, sliding her arms free as he lifted her breasts out of her corset. This was his first time seeing them in proper lighting. *"Oh, Cecilia,"* he said, caressing a nipple with his thumb. They were *perfect*. Big. Round. A delectable shade of cream, with pinkish-brown nipples large enough to fill his mouth.

Nothing roused Marcus like a woman's breasts. And Cecilia Chenoweth's were everything he had been fantasizing about since he was fourteen years old.

The next thing he knew, he had captured both of her wrists in one of his hands and was pinning them to the wall over her head. His mouth was on hers, and his other hand was making free with her exposed breasts, cupping and stroking and rubbing. If she minded this high-handed behavior, she gave no sign of it. Instead, she was mewling with pleasure, rubbing herself against him, demanding more of his attention.

He released her wrists with a growl, ready to shove her back on the bed and give her what she so clearly wanted. But she stayed him, placing her hands on his shoulders. "Marcus." Mischief gleamed in her eyes as she ran her hands down his chest... across his stomach... then came to rest on the bulge that had formed beneath his tunic. "Oh, my. What do we have here?"

Before he could form an answer, she slipped one of her petal-soft hands beneath his tunic and wrapped it around his length, and the only sound he managed to make was a whimper.

She pushed his tunic up, laughing. "Marcus! I can't believe you're not wearing anything beneath this skirt!"

He shook his head. He was breathing hard, and his hands were fumbling with the buckle of his belt, eager to get the damn thing out of the way. "Bastian won't even let me own a pair of drawers. He says they would only ruin the line of my breeches."

His belt and skirt finally gave way. He tossed them aside, then all but ripped his tunic up over his head. He was now naked but for his sandals and leather greaves.

Cecilia looked stunned by the sight of him. She ran a tentative hand across the corded muscles of his stomach. "My God, Marcus," she breathed.

He started to pull her toward the bed, but she stayed him with a hand. "Wait!" She swallowed, and he got the impression that she was gathering up her courage. Slowly, holding his gaze the entire time, she slid down until she was kneeling at his feet. Taking his cock in her hand, she pressed a reverent kiss against his head, then looked back up at him with those captivating brown eyes. "It looks as if Your Grace could use some help with this," she said earnestly, and Marcus wanted her mouth on him so badly he thought he was going to die.

She leaned forward, hesitating for only the slightest instant, and took him into her mouth. Her friend must have told her what to do. She had little technique, but it didn't matter. The sight of Cecilia Chenoweth kneeling at his feet, eyes closed reverently, her gorgeous breasts trembling as she slid her mouth tentatively along his length was more erotic than anything he'd beheld in more than a decade of debauchery.

He slid his hands into her hair. "Use your hand, too," he instructed. "Get it wet... *yes, Cecilia.* Now, grip me harder... Yes, like *that.* My *God,* that feels good."

She had picked up the rhythm, had figured out how to work her hand and mouth in concert. He was already getting close. He'd been anticipating this moment, and anticipating it ravenously, ever since he saw her lose herself in the music at the piano bench, had been chasing this climax for the last week. For even longer, if he was being honest. He'd wanted Cecilia from the first moment he'd laid eyes on her. But he'd never imagined that this passionate creature was hiding inside the meek façade she presented to the world.

She swirled her tongue over the head of his cock, and he moaned. She glanced up to gauge his reaction, and that was his undoing. Because she held his gaze, and the sight of Cecilia Chenoweth's gorgeous brown eyes staring up at him while her mouth was wrapped around his cock undid him completely. Utterly. *Irrevocably.*

He would've barked out a warning had he possessed a single shred of presence of mind. But he didn't, and so what he did instead was make a feral sound in the back of his throat as he flooded her mouth with cum.

He vaguely registered her eyes going wide with surprise for the briefest instant. But she didn't stop working his cock with her hand and mouth, and the pleasure was so overwhelming, Marcus wasn't aware of anything else for a time.

When the room swam back into focus, he found he was slumped against the wall. His cock, which had gone halfway soft, was already twitching, letting him know that it would be up for a second round—literally.

And there was Cecilia, still sitting at his feet, beaming up at him as if sucking him off had been her fondest wish come true.

And really, Marcus had already decided she was going to be his duchess.

But now he felt more sure of his decision than ever. Having this woman by his side, both on his arm and in his bed, would be a pleasure, in every sense of the word.

He reached down, helping her to her feet, then kissed her deeply before ushering her to the bed. He kicked off his sandals and greaves; he didn't want anything coming between him and her petal-soft skin. He proceeded to strip her in record time, groaning as each delectable, curvaceous inch was revealed to his hungry eyes.

Once they were both nude, he took her into his arms, and merciful fuck, if that didn't feel perfect. He tended to be a bit lean, while Cecilia was lush, and it was slightly pathetic how much he liked the feel of her soft curves pressing against him.

"My darling Cecilia." He swept a hand down her side, teasing her nipple with her thumb, and she shuddered against him. "I do believe that was the most intense orgasm I have ever had." He looked her in the eyes and pitched his voice low. "How shall I reward you?"

She was stunned speechless, but Marcus didn't mind. If the way she was squirming against him was any indication, she was every bit as eager for what they were about to do as he was.

If sucking his cock aroused her, then she was going to be very, very aroused in the future, and he was going to be the most happily married man in all of England.

He kissed her, wanting to take his time, to linger over her. But those glorious breasts were filling his hands, and soon he had to have them in his mouth. She made a cry of frustration as his lips broke from hers, but it soon turned into a sound of pleasure as he tugged one of those dusky nipples into his mouth and began to suck.

He soon had her writhing on the bed, sobbing his name and begging him to give her the release her body craved. He couldn't resist lying atop her just for a moment, a delicious preview of what would soon come. It felt *glorious*, having her beneath him. But it was his turn to give her the ultimate pleasure she had so guilelessly given him, so he muttered soothing platitudes as he kissed his way across her stomach, pressing her legs open as he went.

He found her glistening and slick, just for him. The smell of her was indescribably sweet, and he couldn't wait to taste her. Nuzzling her folds apart, he buried his face between her legs, going straight to the little pearl that was the center of her bliss.

As she had been on the balcony, she was immediately overwhelmed by the pleasure he was giving her, unable to control her body's writhing and unaware when she pulled his hair in her desperation to position his mouth over *just* the right spot. Marcus didn't mind a bit. He licked at her pearl with a light, flicking touch, reveling in the way it made her incandescent with pleasure.

Propping himself up on an elbow, he slid a finger inside her, still tonguing her all the while. Ah, there it was, that slightly rough patch that denoted the bundle of nerves on the front wall of her passage.

Cecilia froze at his unexpected invasion, but only for a

second. She immediately came roaring back, digging her nails into his scalp and babbling nonsense.

Marcus could sense she was getting close, so he took her pearl into his mouth and started giving her suction. That was all it took—her back arched, and the sight of her beautiful breasts thrusting out made his cock give an eager pulse. He continued sucking her and rubbing her front wall with his finger while her legs shook around his head. When her thighs clamped around his ears, he let up at last, interpreting that as a signal that she had crossed that threshold where the pleasure was too intense to bear.

He slid up the bed and took her in his arms. She was breathing hard, so he took a few moments to enjoy her soft skin beneath his fingertips and the way she fit perfectly upon his shoulder.

Once her breathing calmed, she chuckled nervously.

"What is it?" he asked.

"Nothing. It's just... you're ready for another round." She flexed her hips, nudging his cock, which had indeed risen to the occasion.

He brushed a stray lock back from her forehead. "I am. What would you like?"

She looked down rather than at him. "It's just... I feel like I should save the act itself for my eventual husband."

Marcus frowned. That was an odd way of phrasing it, but he honestly didn't mind if she wanted to wait until after they were married for him to take her maidenhead.

There were *plenty* of other things they could do tonight.

In fact... glancing at her magnificent breasts resting against his chest, an idea occurred to him that made his cock twitch eagerly against her stomach.

"That's fine. I understand why you might prefer to save that particular act for after the wedding." He sat up, taking a breast in each hand. He couldn't resist caressing her nipples with his thumbs and was gratified when she shuddered.

He was probably going to shock her. Oh, well—she'd best get used to it. He fully intended to fuck this woman a hundred different ways, in every room and against every surface of both Latimer House and Hallane Hall back in Cornwall.

And that was just for starters.

"There's something I've always wanted to try," he began.

"What's that?" she asked, her voice breathless.

He pushed her breasts together, moaning at the sight of the soft, welcoming nest they formed. "Would you let me fuck you here?"

CHAPTER 29

*C*eci blinked up at Marcus as he knelt above her on the bed.

She knew she was an innocent.

But she was feeling especially confused.

"Would I let you fu—" She broke off, embarrassed by what she had almost said. "I'm not sure I understand."

"I will hold your breasts together, like so"—he began sliding a finger back and forth in the pocket he had just created—"and my cock will go here."

"Oh!" Ceci glanced from her breasts to his swollen cock. It was now straining toward the ceiling, and a bead of moisture had formed at its tip. She bit her lip. "And that feels good for you?"

"Yes. That is to say, I think it would."

Her eyes flew to his. "So you've... never done this before?"

He ran a hand down her side, lingering over her breasts, her waist, and her hip. "It's only possible with a woman who has a truly exceptional figure. As you do, Cecilia."

She was struggling to wrap her head around the notion

that he found her figure *exceptional* when he added, "It is the thing I have always longed to try. And I will confess, ever since the very first moment I saw you, I have fantasized about doing it with you."

Ceci sat up, making an incredulous sound. "Really, Marcus! We both know that isn't true."

He stared at her chest, mesmerized. "Oh, but it is."

She hmphed. "The first time you saw me, you reviled me."

He tore his gaze from her breasts to glare at her, offended. "I most certainly did not!"

"You did so! I'll never forget it—it was the most mortifying moment of my life. I was taking tea with Caro, and just as I took a sip, she said something so funny, I"—she swallowed, the humiliation washing over her once more—"I snorted, and tea came out of my nose." She flicked her wrist at him. "And right as I did it, who should come walking into the room but the most handsome man I'd ever seen?"

Marcus frowned. "I don't remember that."

"See?" Ceci jabbed a finger into his stomach, then flinched, shaking her hand. It was as hard as an anvil. "I was so unremarkable you didn't notice me at all."

He narrowed his eyes at her. "The first time I saw you was the day before Lord and Lady Thetford's wedding. You had just come up from the country to see your friend marry. I came to collect Fauconbridge so we could go fence at Angelo's, and the two of you were in the morning room. You were wearing a long-sleeved gown of mustard yellow flocked with brown diamonds."

Ceci blinked up at him, disbelieving. That *was* the gown she'd had on; there was a tiny but stubborn tea stain on the sleeve that she'd never been able to get out. "That... that's right. You even remember my dress."

"Of course, I remember it." He shook his head, his lip

curling. "The neckline came all the way up to your collarbone, *and* you were wearing a fichu. It was a *tragedy*."

"It's a morning dress, Marcus! Most people don't sport a plunging neckline at nine o'clock in the..." She broke off, rubbing her forehead. This was all beside the point. "How is it possible that you remember all of that, but you don't remember me snorting tea out of my nose?"

He shrugged a negligent shoulder. "Well, I don't."

"And what was Caro wearing?"

"I haven't the faintest idea."

Ceci was in a state of disbelief. It made no sense that he had noticed her, but not Caro, who was widely hailed as the most beautiful woman in all of England. "But... you gave me the most derisive look. As if you found me beneath you in every way."

"Oh, I was imagining you beneath me, all right."

"Marcus! Be serious!" She poked him in the chest this time. It went every bit as badly for her as when she'd attempted to poke him in the stomach. Gracious, did he have even an ounce of fat on him?

"I am being serious. Think about it—I sport a derisive sneer upward of ninety percent of the time. It is simply what my face looks like at rest."

Ceci considered his handsome face, which was currently set in... a derisive sneer. He had a point. "So, that's your excuse? That it was merely your"—she gestured to her own face, trying to come up with an appropriate phrase—"resting duke face?"

"Precisely. Although it's entirely possible that I was scowling." His nose wrinkled in distaste. "It still makes me scowl, thinking about that fichu."

She rubbed her temple. "Allow me to make sure I understand. The first time you saw me, you were so preoccupied with staring at my bosom that you did not even notice when I snorted tea out of my nose?"

He cupped one of her breasts. "Who can blame me? Just look at you, Cecilia. You're *magnificent.*"

"And while I was sitting there feeling mortified, you were picturing yourself"—she waved a hand, struggling to find the words—"*thrusting* into my chest?"

"You have it precisely. So," he said, giving her a cheeky smirk, "what do you say?"

She considered his request. On the one hand, she had never imagined herself participating in such a depraved act.

And yet... this was the thing he longed for. He'd been dreaming of it for years but had never done it before, had never had a lover who was built to carry it off. And, as he was planning on being faithful to his future wife, the odds seemed high that this would be his only chance to live out this particular fantasy.

She was even the one he pictured when he imagined doing it.

She felt her enthusiasm building. Yes, she would give him this, a memory to last a lifetime. Even if she could not be his wife, even if they were both married to other people by this time next year, he would always remember her as the one who had made his utmost desire come true.

Recalling Caro's advice that she should act confident and coquettish, even if she felt ridiculous, she sat up, thrusting out her breasts. She flattened her hands upon his thighs and slid them up, deliberately avoiding his straining cock before coming to rest upon his stomach.

It helped her confidence that her clumsy attempt was so obviously working. Marcus was breathing hard, his hands were clenched into fists, and his expression was ravenous.

She pressed her lips reverently against his stomach before

looking up at him and batting her eyes. "You know I would do anything to please Your Grace."

The next thing she knew, she was flat on her back. Marcus growled as he swung a leg over her to straddle her torso. He took a breast in each hand and pressed them together. "Just look at you, Cecilia. If you only knew how I've dreamed of this..." He suddenly released her, reaching toward the side table. "We should use some oil."

Ceci noticed for the first time that a variety of items had been laid out on the bedside table, many of which she didn't recognize, such as the translucent white strips floating in a glass jar. She could guess the purpose of the little flasks of oil. But why was there a length of rope? And... was that a riding crop? What on earth was that doing there?

She glanced up at Marcus and found him arching a questioning eyebrow. "Is anything the matter?"

"No, it's just—someone forgot their riding crop."

That smile, the one that was neither a sneer nor a smirk, the one that was rarer than diamonds, broke across his handsome face.

"What?" she asked, sensing that he was laughing at her.

He bent and kissed her. "Never change, Cecilia."

"But what—"

"I'll tell you later. Right now"—he drizzled a generous portion of oil onto his palm, then slicked it over the valley between her breasts—"I cannot wait another second to have you."

Ceci tried to lie still, but it was difficult not to wriggle, especially when one of his thumbs strayed across her nipple. Marcus didn't seem to have noticed. He was now using his oiled hand to lubricate his cock, his eyes going glassy with pleasure as he slid it up and down his length.

He groaned, pulling his hand away. Taking a breast in each hand, he pressed them together. He slid his cock into the chasm he created, and his eyes rolled back inside his head.

He recovered quickly, his gaze rapt upon her chest as he slid his length back and forth. "My *God*, Cecilia."

"Does it feel good, then?"

"It does," he moaned. "But it's mostly the sight that is so arousing. You are beyond *anything* I could've imagined."

Ceci found she was enjoying this strange act more than she had expected. Marcus's hands, slick from the oil, could not help but slide over her nipples as he pressed her breasts together. The slippery friction felt *so good*, and a cry escaped her lips.

His rhythm faltered, but only for a second. "You like this, too," he breathed, a statement, not a question.

"Y-yes." She bit her lip, trying to stay quiet, but then he started rubbing her nipples with his slick thumbs. "Marcus!"

"Put your hand between your legs," he ordered.

She lifted her head, shocked. "Put my... my..."

"*Do it.*" She could see veins standing out on the side of his neck. Blushing, Ceci complied, and—*oh, merciful heavens*, it felt so good to touch the little pearl he had shown her at the juncture of her thighs! With a whimper, she began tracing little circles over her special spot.

"Rub yourself," he ordered, "in the same place that I..." He glanced over his shoulder and smirked. "You're already doing it." Still pumping his cock between her breasts and working her nipples with his fingers, he drawled, "My dear, sweet, Cecilia, how do you manage to be so perfect? It wasn't enough that you have the body of a goddess. Oh, no— beneath your quiet little shell, you have this magnificently sensuous nature. And now, you're letting me do this. You have destroyed me completely. I will never be the same after tonight. I hope you're satisfied."

His thrusts were becoming faster, more disjointed, and

his voice was growing ragged. Her fingers were flying between her legs, and little sounds of pleasure were burbling from her mouth. "That's it," Marcus grunted. "Let me watch you take your pleasure. Let me see the moment you are overwhelmed. Here, maybe this will help."

He pinched her nipples then, pinched them *hard*, and, indeed, it did help. Suddenly Ceci was on the edge of the knife, where the pleasure was almost too much to bear, but also not enough, not nearly enough. Her fingers slipped as she struggled to move them faster, desperate to bring herself off.

And then, she tumbled headlong into bliss. She could feel her core pulsating against her fingers as her thighs clamped down around her hand. Her head tipped back, and she was crying out, crying his name, crying a bunch of garbled nonsense, truth be told, but how could she be expected to form actual words when she was drowning in a tidal wave of pleasure?

She looked up at Marcus and knew in an instant that she would never forget the way he was looking at her. Any nagging fear or doubt that he might not have really meant it when he referred to her as a goddess was swept away by the raw worship radiating from his eyes. She also saw his pleasure on his face, although clearly, he had not been swept away as she had been. Suddenly she wondered if there was anything she could do to make this even better for him.

She stroked her hands over his thighs, trying to think what she might do. It occurred to her in a flash—with each thrust, the tip of his cock emerged from between the cushion of her breasts. If she tipped her head down, she thought she could manage to kiss him there...

It worked better than she could have imagined; not only did she manage to press her lips against him, but the head of his cock slipped inside her mouth.

His body jerked, and his rhythm faltered. She found him staring down at her with wide eyes. "*Cecilia?*"

She felt her cheeks flush. "Does that feel good? If it does, I can—"

"It feels *incredible*. Don't stop. Please, use your mouth on me too—yes, *yes*, just like that, darling." He had picked up the rhythm again and was thrusting faster than ever. "*Fuck*, that feels amazing, that feels *beyond* amazing, and the fact that you're willing to do this for me... Oh, how I am going to reward you for this. I am going to *worship* your pussy. You are going to beg me to stop licking you there, you're going to be so tender. And then, the second you've recovered, you're going to beg me to do it again, because I am going to make it *so fucking good* for you. You are going to be *exhausted* from the number of orgasms I'm going to give you."

She loved seeing him like this, stripped of his usual reserve, desperate for the pleasure she was giving him. She couldn't say anything back as her mouth was being filled with his cock with each of his strokes, but she ran her fingers up his backside and squeezed his toned buttocks, digging her nails in just a bit, trying to show him that she was as eager for what they were doing as he was.

He was thrusting so quickly she didn't have time to do much other than let the tip of his cock slide between her lips. Although, based on the filthy words that continued to pour from his mouth, he seemed to be enjoying what little she was able to do. With a little experimentation, she realized that she could at least flick the tip of her tongue over the underside of his cock with each stroke.

The effect was instantaneous. "*Fuck, Cecilia!*" he shouted. "*Oh, my fucking*—" Then he was coming, coming in her mouth, coming on her breasts and her neck and even her face as he continued to thrust, shouting all the while about what a very good girl she was and that she was going to pay for this, and the way she was going to pay was by sitting on his face and coming over and over again until she collapsed from sheer exhaustion.

Abruptly, his body sagged, and *he* was the one who collapsed, landing with a thump beside her. His eyes were closed, and his breathing was labored.

Ceci started to pull him to her but stopped when she noticed what a mess she was. Between the oil and the seed he had spilled on her chest, she was well and truly a disaster.

She struggled to sit up without spilling the mess onto the red satin counterpane. Marcus's eyes popped open. "Wait." He pressed a quick kiss to her lips. "Stay right there."

He slid off the bed and padded over to the washbasin, then returned with a pitcher, a stack of towels, and a bar of rose-scented soap. It took some doing to get all of the oil off of her, but five towels later, they declared victory, and Marcus climbed back onto the bed, taking her in his arms.

He kissed her deeply. "That was incredible. *Incredible.* You cannot imagine how I am going to reward you for the exquisite pleasure you just gave me. What would you like? Diamonds? Emeralds?"

Ceci snuggled into his chest. "You don't have to get me anything. I enjoyed it just as much as you did."

"That was the best part about it. I cannot *believe* that I found you. I'm the luckiest damn man in all of Britain. But I am going to get you something." He squeezed her, a devilish grin stealing across his face. "I already got you a pearl necklace."

"Oh!" she said, startled. "You didn't have to do that, Marcus!"

A look of absolute contentment stole across his face. He said nothing, pressing a kiss to her temple.

"What?" she asked, befuddled.

He shook his head. "Someday, sooner than you think, you

are going to understand all of my wicked innuendos. I must confess, I will be a little bit sad when that day comes."

Ceci couldn't imagine this was true. The Season was all but over. Soon, she would be returning to Cheltenham with the Astleys, and he would presumably be going to his estate in Cornwall. They might—*might*—be able to squeeze in another encounter, two if they were lucky, before they were parted. And, in all likelihood, one or both of them would be married to someone else before they saw each other again. So, Ceci didn't know when she was expected to learn all of his wicked innuendos, of which she was discovering there were many. All she could do was enjoy whatever brief time they had left together to the fullest.

Her ruminations were interrupted by Marcus's voice, rumbling beneath her ear. "We'd best get dressed and finish up our business here so I can return you home. You will want to get as much sleep as you can because we will be having the wedding tomorrow."

CHAPTER 30

*C*eci jerked in surprise.

The *wedding?* What *wedding?*

She propped her head up on an elbow. Marcus lay flat on his back, eyes closed, a soft smile upon his handsome face, giving no indication that an explanation of this bizarre statement would be forthcoming.

"What wedding?" she finally asked.

He opened his eyes, surprised. "Why, our wedding, of course."

Suddenly the room was spinning. She had misheard. She had obviously misheard, because there was no possibility, in this world or the one beyond, that *she* was going to marry *Marcus Latimer.*

She couldn't even afford to mend the holes in her slippers. There was no way she was going to be a *duchess.*

She was obviously hallucinating.

"O-our wedding? Wh-what do you... *Tomorrow?*" This was as close as she could get to a complete sentence. Frankly, she was surprised she'd been able to form words at all.

He sat up, taking her hands in his. "I know it's quick, but

we can manage it. I'll obtain a special license first thing in the morning, then head over to my solicitor's office. I'll make them draw up the marriage contract in a rush. Don't worry, you're going to be very pleased with the amount of pin money I'm going to settle on you, and the guarantees I will put in place should anything happen to me." He pressed a kiss to the back of her hands. "You'll never have to worry about anything again." One corner of his mouth pulled up into a smirk. "Other than putting up with me, of course."

Ceci was still having trouble forming words. "But... but... but..."

He laughed, pulling her against his chest. "If you want a new dress for the ceremony, you'll need to go to the modiste's shop first thing. Tell them that if they want the order for your wedding trousseau, then they'll find a way to have it ready by midafternoon. Or skip it if you like. I honestly don't care. Come to the altar in something that covers every inch of your chest if you must. So long as we're man and wife by sunset and you spend tomorrow night in my bed."

She was still at a loss. After a moment, he continued, "If tomorrow is too soon, I will exercise extreme patience and wait a day. Two, at the most." He gave her a ferocious look. "But we are marrying by special license. Don't even think of having them call the banns. We don't have time before the Season ends, and I absolutely will not accept you going back to Gloucestershire with the Astleys. I refuse to be parted from you. I'm taking you back to Cornwall with me, and that's final."

All at once, her ability to speak returned. "But you said you weren't going to marry me! You specifically said you were going to marry someone else!"

He seemed unperturbed. "So I did, yet, as soon as the

words left my mouth, it struck me that they felt wrong, a conviction that continued to grow in the days that followed."

She sat back, freeing herself from his arms so she would have at least some chance of forming a coherent thought. "No one knows that we have been alone together. If you are doing this out of a sense of obligation, because you think that you have compromised me—"

His answer was a *humph*.

She wrung her hands. "I just worry that you believe that I did this to entrap you. I swear, I did not. I never had any expectation that you would marry me—"

He captured her hands in his. "You should've."

She shook her head. "Everything we have done together, I did because I desired you. Because I wanted to have a memory I could look back on years from now, when I'm married to... Well, to someone else."

He rubbed his thumbs over her knuckles. "I know you weren't trying to entrap me. As if that would even work. Really, Cecilia, do you think that you, or anyone else, could force me to do something I did not truly wish to do?"

"Well... no. But—"

"No *buts*. You're the one I want. It's as simple as that."

She peered at him, suspicious. "Did you decide on this just now? Is the reason you want to marry me because I let you..." She waved a hand in front of her chest.

He cast his eyes to the ceiling. "*Think*, Cecilia. Before we entered Paradisium, Thetford was on the brink of calling me out. But then, he reversed course and allowed me to take you off alone. What is the only thing I could've said to him that would bring about such an abrupt change of heart?"

Ceci's spine went ramrod straight. "That you were going to marry me?"

"Precisely. Ask him if you don't believe me."

The room was spinning. Because he meant it. Marcus Latimer actually wanted to marry her!

Her wildest, most impossible dream was going to come true.

"So," he said, "what do you say about tomorrow?"

Ceci looked up at him. She opened her mouth to answer.

And she burst into tears.

∿

To say that this was not the reaction Marcus had expected upon informing a woman that she was going to be his duchess would be a significant understatement.

He would've offered her his handkerchief, except they were naked, and, come to think of it, he didn't have a handkerchief, because his skirt didn't have any pockets. Bloody inconvenient garment.

They'd even used up all of the towels cleaning the oil-cum slurry from Cecilia's chest.

So, he selected the best available option and scooped his crimson linen tunic off the floor, offering it to her. "That bad, is it? The prospect of being married to me?"

She dabbed at her eyes with a sleeve. "It's not bad at all. I'm sorry, I'm just"—she paused to take a gasping breath—"*so* happy!"

Well, now—that was more like it. He pulled her into his arms and let her sniffle against his chest. "You'll change your mind once you see what I'm like. Every time I hear you play the pianoforte, it makes me want to fuck you. You'll be trying to practice, and I'll come in and start drawing up your skirts." He shook his head. "You'll never have a moment's peace."

She gave another sniff, but her eyes were bright as she looked up at him. "Do you promise?"

He kissed her. Her tears had stopped, and they were both laughing as they helped each other to dress.

The strangest feeling settled over Marcus. It was almost as if he were... content.

He didn't mean that in a damning-with-faint-praise sort of way. For a man who had spent most of his life with fear and dread his constant companions, the simple act of feeling content was an unimaginable luxury. And yet somehow, he had arrived at this point. His father was dead. Diana's introduction to society had been an unequivocal success. For the rest of his life, he would be surrounded by the people he cared about, and he would no longer be in a constant state of anxiety that they would come to harm at the hands of his father.

Marcus went to work lacing up her stays, and Cecilia smiled her thanks over her shoulder. Her face was absolutely glowing, and Marcus realized in a flash that he was going to be happy, being married to this woman. It had never occurred to him that such a thing was even possible, that he could have a marriage like the one Fauconbridge had with his new bride.

But he and Cecilia were going to be happy together. He was sure of it. And if something tragic did come to pass, as it would at some point, because, that was just the way of the world, at least he would wake up with her beside him.

He swallowed the lump that had suddenly appeared in his throat. He was... quite looking forward to it.

When they were finished, Marcus's costume looked all right, as the leather breastplate and skirt covered the wrinkles in his tunic. But Cecilia's dress was badly crumpled.

Oh, well. Anyone who took one look at their faces was bound to know they'd spent the last hour fucking, anyway. They were both grinning like two extremely well-satisfied idiots.

"Are we marrying tomorrow, then?" Marcus asked as he helped her adjust her wig.

"I suppose we are." She laughed. "What use would it be to say no? You'd only browbeat me into it. You're very commanding, you know."

"Of course, I'm commanding. I'm a duke." He seized her by the hips, pulling her flush against him. "And you should know that I am ten times as domineering in the bedchamber as I am out of it. Consider this your warning."

She brushed a quick kiss over his lips. "I do not anticipate that I will have any complaints."

"Good." He scooped the black key off the floor and handed it to her. "Shall we actually see what's in this mysterious locker? It is the reason why we're here, after all."

She laughed. "Let's."

They made their way hand-in-hand through the corridors of the club. Marcus remembered vaguely that the room containing the wine lockers was toward the back of the building, and they were able to find it within a couple of minutes.

Two burly men stood guard at the door, an extra precaution as the club was crawling with non-members for the occasion of the masquerade. One of the men recognized Marcus, though, and they were promptly admitted.

The walls of the small room were lined with lockers made from a dark wood, perhaps ebony. The front of each locker was approximately two feet square, and they looked to be about three feet deep. Each one had a plate in the same black metal as the snake key bearing a number.

"Here it is," Marcus whispered, gesturing to a box at the level of his chest, "number four."

Cecilia looked nervous as she fitted the key into the keyhole. She opened the door with trembling fingers and reached inside.

Marcus was eager to see what was in there, too, but this was her moment, so he bit back the urge to crowd in so he could see. She leaned her head inside, and he heard the clank of bottles being shuffled around.

He managed to tamp down his anticipation for thirty seconds before asking, "What are you finding?"

"Mostly just wine," she said from inside the box. "Which is not entirely unsurprising, given that it's a wine locker. There's also a half-empty box of cheroots. I'm just making sure there isn't—*wait*. This... this has to be it."

"What is it?" he asked eagerly as she withdrew her head from the box. Her arms followed, and then, a leather-bound book.

Oh, shit.

Bloody. Fucking. Hell.

Fate was an absolute prig because the item Cecilia held clutched to her chest was one of his father's old journals.

Fauconbridge might be the clever one, but it didn't take a former Senior Wrangler to guess that if locker number four contained the truth about how Cecilia's mother died, and it also contained one of the journals in which his father had chronicled his many misdeeds in excruciating detail, then the old duke had just made a dizzying ascent up the list of suspects.

Cecilia was flipping through the pages with a slight frown, seemingly unaware that his future happiness was receding before his very eyes. Because really, how could he expect that she would agree to marry the son of her mother's murderer?

An eternity in hell was too good for his goddamn fucking father. Just when he thought he was finally rid of him, he somehow found a way to ruin Marcus's life from beyond the grave.

"I can hardly make out a word," Cecilia said, interrupting

his ruminations. "Whoever wrote it had remarkably terrible handwriting."

"He certainly did. There are few who can read it. Just myself and my uncle, as far as I know."

She looked up from the pages, surprised, then clutched his forearm. "Marcus? What's wrong? You've gone as grey as a ghost." She froze, and he could see her processing the words he had just said. "What do you mean, only you and your uncle can read it? You recognize this writing?"

There was no point in lying to her. "It's one of my father's journals. There are a dozen more in that exact binding in the study at Latimer House."

He couldn't make out much of her expression due to her mask, but he saw shock in her expressive brown eyes. "Your... your father? I... Oh, my *God.*"

He nodded tightly. She seemed to understand the implications well enough. "With your permission, as I am able to make out the writing, I will take it with me and read it tonight. That way we'll know for sure."

She squeezed his forearm. "Marcus. Look at me. We don't know that—"

"Let's confirm what it says in the journal before we make any decisions," he said firmly.

It sounded like she was in denial, which was understandable, he supposed. Who would want to accept that the person you had just agreed to marry was the son of your mother's murderer?

She deserved the unvarnished truth, just as soon as he could give it to her. But the journal was an inch thick, and it was painstaking work, picking his way through his father's scribbles. It could very well take him all night to find what he was looking for.

Cecilia apparently held on to hope that the journal might implicate someone else, one of his father's horrible friends, perhaps. But Marcus had learned long ago never to cling to hope where his father was concerned. There was absolutely no point. However despicable you thought the old duke, he always managed to find a new low.

"All right," Cecilia said, handing him the journal. "But, Marcus—"

"Is there anything else of possible use in that locker? We should make absolutely certain before we leave."

She winced but turned back to the locker. After a minute of shifting bottles, she straightened. "No, there's nothing else of interest."

"Let's get out of here, then," he said, his voice sounding gruff to his own ears.

"Here," Cecilia said, pressing something into his hand. He realized it was the key she'd worn around her neck all these months. "It would appear that you are the true owner."

He was. Like so many parts of his father's legacy, he would have preferred not to inherit it. But he reached into the locker and grabbed a bottle. He peered at the label—a 1793 Margaux. An excellent vintage, and one that was all but impossible to get right now due to the war in France.

He grabbed another two bottles, tucking them under his arm before he spun the key in the lock. Considering the task he had ahead of him, he was going to need some kind of courage, liquid or otherwise, if he was going to get through it.

CHAPTER 31

*C*eci waited until ten o'clock the following morning before heading for Latimer House.

She felt no small amount of trepidation as she mounted the stone steps. After finding his father's journal in the wine locker, Marcus's demeanor had changed so abruptly that she wasn't sure what to expect today. Before that moment, he had been uncharacteristically ebullient.

But as soon as he laid eyes upon his father's journal, he had closed himself off entirely. Marcus wasn't what you would call chipper, but he wasn't usually despondent. Yet that was precisely how he had appeared during the hackney carriage ride home, staring sightlessly out the window and saying nothing. When he missed an obvious opening to skewer Lord Thetford with a withering set-down, Ceci really began to worry.

Ceci wondered what was bothering him. Surely he didn't think she would throw him over for something his father did almost twenty years ago? If it was indeed his father who had killed her mother, that would be a strange twist of fate. But Marcus was not responsible for the sins of his father, and she would not hold them against him.

Perhaps he was worried that she would gossip about it, blackening his father's reputation? That didn't seem likely. No one was quicker to abuse his father's name than Marcus himself. On the other hand, he did like to keep his cards close to his chest, even amongst his closest circle of friends, and he certainly worried about anything that might cause Diana distress. That could easily include malicious gossip.

That was probably what it was, then. She would reassure him that she wouldn't breathe a word of this to anyone, not even the Astleys, and hopefully, that would restore him to his sardonic self.

She hadn't been sure whether she would find him here or whether he would be at his solicitor's office as they had originally discussed. But she was informed by the footman who received her that the duke was at home. He led her to a study on the second floor.

She paused in the doorway. He looked awful. Well, awful was relative for Marcus Latimer. But his hair was unkempt, there were dark circles beneath his blue eyes, and he wore naught but a rumpled linen shirt and pair of loose trousers beneath a jade green silk banyan.

He looked… human. Like a man, not a duke.

The sight made her heart squeeze even more than his usual golden perfection.

"Marcus?" she asked, stepping into the room.

He looked up, sadness flaring in his eyes for an instant before the flat effect returned.

"What's wrong?" she asked.

He raked a hand through his hair, then stood. "Come," he said, gesturing to a burgundy-striped sofa in the middle of the room.

He seated her, then sat at the far end of the sofa, leaving a good two feet of space between them. Dread rose in her throat.

He said nothing, staring at the carpet.

She cleared her throat. "So. Did you read any of the journal?"

"I read the whole thing," he said, his voice gravelly. "Stayed up all night. The information I was looking for was on the second-to-last page." He gave a bitter huff. "Leave it to my father to make my life as difficult as possible, even when he's dead."

Ceci's heart was racing, even though she was fairly certain she knew the answer to the question she was about to ask. "And what did it say?"

His shoulders sagged. "It was my father. He was the one who killed your mother. He happened to be passing through the village of Gorran Haven, and he spotted her from the window of his carriage, and—" He looked away, swallowing thickly. "I won't deny you the details if you truly want to know how it happened. But I must forewarn you... It was horrible to read. And once you hear those words, you will never be able to banish them from your mind. I couldn't help but think of how Ellery spared me from having to see my mother lying at the bottom of those stairs. If you will allow me, I would like to spare you these details, which I fear will distress you to no good end."

Ceci nodded. It was bad enough that she knew her mother had died by strangulation. She honestly didn't want to know more. "I think that's probably wise."

So, this was it. She finally knew the truth about what had happened to her mother. She had anticipated this moment for almost a full year, ever since her father pressed that key into her hand. A month ago, she would have guessed she would find this moment overwhelming.

And yet, to her surprise, her overriding emotion was

relief. Because it was over. She had learned the truth and fulfilled her duty to her mother. The person responsible was already dead. There was nothing more to be done. At last, she could lay aside this burden.

Honestly, Marcus seemed to be taking it worse than she was. She scooted over next to him and wrapped her arm around his shoulders.

He flinched, then cast a despondent glance at her hand where it stroked his back. "You don't have to do that," he said, his voice flat.

"You're upset. Of course, I want to comfort you." She studied his downcast face. "It must've been very disturbing. To have to read about such a thing," she added, seeing his brow crease in confusion. "Is that what you find so troubling?"

He gave a humorless laugh. "No. It was a heinous tale, but I'm used to reading my father's journals." At Ceci's quizzical look, he said, "I've been going through them, trying to track down the people he terrorized and make what recompense I am able."

Ceci felt stunned. In spite of his terrible reputation, Marcus really did have a strong moral compass. "That's very good of you, Marcus."

"Hardly," he said, his voice flat.

She squeezed his shoulders. "Well, if it wasn't that, what is it that has you feeling so morose?"

He pushed off the couch and went to stand next to the desk. "I cannot imagine you would feel comfortable marrying the son of your mother's murderer. I will therefore release you from any obligation you feel you have toward me."

Ceci could hardly hear over the sudden roaring in her ears. "Is that what you would prefer?"

He stared out the window behind the desk, refusing to

look at her. "No. As I said last night, you're the one I want. But I know it is too much to... Cecilia? Wh-what are you doing?"

She had stolen up behind him and wrapped her arms around his chest. "No."

"No?" For the first time that morning, his voice contained a hint of its usual vibrancy. "What do you mean, no?"

"I'm not letting you go," she said, squeezing him tight.

"But..." His voice contained a note of hope but also of dread. "But my father killed your mother."

"I know that." She spun him around so he would be forced to look at her. "What does that have to do with you?"

"W-well," he sputtered, which tore at her heart, because sputtering was so unlike him. "Every time you look at me, you'll feel—"

"Like the luckiest woman in the world," she said firmly, looping her arms around his neck.

He studied her, his face cautious. "You're still willing to marry me."

"Not *willing* so much as eager. Determined. Longing." She brushed a kiss over his lips. "You're not getting rid of me that easily. So, let's not have any more of this nonsense about calling off the wedding."

He peered at her as if he scarcely dared to hope that she meant it. Then, all at once, he crushed her to him, burying his face in her hair. "Cecilia. I... I can't believe it."

She stroked her hand over his back. "Believe it."

His voice shook as he said, "I was so scared you would refuse me."

Her heart ached at his admission. She pulled back and framed his face. "You? Scared?"

He swallowed thickly but didn't deny it.

She shook her head. "How I wish we'd spoken about it last night. I would have told you that no matter what it said in that journal, it would not change my feelings for you." She brushed a lock of golden hair back from his forehead. "There was never any need to worry."

He nodded, his lips tight as if he did not trust himself to speak.

"Come." She tugged at his shoulders and started to lead him back to the sofa so she could hold him, but he seized her hand and pulled her past the sofa and out the door.

"Where are you taking me?" she asked, breathless.

He was almost jogging as he pulled her down the corridor. "To a room in which you will be spending a great deal of time."

He opened a door at the end of the hallway and Ceci knew at once that it was the ducal bedchamber.

The room was huge—bigger than the entire cottage Ceci had shared with her father for most of her life. In addition to the gigantic, canopied bed, there was a seating area as large as the morning room at Astley House with its own sofa and cluster of plush chairs, a writing desk in the corner, and even a table and chairs. Light poured in through a dozen tall windows. The walls were dove grey with white plasterwork and wainscoting—elegant, but in a drab sort of way.

That was all right. Ceci was certain she could add a little color to Marcus Latimer's life.

"The duchess's bedchamber is through there," Marcus said, nodding toward a door. "You may decorate it in any way you prefer. Not that you will be spending any significant amount of time there, other than whatever time it takes you to dress."

A smile tugged at the corner of Ceci's mouth. "Will I not?"

"No." He tugged her into his arms and began pressing kisses to her temple. "You're going to be here. With me."

She had a fair idea what was about to happen.

Considering Marcus would be her husband in a few short days, she had no compunctions. Except…

"Will your sister and aunt not be scandalized? If they notice we're alone together in your room."

He was kissing his way across her cheek. "They're not here. They're attending the same house party as the Astleys in Broxbourne."

"Ah. Well, then," were the last words she managed before his lips claimed hers. This kiss felt different from the ones they had shared last night. Then, Marcus had kissed her with absolute confidence.

But this time, his breath was ragged and his hands shook as he pressed her against him. This raw, unexpected show of emotion undid her even more thoroughly than his usual controlled perfection.

He broke the kiss but only to lead her to the foot of the bed. His voice in her ear was as dark as midnight. "I need you to understand something, Cecilia."

"What's that?" she breathed.

"I am about to devour you. You are going to be *mine*. So, if you do not want that, tell me to stop. You may have to clout me in the head to get my attention, but I will stop if you ask me. Do you understand?"

"I understand," she gasped. "And, Marcus?"

He traced a finger down the column of her throat. "Yes?"

"Don't stop."

He growled as he kissed her. Had Ceci been capable of coherent thought, she might have been alarmed at the efficiency with which he undressed her, for he had her naked in a minute flat.

He lay her back upon the counterpane, then knelt above her to shrug out of his banyan and peel off his shirt. It was the first time she'd managed a proper look at him by daylight.

He was as sculpted as a god, not one of the brutish, hulking ones like Zeus or Poseidon, but Apollo, who was lithely powerful, with a deadly grace. Although he carried no extra bulk, muscles stood out in sharp relief everywhere, on his arms and shoulders and chest, which had just a fine dusting of golden hair.

He lowered himself beside her. Ceci couldn't seem to keep her hands off him, and he growled his satisfaction as he filled his hands with her breasts. "You are perfect," he murmured as she arched into him. "Had I been asked to sculpt the ideal woman from clay, like Pygmalion, you would be the result."

He proceeded to torture her by kissing every inch of her upper body other than her breasts. He teased her collarbone, her sternum, the curve of her shoulder, and even her belly button as she clenched handfuls of the counterpane and tried to thrust her breasts into the path of his mouth. Marcus took no pity on her. By the time he finally tugged one of her nipples into his mouth, she was writhing on the bed.

He rewarded her with a nice, deep pull that had her hips bucking up off the mattress. He seemed to take this as a suggestion, letting his hand drift down to sift between her curls. Softly, ever so softly, he found that little nub that was the center of her pleasure and began to tease it with gentle circles.

Ceci was now starting to feel desperate and also eager for what she knew was about to come. She let her hand trace down Marcus's chest, across his rock-hard stomach, and began stroking the prominent bulge through the fabric of his trousers.

He growled his approval, but when she moved to undo one of the buttons, he captured both of her wrists in one hand and pinned them above her head.

"What about you?" she panted.

"Hush," he said, the liquid fire in his eyes belying the harshness of his words as he slid down to settle between her lolling thighs. "This is almost certain to hurt. I need to prepare you as much as is humanly possible before you drive me out of my mind and I fall on you like a rutting animal."

He kissed his way across her stomach, then brought his mouth to the little pearl he'd been adeptly fingering this whole time. He began massaging it with the flat of his tongue, and Ceci reared up halfway on the bed.

He held her hips in place, allowing her no quarter, pleasuring her relentlessly.

Just when she could almost glimpse paradise, he gentled his tongue, giving her only light, teasing flicks. "Please, Marcus. Please!" she cried. He responded by inserting a finger into her trembling passage, stroking her in a steady rhythm. Which felt… interesting. Not as pleasurable as what he'd been doing with his tongue before, but interesting. After a minute, he added a second finger, and she squirmed. It wasn't painful, per se, but she was cognizant of a feeling of tightness. Having seen the size of his member the night before, Ceci began to feel some trepidation, because the part of Marcus's body that would ultimately be going there was *significantly* larger than two of his fingers.

But he kept licking at her gently and rubbing her insides with his fingers. Gradually, the tension eased. By the time he inserted a third finger, Ceci had changed her mind. His fingers inside of her didn't feel interesting. They felt *good*, and she began to grind her hips in time with his hand.

Just as she once again neared the top of the peak, Marcus pulled back with a grunt.

Ceci cried out in frustration, her hands scrambling to hold him in place.

He smirked as he stood and stripped off his trousers. "You're ready." He crawled onto the bed an instant later, coming to rest on top of her. Something felt so *right* about his weight upon her, and she instinctively threaded her arms around his neck.

He kissed his way up her neck and across her jawline before settling upon her lips. "This is probably still going to hurt," he warned her when he raised his head.

She bit him lightly on his ear. "Then let's get it over with, so I'll never have to worry about it again."

"There's my brave girl." He reached down between them and took his cock in hand, lining it up with her entrance. She felt him slide in an inch or two, but then he stopped, his head lolling forward. "*Fuck*, Cecilia."

"What's wrong?" she asked. Even though it didn't hurt, she was gripping his shoulders in nervous anticipation of the moment the pain would come.

He was panting in her ear as he slid in another inch. "You feel like heaven, and I have to—God *damn* it—go slowly."

"You can keep going," she said tightly. "It's not so bad."

He nodded. Cords of muscle stood out on his neck. He pressed forward, and Ceci could not suppress a yelp as she felt a strong pinching sensation.

Marcus froze. "Are you all right?"

She bit her lip. To be sure, she had felt some pain, but not nearly as bad as she had anticipated. "I think…" She wiggled her hips experimentally, and he groaned against her temple. "I think the worst might be over."

Studying her face the whole time, he withdrew most of the way, then pressed forward again. She felt a slight soreness, but no sharp pang, even when he was fully seated.

She stroked her hands over his shoulders. "It's all right. It scarcely hurts."

His jaw remained iron as he slowly withdrew, then slid forward. He repeated the motion three times, watching her face all the while.

Suddenly his body sagged. "Thank *fuck*." He began thrusting with a moderate, steady pace.

It did feel good, especially when he would grind his hips against her at the peak of each thrust. But not to the same degree it had before when his lips had been on that sensitive spot between her legs.

As if he had read her mind, Marcus threaded a hand between their bodies and brought his fingers to that very spot. He began shaking his wrist, his fingers vibrating over her like hummingbirds' wings.

It was exactly what her body needed. All at once the pleasure was upon her again. She dug her fingers into the muscles on his back and heard him chuckle. "What?" she asked, breathlessly.

He continued to thrust and to flutter his fingers over her core. "I am very much looking forward to having you as my wife, Cecilia."

"You are?"

She could hear the smile in his voice as he pressed a kiss against her temple. "I am. I must endeavor to somehow get into heaven because one lifetime with you could never be enough."

Ceci's emotions were already floating right at the surface, and with these words, they began to swell. Who would have thought that Marcus Latimer, the most cynical man in all of London, had it in him to be tender? Suddenly she felt as if her heart might burst, and it turned out that this swell of emotion was more devastating than any depraved act he might perform with his tongue. Her thighs began to tremble, and her lips, and her heart, as well. She gasped his name, knowing that any second now, she was going to come.

He lifted his head and looked at her, and when she saw real affection in his eyes, mixed in with the desire?

Ceci didn't stand a chance.

Suddenly she was coming, her entire body shaking, her core throbbing around him, mindless with pleasure. Her vision scrambled, but she was dimly aware of him saying her name, of his lips upon her throat as she clung to his shoulders.

Marcus withdrew his hand just as the little nub between her legs became exquisitely sensitive. As he swam back into focus, she saw that his jaw was clenched, and corded muscles stood out along his neck. He was thrusting into her with abandon, eyes closed, forehead creased with tension.

A wave of tenderness washed over her for this man who was so much more than the impeccable duke he showed to the world. She reached up and brushed a lock of pale golden hair back from his forehead, and he looked at her. His eyes were unfocused with pleasure, but as his gaze swept over her face, tenderness washed through them.

"Cecilia," he gasped as his body hardened to stone, and then it was his turn to cry out, his turn to tremble in her arms as the pleasure took him.

He collapsed on top of her. She traced patterns over the smooth skin of his back while his breathing returned to normal.

Yawning, he rolled off her. Without opening his eyes, he settled on his side, pulling her close so her body spooned against his.

"I should probably go," she murmured.

"Stay," he said sleepily as he drew the counterpane up over them.

"It will cause a terrible scandal if I'm missed. And I have—"

"A piano lesson," he said, anticipating her words. He tightened his grip around her waist. "Who cares if there's a scandal? By this time tomorrow, you're going to be the

Duchess of Trevissick. And you're never going to have to teach another piano lesson."

Ceci's eyes were already drifting shut. She hadn't slept much, either, after their late night at Paradisium. And it felt indescribably wonderful to lie there in bed with Marcus's arms around her.

The thought crossed her sleepy brain that it wasn't merely the physical comforts around her—the warm, plush bed, the luxuriously soft sheets, or even the pleasure of feeling Marcus's body pressed against hers.

It was the fact that, for the first time since her father's death, she had a feeling of *rightness*. That, after a year of wandering, she had finally found the place where she belonged.

"Stay," Marcus whispered in her ear. "Stay with me."

And she did.

CHAPTER 33

*T*he pounding at the door would not stop.

Marcus scowled as he forced his eyes open. Judging by the light slanting through the windows, it was late afternoon.

He made a quick inventory of his situation. He was in the ducal bedchamber. He'd likely slept for the better part of six hours.

And, much to his delight, Cecilia was in his arms.

And not just any variation of Cecilia.

This was *naked* Cecilia.

Now that he wasn't exhausted to the point of dropping, he could think of all manner of things he wanted to do with naked Cecilia.

But first, the knocking needed to stop.

"Go away," he called toward the door, sweeping her hair back so he could press kisses against her neck.

"I'm sorry, Your Grace," Bastian answered. "But I must speak with you."

"Not now." His hand reached up to cup one of her

magnificent breasts, and he was gratified when she squirmed against him.

"I'm terribly sorry. I would not dream of disturbing Your Grace were it not of the utmost urgency."

"Don't make me dismiss you." Marcus stroked his hand across her trembling stomach. When he reached the soft curls at the juncture of her thighs, she parted her legs for him. He found her freshly wet. *God*, but she was perfect…

"Please, Your Grace," Bastian called from outside the door. "It's Ellery."

"I know damn well it's not Ellery." Marcus delved between Cecilia's thighs, savoring her sweet sigh as he found her bud swollen and eager for him. "I know Ellery's voice as well as I know yours, Bastian."

"It's about Ellery," Bastian clarified. "I'm so sorry, Your Grace. But we just received the note. Ellery is in danger."

Marcus froze. This was one of a vanishingly small number of things Bastian could have said that could motivate him to stop the very pleasant activities in which he was presently engaged. "Ellery? In danger?" he asked sharply.

He was already halfway off the bed. Beside him, Cecilia sat up, drawing the blankets up to cover her chest. Marcus scooped his banyan off the floor and tossed it to her, then hastily pulled on his trousers.

He padded over to the door and opened it a crack. Bastian thrust a note through. "This is what we received."

He sat down on the end of the bed and started to read.

Your Grace,

I pray this note will reach you, as the previous three clearly did not. I did not make it onto the carriage. I was inside the inn, awaiting the time of my departure when I was accosted by a pair of constables. They arrested me and took me to Newgate Prison, where I have been ever since. I have been charged with being an accessory to murder after the fact. Apparently, it is in connection to some crime perpetrated by your father. I know not which one. I have been permitted to examine the evidence against me, but it consists of one of his old journals, and I cannot make out the writing.

The trial is to commence three days hence. I pray this will reach Your Grace, as I will surely hang for this if my situation does not change, and I know you would not abandon me to this fate.

Yours faithfully,

J. Ellery

Marcus's vision swam. Here he had thought Ellery was safe in Holywell, visiting the nieces and nephews he hadn't seen in twenty years.

Instead, the man who had raised him, the person who had sacrificed his own life and family to protect him and Diana from their father's wrath, had spent the last three days lying forlorn and forgotten in a dank cell in the most dangerous prison in all of Britain.

Shame washed over him and intermingled with his fury. How could he have allowed this to happen? And to *Ellery*, of all people, the man to whom he owed everything?

He felt the mattress sag as Cecilia sat beside him, felt her arm loop around his shoulders. "What is it, Marcus? What's wrong?"

He thrust the note at her, unable to speak, and rose to pace the room. She gasped as she scanned its contents.

He raked a hand through his hair. "I must go and speak to my barrister. At once." He cringed as he turned to face her. "I was going to secure a special license this afternoon, so we could marry tomorrow. But—"

She crossed the room and squeezed his arm. "Don't

worry about that. We'll hold the wedding as soon as this is resolved. Naturally, Ellery's situation must take priority."

He nodded tightly. "Thank you for understanding."

"Of course." She gazed up at him, brow creased with concern. "It will be all right, Marcus. Now that you know what has happened, you will be able to fix this."

"I will," he said, pushing back the voice in his head that countered, *but what if you can't?* Ellery had been accused of a capital crime. Should he fail, Ellery could very well hang...

He could not bear even to think about that. "I absolutely will."

Cecilia was gathering her crumpled garments from the floor. She tilted her head toward the door connecting his bedchamber to the duchess's suite. "I'll go next door and make myself presentable. That way Bastian can start getting you dressed right away."

She really was wonderful. So understanding, even just a few hours after he'd taken her innocence. "Thank you. Would you like a maid to assist you, or—"

She brushed a kiss across his lips. "I'll manage. And I'll stop by tomorrow to see how you're doing."

He framed her face and gave her a reverent kiss. "Thank you, Cecilia."

She hurried toward the connecting door, and he strode across the room to let Bastian in.

CHAPTER 34

arcus was out when Ceci called on him the following morning as well as when she stopped by after luncheon. Bastian kindly offered to send her word once he returned, and that was how she managed to catch him in the late afternoon.

Bastian led her to the study, where she found Marcus seated at the desk, fully absorbed in the letter he was penning. He looked much as he had yesterday after he'd stayed up all night reading his father's journal, with bluish circles beneath his eyes and a dull cast to his skin. It made her heart squeeze to see him under such obvious strain.

She rapped lightly against the doorframe as she stepped inside.

He looked up, his expression blank, then rubbed his forehead. "Cecilia. Come in." He gestured to the burgundy-striped sofa, rising from the desk and meeting her there.

"How is Ellery? Were you able to meet with him?"

"I was," he said, taking the seat beside her. "Believe me when I say that Newgate Prison is no place for a seventy-three-year-old man. He was filthy, shivering, and huddled in the corner when I found him. But I was able to pay to have him moved to one of the private rooms, so at least he is now safe and more physically comfortable."

She wrapped an arm around him, rubbing his back. "Did you learn anything about the charges against him?"

"I did. As Ellery stated in his letter, the prosecution has somehow got hold of one of my father's old journals. In it, my father details stabbing to death a man who had the audacity to try to stop him from raping his wife. He wrote how he came home covered in blood, and Ellery helped him get cleaned up."

"How on earth did they get one of your father's journals?"

Marcus grimaced. "I expect my uncle is the one behind it. I cut off his allowance, as he was one of the people who refused to shelter Diana years ago. He came here to confront me about it, and I left the room to summon a footman to throw him out. So, he not only has a motive, he had a prime opportunity to take one of the journals. I suppose it could be someone else. Lord knows I have enemies aplenty. But he is my leading suspect. And make no mistake, although Ellery is the one who was arrested, I am the target of his wrath."

"Well, your uncle sounds despicable. And yet..." Ceci tilted her head. "Is that all they have? Certainly, coming home covered in blood is suspicious. But the evidence seems rather circumstantial."

Marcus raked a hand through his hair. "Unfortunately, that is not all they have. If you recall, the letter I received yesterday said that it was Ellery's fourth attempt to write to me. It is common for loose women to enter Newgate under the guise of visiting a 'husband.' It was these women whom Ellery asked to smuggle his note outside. Unfortunately, my uncle—or whoever is behind this—must've made it known that he would pay handsomely for any information relating to Ellery's case. And another one of Ellery's letters, one he attempted to send later, after he had received more information about the charges against him, made its way into the prosecution's hands."

"What did it say?" Ceci whispered, dreading the answer.

"Ellery wrote that he feared the charges were true. That he remembered a number of similar incidents, in which my father returned home in a highly questionable state, and invariably the next day, the parish would be abuzz with news of a death under mysterious circumstances."

Ceci squeezed her eyes shut. "He effectively confessed."

"Precisely." Marcus rubbed at one eye with a knuckle. "I hired a team of barristers, and they've moved to have the note disallowed as evidence. But they say it's bad. It's very bad."

Ceci rubbed Marcus's back. "It seems to me that the best option might be to tell the truth. The incident looks bad on its own. But once you understand the full picture, that the reason he had to look the other way and maintain his post at all costs was so he would be around to protect you and Diana, it is impossible not to be sympathetic."

"You sound like my barristers," Marcus grumbled.

"They're suggesting the same approach?"

"Yes," he said tightly.

Ceci took in his drawn brow and his hunched shoulders. "You don't seem pleased with their recommendation."

He rose abruptly, pacing the room. "Do you have any idea how bad the scandal will be if we detail the reasons Diana and I needed protection from my father in a court of law? The transcript of the trial will be a public record. Absolutely *everyone* will read it."

Ceci stood. She laid her hand upon his arm, but he shook her off. "Marcus, there are already rumors about your father."

He snorted. "Those rumors do not encompass a tenth of

what would come out in this trial. Do not mistake me—I don't give a damn for my own sake. Let them say whatever they want behind my back. I don't care if the whole world knows. Save for one person. Diana." He stopped his pacing, gazing into the fire.

Ceci came up beside him. This time, he allowed her to take his hand. "Diana already knows your father was a monster. She watched your aunt Griselda shoot him with a blunderbuss and did not seem the least bit perturbed."

He looked at her, his eyes wary. "She knows in a general sense, yes. But if we take the 'tell the full truth' approach, it would be necessary to explain the primary reason that Diana and I needed to be protected from my father."

"You mean… the fact that he killed your mother."

"Yes," Marcus said tightly.

He did not elaborate. After a moment, Ceci asked, "Why, exactly, does that pose a problem?"

He wouldn't meet her eyes. "You know I would do anything to protect my sister."

She stroked the back of his hand with her thumb. "Of course, you would."

He swallowed. "I have therefore tried to shield her from the most disturbing of my father's misdeeds."

"Which is a noble impulse, but I don't see what—" She froze as something occurred to her. "Wait. Surely you're not saying that Diana doesn't know how her own mother died?"

"She does not know." His eyes were icy. "Nor does she need to."

She blinked up at him, disbelieving. "You cannot mean that!"

He whirled away, stalking to the far side of the room. "Diana was two when our mother died. Two! What would you have had me do? Tell my two-year-old sister about our mother's last moments? How she died screaming for help as she plunged down the stairs before breaking her neck?"

She held her hands up, placatingly. "Of course not. But—"

"What was the right age, then? Six? Nine?"

"Nineteen seems fairly reasonable to me," Ceci snapped. "Especially when the cost of keeping this particular secret might be Ellery's life!"

Marcus rounded on her, narrowing his eyes. "I would never let anything happen to Ellery. *Never*. He will be found innocent. I will make sure of it!"

"And how, exactly, are you going to do that?"

"Firstly, I'm going to get that letter stricken from the record."

She crossed her arms. "And if the judge admits it? What then?"

He made a slashing motion as if he could physically strike down the possibility. "I will pay whatever bribes are necessary to make this go away."

She crossed the room to stand in front of him. "You have no way of knowing if that will work. As it says in the Bible, the truth will set him free. Ellery has done nothing wrong. It is plain to see that the best way to win his safety is to present the whole story to the jury. They cannot possibly judge him once they understand the entirety of the situation. Your own barristers have said as much!"

"My way will work." He turned toward the sideboard and reached for a decanter. "You'll see."

His fingers fumbled with the stopper, and he cursed under his breath. It was unlike him to be less than perfectly graceful. Her eyes drifted up to his face as he struggled to conceal a yawn.

Her heart softened. "Did you get any sleep at all last night?"

He shrugged. "An hour. Maybe two."

Her outrage melted away. No wonder he wasn't thinking clearly.

She took his hands in hers, removing them from the decanter. "I won't argue with you about it now, then. And I don't think the thing you need is a drink. Please, Marcus. Get some rest. You need to be at your sharpest if you're going to help Ellery. The trial is in what, two days?"

"Two days," he agreed, trying and failing to suppress another yawn. "You're probably right," he muttered.

She looped her arms around his neck. "If you promise me you'll go straight to bed, I'll quit badgering you. For now," she amended.

He rested his head atop hers. "I'm too tired to even attempt to debauch you."

"One of the signs of the end times, I'm sure." He gave a weak chuckle. "Go. Rest. We'll talk about it tomorrow."

He pressed his forehead against hers. "Thank you, Cecilia."

He staggered off toward his bedroom as she made her way downstairs.

She would return tomorrow and again explain the importance of telling Diana the truth. Not just because it was Ellery's best chance. But because the situation was strangely reminiscent of her own, in which her father had concealed the truth about her mother's death until the last possible moment.

Diana would want to know the truth, even if it was painful. She was certain of it.

Once Marcus was properly rested, he would see that she was right.

CHAPTER 35

$\mathcal{B}$ut the following day, Marcus was not at Latimer House any of the three times Ceci stopped by.

Bastian again offered to send a note upon the duke's return, but no word came, and when she returned in the late afternoon, the valet reluctantly admitted that Marcus had briefly returned home. "I apologize for not sending word as I promised. But His Grace was in such a foul temper that I could not imagine you would have wished to speak with him."

Ceci felt the color drain from her face. "What has happened that has put him in such a mood?"

Bastian's eyes were full of consternation. "The judge denied the motion to strike Ellery's letter from the evidence."

Ceci winced. "He will have no choice, then, but to present the unvarnished truth and hope the jury is sympathetic."

Bastian said nothing, but his handsome brow furrowed.

Ceci studied him. "The duke has agreed to adopt the recommendations of his barristers, has he not?"

Bastian sighed. "He is still clinging to hope that he can avoid the manner of his mother's death becoming public."

Ceci made a sound of frustration. "That is folly. He must accept that this is Ellery's best... probably his only chance. It isn't too late. Lady Diana is only in Broxbourne. He can send a carriage to fetch her tonight and tell her the truth before she reads about it in the evening papers tomorrow."

Bastian wrung his hands. "Would you write him a note, telling him as much, Miss Chenoweth? He was quite snappish with me when I suggested the same. But I hold out some hope that he might listen to you."

"Certainly, I will."

She followed Bastian to a parlor and took a seat at the writing desk he indicated. How she wished that Fauconbridge and Lady Cheltenham were in town. Marcus held them in high esteem. Surely they would have been able to force him to see reason. To say nothing of Lady Griselda, who would have probably boxed him on the ear and taken matters into her own hands.

But they were all at the house party in Broxbourne, and so Ceci was on her own.

Still, she wrote the best letter she could, explaining in no uncertain terms that Ellery's only hope lay in transparency.

"Thank you, miss," Bastian said when she rose from the writing desk. "I will make sure he receives it."

"Thank you. I will come again tomorrow to see if I can be of assistance."

Bastian bowed. "Thank you, Miss Chenoweth."

The trial was scheduled for the following day. Ceci called first thing the following morning but found Marcus had already departed for his barrister's office. Bastian reported that a letter had arrived that morning, and although the duke had read it in silence, whatever it said had prompted him to shout a string of curses before he stormed out the door. Bastian also confirmed that, although he had presented the duke with Ceci's letter, he had said nothing upon reading it, and the carriage had not been dispatched to Broxbourne to collect Diana.

Feeling sick with nerves, Ceci returned at ten o'clock. This time, Marcus was home. Bastian led her up to the study, whispering a warning that his mood had not improved.

She found him pacing the room like a caged lion. His hair was disheveled, and the circles under his eyes were now black. Somehow, he still managed to look handsome.

"Tell me what's happened," she said, striding into the room.

There was real panic in his eyes as he said, "He's taken out my barristers."

Ceci recoiled. "Taken out your... Who are you talking about? And what do you mean, taken out your—"

"My uncle." He wheeled around as he reached the fireplace and paced back toward the other side of the room. "This is his doing. I'm sure of it. I—"

"Marcus, stop." She crossed the room, captured his hands in hers, and led him to the sofa. "Tell me everything."

He allowed her to pull him down onto the cushions. "Last night, my barristers were working late, preparing for the case, when servants from the inn down the street arrived, bearing supper."

"Umm... all right?" Ceci said, unsure how this was relevant.

Marcus raked a hand through his hair, causing it to stick up even more. "They claimed that I had purchased the food and arranged for it to be sent over."

A chill of foreboding swept through her. "But you did not?"

He shook his head. "I did not, nor did the inn know

anything about it. Within an hour, every one of them was stricken with an extremely urgent, extremely pernicious case of stomach upset."

"They were *poisoned*?" Ceci asked, disbelieving.

Marcus nodded grimly. "That is what the physician says. They are all mending, but... I'm trying to think of a delicate way to say this... There is no possibility of any of them appearing in a court of law by two o'clock today. They are not fit to be seen in public."

"My God, Marcus! That's... that's awful!"

"And it gets worse, if you can countenance it. After learning what happened, I went straight to the judge's office this morning to request a continuance." He gave a mirthless laugh. "My request was denied, on the basis that an innocent man has no need of a defense attorney. The trial will therefore proceed this afternoon, with Ellery being expected to defend himself!"

Ceci squeezed his hand. "You've got to find a new barrister."

"I am aware," he said in a clipped voice. "I have, in fact, spent the last hour and a half knocking on every door at the Inns of Court trying to convince someone to take the case. It was already an unappealing prospect, as the trial starts in four hours. But apparently, no sum will tempt a man to take on such a case when word has spread like wildfire that the previous barristers were all *poisoned*." He rubbed his forehead. "It's hopeless. I must've asked fifty men. They turned me down, every one. I feel like I'm going to be sick myself. I can't let Ellery down. I cannot. But..."

Ceci sat bolt upright as something occurred to her. "Samuel Branton is a barrister!"

Mr. Branton served with them on the board of the Ladies' Society, as vice president of legal affairs. Hope dawned on Marcus's face. "Branton! Why didn't I think of him?"

"Because you've scarcely slept in three days. Mr. Branton does not work in criminal defense," Ceci cautioned. "I believe most of his work is before the Admiralty Courts."

Marcus rose swiftly. "But he will be a thousand times better than Ellery could do on his own. And he may know someone who specializes in criminal defense who could be persuaded to join us." He brushed a kiss across Ceci's lips. "I must go to him at once."

She caught his hand as he turned to go. "Marcus, wait. Did you send word to Diana?"

His brow descended. "No. We've already discussed this."

"It will be better for her to hear the truth about how your mother died from you than to read about it in the papers."

"It will be better for her not to hear about it at all," he retorted. "And she won't. Because that will *not* be a part of our legal defense."

"It *must* be a part of Ellery's defense. The judge has admitted his letter into evidence. He confessed that the charges were probably true and that he had done a number of unsavory things in your father's employ. The jury will immediately ask why he did not simply leave if he was not truly a villain. You have to give them an answer to that question. And that answer is you and Diana. But you are going to have to explain *why* the two of you needed protection. There is no other way!"

"There will be another way!" he snapped. "Because I will not countenance your way. I will not permit Diana to be hurt in this manner!"

"And I cannot countenance your hiding the truth from Diana," she shot back. "Even if it were not material to Ellery's case, she has the right to know what happened to her mother."

"It would distress her. And it is my duty as her brother to

protect her from distressing things." He turned and started for the door. "You wouldn't understand."

She snagged his elbow. "Oh, I understand, all right. I understand far better than you do, in fact! Because I have been in Diana's position. My father thought he was protecting me by concealing the truth about my mother's death. But the truth came out in the end, and when it did, it hurt so much worse because he had kept it from me."

"Just because your father failed does not mean that I will," he shot back. "Had it never come out, you would have been spared that pain. And I am going to spare Diana!"

Ceci shook her head violently. "The truth has a way of coming out, whether you wish it to or not. And Diana is strong—"

"I know she is strong!" Marcus snapped. "It makes no difference. I am strong, and I can tell you—knowing the details about my mother's death is *horrible*. I will not subject my sister to that!"

Ceci cringed. As strongly as she disagreed with him, Marcus's intentions were noble. "She strikes me as the type of person who *hates* being coddled. Even if the truth is painful, I feel certain that she would rather know it. You must trust me in this."

He narrowed his eyes at her. "You have the audacity to stand there and lecture me on what is best for *my* sister?"

"If I see you making a mistake, then yes. And this is a mistake, Marcus. One that could cost Ellery his life and permanently damage your relationship with Diana. You *must* tell her."

His eyes were wild, darting about the room and showing as much white as blue. "For the past seventeen years, I have done whatever it took to protect my sister. You have *no idea* the lengths to which I have gone! You would be *appalled* by some of the things I have done! And if you think I am going to throw all of that away—"

"She no longer needs your protection!" Ceci shot back. "She is no longer a girl of four. What Diana needs now is your respect."

"Enough!" He jerked his arm from her grasp. "I do not have time to stand here and argue with you. Ellery's trial starts in four hours, and I need to find him a barrister."

He had almost made it to the door when Ceci said, "If you don't tell her, then I will."

He froze in the doorframe, then slowly turned. He looked shocked that she had said it. Frankly, Ceci was as shocked as he was. Two weeks ago, she hadn't been able to look this man in the eye while muttering good morning. Had she truly just *threatened* him?

When he spoke, his voice was quiet, but make no mistake —that hushed tone was ten times more frightening than if he had been shouting. "You did not just say that."

She would never know where the courage came from, but she lifted her chin. "I did. And I meant it. For Ellery's sake. And for Diana's as well."

His voice shook as he said, "If you do anything that hurts my sister, you will be *dead* to me. I will never be able to so much as look at you."

She swallowed thickly. "I understand."

He left without saying a word.

She collapsed upon the sofa, gasping for breath. She should have known this past week was all a dream, that it was too good to be true. Why had she even dreamed that *she* would marry Marcus Latimer?

He was going to hate her.

Because, as much as she wanted to marry him, it did not change what she had to do.

A man's life hung in the balance. A good man's.

And she would not abandon him, not even for a duchess's coronet.

On the carriage ride back to Astley House, she turned over the question of how she was going to get word to Diana. Broxbourne was some twenty miles away. It was unlikely that she could convince a hackney driver to take her that far out of town for any price.

It seemed unlikely that a stagecoach would get her there in time. The schedule would have to be perfect. But she had to try, so she jogged up the stairs to count the money she'd saved from her music lessons, to see if she would even have enough to pay the fare.

Halfway up the stairs, she encountered Harrington Astley, who was on his way down. "Morning, Ceci," he said, giving a jaunty salute. He paused, studying her face. "I say, is something wrong?"

She grabbed his forearm. "I am about to ask you for the most terrible favor."

His brown eyes were full of concern. "What's that?"

She swallowed thickly. "Order your curricle. I'll explain on the way."

CHAPTER 36

When Marcus arrived at Samuel Branton's office at the Inns of Court, the clerk informed him that his employer had just returned from the Admiralty and could see him immediately.

When Marcus walked into his office, Branton had his back to him. They knew each other reasonably well from their work for the Ladies' Society. Marcus knew that Branton had been born in Jamaica, but more than a decade of living and working in London had erased all but a trace of his original accent. He was a black man of around Marcus's same age and height. He had warm brown skin, dark brown eyes, and kept his coiled hair tightly cropped to accommodate the barrister's wig he was currently arranging on its stand in the corner. From their time spent together on the Ladies' Society's board, Marcus knew him to be highly intelligent and impeccably turned out. Marcus actually liked him, a statement he could make about vanishingly few people.

"Trevissick," Branton said warmly, brushing his hands

together to dust off the powder from his wig, "to what do I owe the plea—"

He jerked in surprise as he turned around. Marcus supposed he must look about as awful as he felt, judging by the way Branton was gaping at him.

"I need to ask you for a tremendous favor," Marcus said. There was no point in beating around the bush. "I'm desperate."

"Of course." Branton gestured to a chair. "Please, sit. Let me get you a drink. You, er… look as though you could use one."

Branton started to reach for the decanter sitting atop the sideboard. Frowning, he opened the cabinet below and pulled out a different bottle. He poured two glasses, handing one to Marcus, then took the seat opposite him.

Marcus took a sip and immediately felt better. "Chateau Margaux Bordeaux. An excellent vintage. The 1792, unless I am mistaken."

Raising an eyebrow, Branton consulted the label. His eyes widened. "That's right." He took a sip from his own glass and folded his hands on the desk before him. "So, what is the cause of your desperation?"

Marcus gave him the briefest summary of events. It came out a bit garbled to his own ears, but he'd hardly slept in three days, and he could tell it was affecting his mind.

"And the trial is at two o'clock?" Branton asked.

"Two o'clock," Marcus confirmed.

Branton rose and began pacing the room. "Then we haven't much time. We need to formulate a plan."

Marcus gazed at him blearily, scarcely daring to hope he had understood correctly. "You'll help me, then?"

Branton gave him a strange look. "Of course, I will."

"Even though the last set of barristers were all poisoned?"

"Well, I'm certainly not going to eat any strange food that

arrives at my office. But yes. Ellery sounds like a good man. We cannot abandon him in his hour of need."

"Thank you," Marcus said, his voice rich with feeling. "If you're worried about the food, you can dine at Trevissick House for the next month... year... make that the rest of your life."

Branton came around the desk and took the chair next to Marcus's. He turned it to face him, then took a seat. "That won't be necessary. Now, we need to figure out who is behind this." He gave Marcus a searching look. "Do you have any enemies?"

Marcus blinked at him. "Do I have any enemies?" What kind of question was that? He was a *Latimer*, for God's sake. "Let's see, there is... my entire family, excepting my sister Diana and my great-aunt Griselda. There are the three dozen servants I recently sacked, on account of their being my father's sycophants. There are dozens, if not hundreds, of people who were wronged by my father, including a couple I recently encountered. I informed them that if they caused a scandal that ruined Diana's season, their friends would have to clean up what's left of them with a rag."

Branton was giving him a strange look. "Were they demanding a bribe for their silence?"

"No. I sought them out. In order to apologize for my father's past misdeeds."

Branton rubbed his forehead. "Are you familiar with how apologies work? Never mind. Don't answer that. We haven't got time. Anyone else?"

"Let's see... There was also the man I threatened to murder four days ago, in the middle of the junction of Broad Street and Monmouth, before two hundred witnesses."

At Branton's incredulous look, Marcus added, "He was beating his children in a drunken rage. What was I supposed to do, drive by?"

Branton's face softened. "Ah. That's different, then."

"They're now staying at the Ladies' Society. In summary, it might be more efficient to make a list of people who are *not* my enemies. But, ultimately, unnecessary. I am all but certain that my uncle is the one behind Ellery's arrest."

"Your uncle. Good." Branton reached across the desk, snagged the bottle of Chateau Margaux, and refilled both of their glasses. "Now, I need you to tell me *everything*. Hold nothing back. As your barrister, you may trust that I will keep it in the strictest confidence. But if we're to have any chance of getting Ellery acquitted, I must not face any surprises in there."

Marcus nodded gravely. "Very well."

He proceeded to tell Branton everything.

Even the ugly bits.

And there were *a lot* of ugly bits.

A half-hour later, when he finished, Branton nodded. "All right. This is what we need to do."

"But I cannot tell the truth!" Marcus snapped.

"It's the only way," Branton countered. "And Ellery's only hope."

Marcus narrowed his eyes. Why did everyone keep saying that? "It is not the only way. I am a *duke*. The jury will naturally be influenced by me."

Branton snorted. "Yes, influenced to stick it to the posh nob who thinks he's better than them."

Marcus gave him an affronted glare.

Branton held up his hands, placatingly. "Were you the one on trial, you'd be facing a jury of your peers in the House of Lords. No doubt *they* would be eager to curry favor with you. But Ellery will be facing a jury of *his* peers.

And, believe me, the fact that you're a duke is a point against you."

Marcus pinched the bridge of his nose. "Then I will pay whatever bribes are necessary to the jury."

"No client of mine is going to bribe a jury, so don't mention that again. But even if I were the type of unscrupulous barrister who would go along with it, you haven't got time. The trial starts in two hours, and we have no idea who the members of the jury might be or how to get in contact with them."

Marcus's shoulders sagged. The finer logistics of bribing a jury had slipped his mind. "But if I tell the truth in open court, my sister will learn how our mother died. She would be devastated. I have been so careful to spare her from this."

Branton's face was a portrait of skepticism. "You speak of Lady Diana? The same girl who publicly annihilated Lady Pritchard Monday last?"

Marcus stiffened. "I don't see what that has to do with anything."

"I'm not sure that your sister is the shrinking violet you believe her to be." Branton's eyes were sympathetic. "Look, Trevissick. I'm sure you're used to dealing with things by acting superior and throwing your weight around. But that's not going to work this time. You need to show a little humanity. The jury will have no sympathy for the all-powerful duke. But the boy whose mother died? Who only cared about protecting his little sister? And who is damn near killing himself to save a beloved servant? *That* is a character a jury can get behind."

"I am not some character in a book," Marcus snapped. "This is my life, not the melodramatic plot of some penny dreadful."

"But make no mistake—you're telling a story to that jury. And the story of a butler who would go to any lengths to protect two helpless children? That is the story you want to spoon-feed to that jury."

Marcus could understand the logic of this. Because, when the story wasn't about your own mother, it tugged at your heartstrings for all of five minutes before your thoughts moved on and you started to wonder what was for supper.

But Marcus knew all too well that when the story was about your own mother, it wasn't just a story. The jury would wince sympathetically when Marcus told them his sad tale, then move on with their day.

But it would be different for Diana. Those same details—their mother's scream, the way she'd begged for her life, the horrible and sudden silence after she fell—would haunt her every moment, both waking and sleeping. It was nigh impossible not to fixate on them. Even now, all these years later, Marcus's heart was racing at the memory of them.

Marcus was the only one who understood that telling Diana these truths was no simple matter. This was Pandora's Box they were asking him to open, and once you peeked beneath that lid, you could never go back to the innocence of not knowing.

Nobody understood what a horrible thing it was that they were asking him to do to his own sister. If they truly understood, they would not have even suggested it.

The notion of describing the worst moment of his life, out loud before a packed courtroom, and then having it printed in the evening papers, so that absolutely everyone he encountered for the rest of his life would know his deepest, darkest secrets, made him break out in a cold sweat. But Marcus would have done it. In order to save Ellery, he would have forever destroyed his façade of being the perfect duke living the perfect life without the slightest hesitation.

But hurting Diana, exposing her to a lifetime of pain... He

had vowed from an early age that he would protect her. That he would shield her from the horrors of the world.

He could not go back on that vow.

He shook his head. "Out of the question."

Branton shook his head. "This is all beside the point. *You* are not the one about to go on trial. Ellery is. And he should be the one to choose what defense will be presented on his behalf. Come." Branton rose. "I need to speak with my client."

It was less than a mile to Newgate Prison. They took Marcus's carriage and met with Ellery in his new private room. Ellery looked better than he had when Marcus had first found him. At least he'd been able to clean himself up. But he still looked drawn and scared, and as if he hadn't slept much. Here in this tiny stone room, lit only by what autumn light made its way through the slit of a window high above, Ellery was stripped of his usual air of command, and he looked every one of his seventy-three years.

Marcus sat next to Ellery on the narrow bed while Branton explained his various options for mounting his defense. As expected, Branton pushed hard for full disclosure.

"I think we should adopt the duke's strategy," Ellery said once Branton had finished.

Branton cringed. "Are you quite sure? I feel you would stand a better chance by laying all of your cards on the table."

Ellery shook his head. "It is bad enough that His Grace knows the horrible truth. I would not have Lady Diana experience that pain, not for all the world."

Marcus placed a hand on Ellery's knee and gave it a gentle squeeze. Of course, Ellery the only one who understood. He had been there that day.

He knew that knowing the truth was not always a simple matter. Sometimes, the truth had consequences.

Branton's expression was that of a man who'd bitten into

a lemon, but he nodded. "Very well, then. Let's go over your testimony."

While they rehearsed, Marcus tried to ignore the queasy feeling in his stomach.

He knew he was doing the right thing. The only thing.

And Ellery had placed his trust in him.

Soon, Ellery's fate would be in the jury's hands.

CHAPTER 37

*A*t two o'clock sharp, the judge entered the courtroom in the Old Bailey through a side door.

"All rise," the bailiff called, and Marcus complied on wooden legs. Out of the corner of his eye, he caught sight of Uncle Eustace standing just behind the prosecution's bench.

So, his instinct that his uncle was the one behind this had been correct. He exchanged a glower with his uncle, already plotting a dozen things he would do the second this trial was over to exact his revenge.

"You may be seated," the judge said. "Before we begin, I would like to say a few words to the jury."

The judge began a pat speech emphasizing the importance of the duty they were about to undertake and the sanctity of the judicial process. It was rich, coming from a man who had probably accepted a handsome bribe from his uncle.

Marcus glanced at the jury box to study the men who would be deciding Ellery's fate and all but fell off the bench.

Sitting in the front row, in the place reserved for the foreman of the jury, was none other than the man he had visited in Whitechapel a week ago, the husband of the woman who had been raped by Marcus's father.

Kimbrell—that was his name.

Fucking hell. Of all the bloody bad luck. How he wished he could take back the part where he had said his friends would have to clean him up with a rag.

Well, there was nothing he could do about it now. The judge finished droning about what a solemn undertaking this farce of a trial was, and the prosecutor rose to present his case.

It was as bad as Marcus had feared. He read a passage aloud from his father's journal in which the old duke described in a mocking tone how Ellery was so cowed that he didn't even bother to ask about the blood soaking his clothing after he had stabbed a man to death behind a roadside inn. By the time the letter in which Ellery effectively confessed was read aloud, half the men in the jury box were openly glaring at the defense table.

Uncle Eustace even took the witness stand and testified very solemnly that, although his brother had always been troubled, he believed he might have been able to repress some of his worst impulses had he been surrounded by better people.

That absolute *fucker*. As if Uncle Eustace cared about anything but maintaining his allowance! Marcus was going to go over the rest of his father's journals with a fine-toothed comb to see if there wasn't some mention of his uncle. What was sauce for the goose was sauce for the gander, and they would see if Uncle Eustace could stand up to the level of scrutiny he was leveling upon Ellery.

Then it was time for them to present Ellery's defense. They had determined that Marcus would be the first to testify, in order to set the tone. God, he felt like he might be physically ill right there in the middle of the courtroom.

The judge asked for the name of the first witness. Branton gave him a firm nod.

Marcus was just rising to his feet when the doors to the courtroom flew open, slamming into the wall with a sharp bang. "Stop the trial!" a high-pitched voice screeched.

Marcus turned, along with everyone in the courtroom, to see one of the Astley twins—the dark-haired one, the one who was deranged—striding down the aisle.

Following just behind her were her sister, Lady Cheltenham, Aunt Griselda, Lord and Lady Fauconbridge, and, finally, Cecilia Chenoweth, trying to hide at the back of the group and keeping her eyes fixed upon the floor.

Marcus scowled at her ferociously, but she refused to meet his eye.

They made their way to the front of the courtroom, where Lady Lucy fixed the reporters sitting in the pew just behind the defense's table with a hopeful smile. "Could we sit here?"

Six out of the seven men occupying the bench went scrambling out of the way, unable to deny the blonde beauty. The seventh frowned, hesitating.

"Move!" Aunt Griselda barked, shouldering her way onto the bench. The Astley party took their seats, Cecilia still keeping her eyes downcast.

There was a click of boots at the back of the room. Every head once again swiveled, this time to see an officer in a green coat escorting a slight young lady.

Marcus rolled his eyes at this carefully staged entrance. Harrington Astley, the man who had once stolen all of Marcus's quills, replacing them with ostrich feathers to make him look like a ridiculous fop, was the officer.

And the girl clinging to his arm as if she would blow away in a stiff breeze was Diana.

She wore a pale pink traveling costume with a matching

hat and reticule and one cream kidskin glove. Her lips were pursed in a moue, and her eyebrows sloped in an expression of studied distress he had never seen upon his sister's face, not once in his life. Meanwhile, Astley rested his gloved hand gently atop her forearm where it looped through his as if he were fearful that she might faint away.

They reached the front of the aisle. Diana drew in an unsteady breath, and Marcus wondered if he might be wrong, and she was truly in distress. The news that Ellery was being tried for a capital offense was highly distressing, after all.

For the briefest instant, her eyes met his, and he saw a spark of annoyance flare. Aha! There was the sister he knew so well. This wilting flower business was all a front.

Diana turned to their barrister. "Mr. Branton, I hope you will forgive me, as I can see you had planned to question my brother next. But would there be any chance I could go first? I wish to testify"—she closed her eyes and pressed the back of her hand against her forehead—"while I still have the strength."

While she still had the strength. It was all Marcus could do not to snort. Diana had been raised by *Aunt Griselda.* Under Aunt Griselda's guidance, Marcus had seen his sister tramp across the moors from dawn until dusk, shooting a pheasant for her luncheon which she was required to pluck, gut, and roast over an open fire without the slightest assistance.

Some wilting flower. There were plough horses out there who envied Diana her constitution.

But the jury did not know that. They saw only that she was young and blonde, pretty and slight, and they were eating up this melodramatic display. And no one looked more pleased than Samuel Branton, whose expression could be summarized as, *finally, something I can work with.* Branton nodded his thanks to Astley as he gingerly took Diana's arm, helping her into the witness box with such a degree of care that one would have thought she was a newborn fawn who had not yet mastered the art of walking on her own.

Marcus turned to glower at Cecilia, but she still wouldn't look at him. He had to settle for glaring at Harrington Astley, who had taken the seat beside her. Astley responded with a cheerful wink.

Up on the stand, Diana tremulously took her oath, then accepted Branton's handkerchief, pre-emptively dabbing at her eyes.

"My lady," Branton began, "I assume you are familiar with the charges against Mr. Ellery?"

"I have been informed of them, yes."

"And you are aware of the letter Mr. Ellery wrote, confessing that he had to do a number of unsavory things while in your father's employ?"

Diana turned to speak directly to the jury, her eyes entreating. "What you must understand is that everything Ellery did, he did only for the sake of my brother and me. Had he crossed my father, he would have lost his post. And then, there would have been no one there to protect us."

"To protect you," Branton said. "A curious choice of words. From what did you need protection?"

Diana wrung the handkerchief with her gloved hand. "I fear it was not so much from *what* as from *whom*, Mr. Branton. And the person we required protection from was my father."

Branton's voice was soothing as he asked, "And why did you require protection from your father, my lady?"

"The truth is…" Diana closed her eyes as if she were gathering all of her strength, and maybe she was. She opened her eyes and looked straight at the jury box. "It was my father. He was the one who killed my mother."

CHAPTER 38

The courtroom exploded in conversation after Diana made her revelation.

Ceci glanced surreptitiously at Marcus. His spine was stiff, his shoulders raised almost to his ears. He did not turn, so it was difficult to gauge his reaction. Shock, perhaps?

That he was furious with her, she was certain. How she wished she could speak to him. He was probably imagining that she had told Diana the horrifying truth about how her mother died.

But it turned out that Diana had always known. She had been impressively stoic upon receiving the news that one of her few childhood protectors was going on trial for a capital offense. The strongest emotion she had shown was annoyance at her brother for not sending for her at once. They had spent the entirety of the carriage ride from Broxbourne to London strategizing. Diana would be Ellery's most sympathetic witness by far, and Lady Cheltenham had coached her in exactly how she should present herself to the jury. Diana had listened to her advice with a steely determination.

But, as soon as she stepped into that courtroom, she had become the very picture of feminine frailty.

And the jury was entranced. It took a full minute for the judge to restore some semblance of order.

Once the room was silent, Mr. Branton asked, "You say your father killed your mother."

Diana nodded tremulously. "That is correct."

"Were you witness to this event?" Mr. Branton asked.

"No. I was but two years old when she died, so I imagine I was in the nursery." She gestured toward the defense's table. "But Ellery was there, as was my brother. They can provide you with the details."

"Did your father face trial for your mother's death?"

Diana shook her head mournfully. "No. He escaped all consequences."

"Did anyone report him to the magistrate?" Mr. Branton asked.

From her place in the audience, Lady Griselda shouted, "I did! I tried to have that worthless *Schietbüddel* held accountable, but—"

The judge pounded his gavel against the podium. "Order! Order!"

Mr. Branton had turned to face the audience, eyes wide with surprise. Ceci felt a pang of pity for him, trying to conduct a trial without having had the opportunity to interview the majority of the witnesses. But, quick on his feet, he turned to face the jury. "You will hear Lady Griselda's testimony presently." He turned back toward Diana. "Did you have any other reasons to fear your father?"

Diana dabbed at her eyes. "After my mother's death, he left for a time. I don't know where he went. There are a great number of properties associated with the dukedom where he could have been. But he absented himself for around two years. When he returned…" She paused to draw in a breath, and it struck Ceci that Diana was not entirely performing for the jury, that it was genuinely difficult for her to recount these memories. "I was the one who became the focus of his wrath."

One of the jurors, a baker, judging by the fine layer of flour coating his red beard, was not able to contain himself. "Is that what happened to yer arm?"

Diana turned to address the juror directly. Although she had developed a reputation amongst the *ton* for being something of an ice queen following her evisceration of Lady Pritchard, her manner could not have been warmer as she said, "No, sir. I was born like this."

The juror nodded sympathetically.

Mr. Branton cleared his throat. "Lady Diana, I must apologize for asking an indelicate question. But could you explain what you mean when you say that you became the focus of your father's wrath?"

She nodded, setting her jaw. "He would scream at me constantly. Sometimes, he would hit me." She swallowed thickly. "I was only four, but I have a distinct memory of him grabbing me by the hair and throwing me into the wall."

Murmurs broke out throughout the courtroom. Once they had died down, Mr. Branton asked, "And what did Mr. Ellery do during this time?"

"Several things," Diana said quickly. "He did everything within his power to distract my father and keep him away from me. I also remember him following my father around the house, loudly addressing him as 'Your Grace,' so I would know he was coming and have a chance to hide. And, of course, he was the one who sent for my brother. Marcus was the one who forced my father to give me up. He arranged it so I could live with Aunt Griselda instead."

"You say your brother forced him to give you up. How did he do that?"

Diana tilted her head to the side. "I don't actually know. But Marcus can tell you."

Mr. Branton bowed. "Thank you, my lady. No further questions."

~

Marcus watched the prosecutor attempt to cross-examine Diana for all of two minutes.

"You were four years old when your father returned?" he asked.

"That is correct," she replied.

He stroked his chin. "That's very young. Is there not a possibility, Lady Diana, that you could be misremembering some of these incidents?"

She shook her head sadly. "No, sir. How I wish I could forget them! But I fear they are seared into my memory."

"And you are certain that, over time, your mind has not twisted them into something they are not?"

Diana made a wounded sound. When she spoke, her voice was very quiet. "I hope, sir, you do not truly think me a liar?"

Several members of the jury scowled, and the prosecutor was not an idiot. He recognized that attacking such a sympathetic witness could do nothing but backfire. "No further questions, Your Honor."

Aunt Griselda went next. Marcus had not realized the lengths to which she had gone in an attempt to have his father held responsible for his mother's death. Her testimony certainly helped Ellery's cause, establishing that his father had all of the local officials in his pocket, such that even someone as wealthy, well-connected, and determined as Aunt Griselda had been unable to obtain justice for her beloved niece.

Then it was Marcus's turn to take the stand. Although it

was anathema to say such things out loud, in public, Marcus forced himself to recount the events leading up to his mother's death in excruciating detail. How protecting her had been his motivation in learning to fence. How he had forgotten his sword that morning and had been sprinting toward the stairs, trying desperately to get there in time.

When he reached the part where Ellery came charging up the stairs, catching Marcus in a bear hug and preventing him from seeing his mother's broken body lying on the floor below, the baker blew his nose into his apron. Indeed, there was scarcely a dry eye in the jury box, and Marcus was starting to congratulate himself on a job well done when the prosecutor rose to perform his cross-examination.

"What a moving tale you have spun for us today, Your Grace." The prosecutor fixed Marcus with a predatory gaze. "Perhaps a bit too moving to be believed."

Marcus understood in an instant that because the prosecutor had been unable to attack Diana without damaging his own case, he had saved his powder and would now be levying those blows against him.

He could not rise to the bait. The only thing that mattered right now was presenting Ellery in the most sympathetic light possible. For once in his life, he could not come across as an arrogant ass. So, Marcus answered blandly, "Allow me to assure you that every word is true."

The prosecutor regarded him skeptically. "How old were you when your father returned?"

"Thirteen years old."

"Why were you not home to begin with?"

"I was sent to Eton at age twelve."

"And how did you get back from Eton after receiving this alleged letter from Ellery?"

Calm. Marcus had to remain calm at all costs. "I had my own horse stabled at a local mews. I rode him as far as he would carry me, then hired saddle horses the rest of the way back."

The prosecutor looked openly skeptical. "How long did the journey take you?"

"I arrived home the following evening," Marcus said evenly.

The prosecutor turned to the jury. "He expects us to believe he traveled more than 250 miles in one day."

"He does," Marcus snapped, frustration seeping into his voice, "because when you receive a letter informing you that your father is about to kill your little sister, the same way he killed your mother, you change horses every ten miles and ride through the night."

Two members of the jury nodded. Good. He hadn't lost them—yet. But Marcus was cognizant of the fact that his temper was starting to flare, and that was not what Ellery needed right now.

The prosecutor looked him up and down, baldly skeptical. "And how did a boy of thirteen force the hand of a duke? A duke whom, we have been told, was so all-powerful he was above the very law?"

Oh, hell. He would ask this, the one question Marcus wanted to avoid answering above all others. "It does not make for very pleasant hearing," he said, his voice clipped. "It is certainly not a tale I should like to recount in front of the ladies who are present."

The prosecutor snorted as he spun to face the jury. "How very convenient. You see, this is nothing more than an excuse. The truth is, the duke and his sister were never in any danger from their father. The old duke could be very cruel. We have heard as much from his journals. But, as is often the case, he reserved this cruelty for those he considered below him. Not for his own children."

"Objection!" Branton bellowed.

"Sustained," the judge said. "You will have the opportunity to make your closing remarks, Mr. Dixon. *Later*. Right now, you will direct your questions toward the witness."

The prosecutor turned to face Marcus in the witness box. "If it is true, if your father was so depraved, and such a danger to your sister that he had to be *forced* into giving her up, then it follows that there must be some means by which you forced him. If you cannot tell us what that was, then what are we left to conclude?"

"Fine!" Marcus snapped. He could not believe he was about to speak these words out loud, in a public courtroom, so that they would appear on the front page of every evening paper. Yet, as he looked at Ellery, sitting frail and forlorn at the defense table, he knew he would not have any regrets.

He avoided Diana's gaze, staring instead at the far wall as he said, "I told my father that if he would not let Diana go, then I would kill myself."

The silence in the courtroom was absolute, as if what he had just said was so shocking, it had knocked the air from everyone's lungs.

The prosecutor was the first to recover. "K-kill yourself? Why would that motivate your father?"

"Because I was his flesh and blood. You see"—Marcus winced at what he was about to say in front of a half-dozen ladies—"my father had certain *diseases* that made it difficult for him to father children. And, as those *diseases* progressed, it became increasingly clear that Diana and I would be the only children he would ever sire. He did not care about her, because she was a girl. But I was his son and heir, the one who would ensure that his own blood continued through the ducal line. So, paradoxically, although I despised him, I was the one person he truly liked. He never raised a hand against me. Not even once."

The courtroom was still stunned silent, so Marcus

continued, "That is why my threat was so potent. Had something happened to me, the dukedom would have gone to his brother"—Marcus fixed his uncle with a vindictive glare—"a weakling who came to him every month, begging for his allowance. A pathetic creature not capable of standing on his own." Marcus shook his head. "The mere thought revolted him. The day I came to understand how important I was to my father was the day I realized my own power. I did not merely hold the ace of spades in my hand; I *was* the ace of spades. I had the power to protect Diana. But only by bringing myself into play."

The prosecutor shook himself. "But why would your father acquiesce? We would expect such a monster as you describe to lock you in a cell. To chain you to the wall, so you had no means of harming yourself."

Marcus shook his head. "There is a certain futility in attempting to ascribe logical motives to a man such as my father. As I said, he despised weakness above all things. And here was his son, his own flesh and blood, displaying such strength of will. I remember how he smiled at me when I placed my sword at my own throat. It pleased him beyond measure to see such ruthlessness in his son. I think he fancied he was seeing himself in me. And perhaps he was." He fixed the prosecutor with a hard look. "I, too, can be utterly ruthless."

The prosecutor's brow was drawn. "Suicide is a mortal sin. Those guilty of such a sin abandon all hope of grace and salvation."

"I am aware," Marcus said tightly. "The words were not spoken lightly."

"And yet, you expect us to believe that you risked your mortal soul?"

"Of course, I did. If it meant Diana would live…" He trailed off, his gaze finally falling upon his sister.

She was quietly sobbing into her handkerchief, Aunt Griselda's arm around her shoulders.

Marcus fixed the prosecutor with his blackest scowl. "Look what you've done—you've made my sister cry, you absolute piece of—" He broke off before he could say something he would regret in front of the jury. "I hope you are satisfied, *sir*. Is there anything else?"

Mr. Dixon's face was tight as he said, "The prosecution rests, Your Honor."

As Marcus resumed his seat on the bench next to Ellery, Fauconbridge leaned forward and squeezed Marcus on the shoulder. It suddenly struck Marcus that he could've spoken to Fauconbridge about all of this, if not at the time it was occurring, then certainly in the years that had followed, as their friendship had deepened. That... perhaps he should've. That it might have helped.

Then, it was Ellery's turn.

Much of the information he recounted was similar to what Marcus and Diana had related. But, having spent a great deal of time in their father's presence, Ellery had a number of additional horrors to relate. "The old duke was constantly in a drunken state. There was nothing I could do to make him sober. I therefore plied him with wine, as keeping him so drunk he was insensible seemed like the best of a number of bad options." Ellery paused, biting his lip. "At one point, he laid the poker in the fireplace. Once the tip became red hot, he removed it, calling, 'Where is Diana?'" He squeezed his eyes shut. "I confess that I handed him a glass of brandy laced with a heavy dose of laudanum. Perhaps that was wrong, but I could not think of any other way to prevent him from doing her ladyship serious harm. It worked. He fell asleep right there on the hearth rug, and while he was passed out, I had the footmen gather every poker in the house so I could lock them away in the butler's pantry."

When it was the prosecutor's turn to perform his cross-examination, he went through a laundry list of the old duke's misdeeds, some from the day's testimony, and some from the journal. He asked if Ellery had known about each one. Ellery somberly admitted that he had known about most of them.

"And you never reported him to the authorities?" the prosecutor asked.

"No, sir," Ellery said solemnly. "It was well known that the old duke had all the local officials in his pocket—the magistrate, the coroner, the bailiff. He even had spies in the posting inn in the local village, watching the outgoing mail for him. I had to walk to the neighboring village in the dead of night to send the letter regarding his father's return to His Grace the present duke. I did not dare anger the old duke. It was imperative that I maintain my position so there would be someone to watch over the children."

The prosecutor looked skeptical. "But, had you lost your position, would your successor not have watched out for them?"

"They might have," Ellery acknowledged. "There were many other servants whom I know looked out for them. But the old duke tended to attract a certain type of servant. Ones who shared his base proclivities, who knew he would look the other way when it came to their own bad behavior. His Grace the present duke had to dismiss a good third of our household staff in order to rid ourselves of that element. I could not trust that my successor would have their best interests at heart."

"But surely after Lady Diana went to live with her aunt, you could have absented yourself from a household in which so much illegal activity was taking place. That is, if you truly objected to that illegal activity and were not a party to it."

Ellery fell quiet. "You must keep in mind that His Grace the present duke still had to come back to that house during his school holidays and that he was but a boy of thirteen. I know it is hard to countenance, seeing him so masterful and confident today." Ellery shook his head. "But a boy he was, and he deserved to have someone who would watch over him. It was bad enough that he had to grow up as quickly as he did."

"But did he truly need someone to watch over him?" the prosecutor pressed. "He testified himself that his father never raised a hand against him."

Ellery tugged at his collar. Marcus fancied he saw a faint blush spreading across his cheeks. "The, er, *diseases* that His Grace alluded to earlier grew more severe with each passing year. And one of the symptoms was madness. Who knows— the old duke might never have raised a hand against his son and heir. But his mind was disturbed at the best of times and growing more so every day. I was not about to assume that his son would always be safe."

The prosecutor eventually rested. Closing statements were made, and the judge gave his instructions to the jurors.

Soon, they would learn Ellery's fate. Until then, all they could do was wait.

CHAPTER 39

*S*amuel Branton warned them that the jury might deliberate for an hour or more. Marcus was pumping his hand, thanking him for doing such an exemplary job on such short notice when the jurors filed back into the room a mere two minutes after they had recused themselves.

They hastily resumed their seats. "Is it normal for the jury to take so little time?" Marcus whispered to Branton.

"Not *this* little," he murmured.

"What does it mean?" Marcus hissed. The thought that, in mere moments, Ellery might be convicted, might be sentenced to transportation or even death, had Marcus's pulse flying.

"I don't know," Branton whispered.

They were prevented from further conversation as the judge opened the proceedings. "You have reached a verdict?"

"We have, yer honor," said Mr. Kimbrell. Marcus felt his heart sink further as he recalled who was serving as the foreman of the jury.

"And what is your decision?" the judge asked.

Mr. Kimbrell kept his eyes fixed upon the judge. "Not guilty, yer honor."

The murmurs that broke out across the courtroom were nothing compared to the roaring in Marcus's ears. Not guilty —those were surely the sweetest words in the English language.

The room around him swam. When his vision cleared, Mr. Branton was pumping his hand and Fauconbridge was squeezing his shoulder. Diana wrapped her arms around Ellery's neck right there in the middle of the courtroom.

"On all counts?" the judge asked.

"On all counts," Mr. Kimbrell confirmed.

"Very good." The judge lifted his gavel. "The jury has entered a verdict of—"

"What do you mean, not guilty?" Uncle Eustace snapped. "He wrote out a signed confession!"

Into the stunned silence that followed, Mr. Kimbrell said, "He said he couldn't remember this specific incident, and there weren't no details. So the old duke came home with some blood on him. So what? That could've been anything. He could've been butchering a hog, or—"

"You think the *Duke of Trevissick* was *butchering a hog?*" Uncle Eustace screeched.

Mr. Kimbrell's brow lowered into an angry vee. "He might've been!"

"Or hunting," Diana interjected, giving Mr. Kimbrell a brilliant smile. "After all, what gentleman does not hunt? And many men prefer to clean their own game. My own brother, the duke, often performs that task."

This happened to be true, but only because Aunt Griselda insisted that both he and Diana clean their own game. But now was not the moment to mention this detail.

Marcus nodded gravely. "So I do. And it can be quite a messy business."

Uncle Eustace was still glaring at Mr. Kimbrell. "There was a mountain of evidence!"

"Well, we didn't find it very compelling!" Mr. Kimbrell snapped.

The judge pounded his gavel. "Order, order. Mr. Ellery has been found not guilty. This court is adjourned."

"All rise," the bailiff called. They all stood, the judge filed out of the room, and the nightmare was finally over.

A cluster of well-wishers formed around Ellery, and another around Samuel Branton. Marcus glanced around their party, looking for Cecilia. He was still feeling annoyed that she had gone against his express instructions and told Diana the truth about their mother's death.

But he had to acknowledge that her strategy had worked, and Diana seemed to be bearing up for the moment. Perhaps she had been right all along. Hell, he didn't know. He wasn't sure what he was going to say. But he knew they needed to talk. Now that the excitement of the trial had worn off, a crushing exhaustion descended upon him. All he wanted to do was go back to Trevissick House and sleep for the next twelve hours.

It was a moot point, as it appeared she had slipped from the room.

Well. He would work things out with Cecilia Chenoweth. Tomorrow, once he could think straight and would not worsen the situation by saying something he would regret.

As soon as he was ensconced in the Trevissick carriage with Ellery, Diana, and Aunt Griselda, Marcus slumped against the padded wall and closed his eyes.

He was already fading when a sharp finger jabbed him in the arm. "Marcus! Wake up!"

"What is it?" he asked groggily. He found Diana glaring at him with tears in her eyes.

"I am trying to decide," she said, her voice shaking,

"whether I should hug you or throttle you. I never knew that was how you convinced Father to let me go live with Aunt Griselda. That you... that you..."

"I never told anyone," Marcus said, fishing his handkerchief out of his pocket and handing it to Diana. "I never intended for you to find out."

Diana dabbed at her nose. "Which brings me to the reason I want to throttle you! What on earth were you thinking, Marcus? You should have sent for me the second you received word of Ellery's arrest!"

His jaw tightened. "I only sought to spare you from distressing news."

There was a pleading frustration in her eyes. "I know that. You always want what's best for me, and you're always so certain that you know what that is. But you don't! Because the thing I want above all else is to chart my own course."

"I let you chart your own course," he protested.

She glowered at him. "As you did at my debut ball when you chose *all* of my partners?"

"Be fair, Diana. I know those men. I know which ones are scoundrels, and—"

"Yes, you do! Which is why I would have wanted to *have a conversation* with you about my prospective partners. I would have appreciated your advice, and I would have heeded it the majority of the time. But that isn't what you did. You just went and arranged everything to your own liking, without so much as consulting me!"

"I... I..." Marcus tried to think of a counterargument, but it was difficult when his brain was feeling so sluggish.

And also, a waspish voice inside his head added, *when your sister is entirely correct.*

"I am sorry," he finally said. "I was so wrapped up in trying to make sure your debut was perfect, I did not realize how overbearing I was being. I will certainly consult you should a similar situation arise in the future."

The thin line of Diana's lips did not soften. "While I do appreciate that, the matter of my dancing partners is the merest trifle compared to today. Ellery could have been convicted! He could have hung!"

Ellery, who had up until this point opted to observe the squabbling siblings in silence, held up both hands. "You mustn't distress yourself, my lady. It all came out right in the end."

"It came out right thanks to *me*," Diana insisted, glaring at her brother. "The merest child could have seen that I was our most sympathetic witness. Yet, had Marcus had his way, I would have been twirling my thumbs in Broxbourne, oblivious to the fact that Ellery was in danger." She huffed. "Thank goodness for Miss Chenoweth!"

"I am still vexed with Miss Chenoweth," Marcus grumbled.

"I should like to know why," Diana shot back. "It was thanks to her intervention that Ellery was acquitted."

"He might very well have won without it."

Aunt Griselda snorted. "Unlikely."

"He might have," Marcus insisted. "We had a good plan."

Diana crossed her arms. "What did the barristers think of your plan? Because, unless I am very much mistaken, Mr. Branton was enormously relieved when I walked into that courtroom."

When Marcus's only response was to narrow his eyes, Diana poked him again. "Well?"

Marcus slouched against the squabs. "They all recommended a plan similar to yours."

"Then why on earth didn't you listen?" Diana snapped.

"Because I was hoping I could find a way to spare you."

She looked genuinely perplexed. "Spare me? From what?"

He pinched the bridge of his nose. "From having to learn the truth about how our mother died."

Marcus had imagined a range of ways Diana might react to that statement, but he had never considered that she might burst out laughing.

"Surely you did not believe…" She trailed off, studying his face. "You did. You thought I didn't know that the old duke killed our mother. Marcus!" She cast her eyes heavenward. "I have always known. How is it possible that you imagined otherwise?"

"You could not have always known. You were two years old when it happened!" He leaned forward, angry that someone had exposed his young sister to this painful truth. "Who told you?"

"I honestly don't know. It was after Father returned. I spent a great deal of time hiding in the weeks before you arrived. I overheard a pair of housemaids talking about it while I was hiding behind some curtains." She shook her head. "Frankly, it did not come as a great shock."

He shook his head. It did not have the effect of clearing his murky brain. "I… I didn't realize you knew."

"I did. But even had I not, Marcus, surely this would have been the occasion to tell me. Ellery's life was at stake! Frankly, you should have told me as soon as I came of age. I would rather know the truth, even if it is difficult to hear."

Which was exactly what Cecilia had said. Marcus sighed. "I was only trying to protect you—"

"By keeping me sheltered like a hothouse flower." Diana snorted. "Let this be the turning of a new page. Going forward, you are going to discuss things with me. We are going to talk about the past, and you are not going to hide the truth just because you think it will be difficult."

"But—"

"And I expect you to consult me on matters concerning my life going forward."

"I will, but—"

"And you are *not* to go out and betroth me to whatever man *you* deem fit. I am going to choose my own husband, Marcus. I mean it."

Marcus tried and failed to suppress a yawn. "But what if I know the man you choose to be a reprobate?"

"I will always listen to your advice. But the final decision will rest with *me*."

He sighed. "I suppose—"

She shook her head so hard the curls peeking from the sides of her bonnet trembled. "Don't suppose. I want your promise."

"But—"

"Give me your word!"

"Fine," he grumbled. "I promise that you will have the final say regarding the man you marry. And I will strive to do better going forward."

"Good." Diana peered out the carriage window. "Ah, here we are. Go and get some sleep. You look *dreadful*."

"Thank you ever so much," Marcus said dryly.

But his sister was right—he was utterly exhausted. He managed to stagger up the stairs to the ducal bedchamber, where he proceeded to fall asleep face-down on top of the counterpane with his boots hanging off the end of the bed.

CHAPTER 40

*W*hen Marcus awoke, afternoon light was streaming through the windows.

He sat up, rubbing his neck. God, he must've slept for the better part of twenty-four hours. Bastian had apparently attended to him at some point, because someone had removed his boots, cravat, and trousers, and tucked him under the covers.

Speaking of Bastian, Marcus became cognizant of a light knocking at the door. "Your Grace," Bastian called. "Are you awake?"

"You may enter," Marcus said, flopping back against the pillows and staring up at the crisp white plasterwork on the ceiling. He snorted. "The last time you came barging into my room, it was with the news that Ellery had been arrested. You'd better not have any bad news for me this time."

He heard rather than saw Bastian freeze. Propping himself up on one elbow, Marcus frowned. "What could have possibly happened this time?"

Bastian was wringing his hands. "It's Miss Chenoweth, Your Grace. She's been ruined."

∼

Bastian filled him in while getting him dressed. "You see, when she went to Broxbourne to fetch Lady Diana, she traveled with Lieutenant Astley in an open carriage."

Marcus lifted his chin so Bastian could shave his neck. "If it was an open carriage, there shouldn't be any problem."

Bastian paused to rinse the blade. "It wouldn't have been a problem had their destination been Hyde Park. But they were spotted by Lady Melville as they were leaving Tottenham. No young lady can be seen alone with a gentleman that far afield, open carriage or no."

"And Lady Melville has no doubt told everyone," Marcus said as Bastian wiped off the last bits of shaving soap with a warm towel. "Well, no matter. I was already planning to marry her. That will quash any rumors."

"Yes, Your Grace," Bastian said, dabbing Marcus's custom blend of shaving tonic onto his face. "I just thought that, given the lovers' quarrel the two of you had the last time you were here, you would want to reassure Miss Chenoweth at the first opportunity that your intentions have not changed."

Marcus sighed. It shouldn't come as a surprise that his entire household staff was aware of the most minute details of his relationship with Cecilia. He hadn't been particularly discreet. "You are correct. I'll head over to Astley House as soon as you're done with me. I should let Diana know of my plans. Where is she?"

"Last I saw, she and Lady Griselda were exercising the pointers in the back garden. I will inform them that you're heading out."

Marcus had the housekeeper empty the hothouse of pink dahlias and make up an impressive bouquet. Upon further reflection, and especially in light of his conversation with

Diana yesterday, he had to own that he owed Cecilia an apology. He may as well do it properly.

As he awaited the carriage, Diana came striding onto the front portico, Aunt Griselda trailing after her. "So long as you're heading to Astley House, I'd like to call upon Lucy and Izzie. I probably won't have too many chances to see them before the end of the Season." At Marcus's sour look, she held up her hand. "I promise not to intrude upon your tete-a-tete with Miss Chenoweth." She gave him a sideways look as the carriage drew near. "As tempting as it will be to listen at the door to hear you groveling."

Marcus sighed. "I must insist that you not listen at the door. This will be bad enough as it is. But she deserves an apology."

After the short carriage ride across Mayfair, they were admitted to Astley House by the butler, Yarwood, only to learn that the people they sought were not present. "The Astleys decided to go to Vauxhall, as tonight is the last night the gardens will be open for the Season." Yarwood frowned. "A note was dispatched to Latimer House several hours ago to see if Your Grace, her ladyship, and her ladyship might care to join their party. I wonder that you did not receive it."

Marcus waved this off. "I'm sure you heard about Ellery's ordeal."

Yarwood bowed. "Yes, Your Grace."

"I insisted he take a few days to rest and recover. So, perhaps it is not surprising that things at the front of the house are not running with their customary efficiency." Marcus flicked a speck of pollen off of his cuff. "No matter. We will head to Vauxhall and find them there."

Yarwood's expression was pained, and his gaze was fixed upon the bouquet of dahlias. "May I ask Your Grace a presumptuous question?"

"Please do. I am all curiosity."

"I could not help but notice your rather impressive bouquet. Am I correct in my assumption that you intend to mend things with Miss Chenoweth?"

Marcus cleared his throat. Damn, but this was awkward, but a duke did not blush. "Just so, Yarwood, but no matter. I will speak to her at Vauxhall."

The butler cringed, rubbing his brow. "Why does this always happen on my watch?"

Marcus frowned. "Why does what always happen? What do you mean?"

"First it was Lord Morsley and Lady Anne, and now—" Yarwood broke off with a sound of disgust. "I am not sure if Your Grace is aware, but Miss Chenoweth was seen yesterday leaving Town in an open carriage along with Master Harrington. It will come as no surprise that word has traveled fast, and her reputation is now in tatters."

Marcus nodded gravely. "I have been informed, but there is no cause for distress. By this time tomorrow, Miss Chenoweth will be the Duchess of Trevissick. That should silence any gossip."

Yarwood made a bleak sound. "If you don't hurry, by this time tomorrow, Miss Chenoweth will be Mrs. Nettlethorpe-Ogilvy."

The room around him spun. "*What*? That... that is not possible. I have already informed her that we were to be married!"

Diana squinted at him. "You... *informed* her? Do you not mean that you *asked* her to marry you?"

Marcus reflected upon that particular conversation. "It would be more accurate to say that I informed her," he muttered.

"Marcus!" Diana snapped. "What is *wrong* with you?"

"Let us save the cataloging of my many failings for a less urgent moment." He turned back to Yarwood. "The point is, there should be no possibility of Miss Chenoweth accepting Nettlethorpe-Ogilvy, as she has already accepted me."

Yarwood wrung his hands. "I am sorry to be the one to inform Your Grace that everyone is under the impression that your offer has been rescinded. And that the present situation is most urgent. Lady Cheltenham spelled it out in her note—the one you did not receive. Miss Chenoweth must marry post haste. If the Astleys offer shelter to a woman who has been so publicly ruined, it will destroy the reputations of not only Miss Chenoweth but also Lady Lucy and Lady Isabella. I am not sure what it was precisely Your Grace said that gave the impression that your intentions toward Miss Chenoweth had changed—"

You will be dead to me. That would just about do it. *God,* but he was an idiot.

"—but Lady Cheltenham wanted to be sure there was not a misunderstanding. Hence the note she sent to Latimer House, saying that, if it is still your wish to marry her, you should reassure Miss Chenoweth with all possible speed. But if not..."

Yarwood trailed off, swallowing.

"If not, what?" Marcus asked, dreading the answer.

"Mr. Nettlethorpe-Ogilvy came as soon as he heard about the rumors. He intended to propose on the spot, but Lady Cheltenham asked him to hold off, so they could see if your offer still stood." Yarwood shook his head in disbelief. "I have never seen a man display such fundamental *decency.* But they agreed that if they did not hear from you..." Yarwood trailed off, cringing.

Marcus's heart was thundering in his ears. "If they did not hear from me, then what?"

Yarwood's eyes brimmed with sympathy. "If they did not hear from you by the time the fireworks begin at Vauxhall, then Mr. Nettlethorpe-Ogilvy would issue his proposal."

CHAPTER 41

"Can't you row this thing any faster?"

Surprisingly, the question had come not from Marcus, who was slumped in the prow of the wherry making its way ever so slowly across the Thames, but from Aunt Griselda.

"We must make it to Vauxhall before the fireworks begin!" Aunt Griselda insisted.

"You'll have a lovely view of the fireworks from the river," the wherryman said firmly, not exerting himself an extra whit.

"We do not care about the fireworks themselves," Aunt Griselda explained. "It's what's going to happen when the fireworks display begins."

The wherryman did not trouble to sound overly interested. "And what's going to happen when the fireworks begin?"

She pointed toward Marcus. "The woman he loves is going to agree to marry someone else! This man is planning to propose beneath the fireworks. Do you see?"

Based on the way he rolled his eyes, the wherryman did

not seem overly impressed. "Is this the plot of some penny dreadful?"

"No," Marcus muttered. "It's just my life."

Diana, who was seated next to Marcus, squeezed his arm. He watched as she purposefully wiped the haughty expression characteristic of the Latimer family from her face, donning the pathetic, doe-eyed mien she had used in court yesterday as easily as she might change her bonnet. "Oh, please, sir, won't you help my brother? His situation is, how you say..." She waved her hand, searching for the right word.

"Pathetic," Aunt Griselda supplied.

"I fear *pathetic* is an apt descriptor," Diana agreed. "You see, my brother is horrifically imperious."

"Overbearing," Aunt Griselda added. "Despotic, even."

"Just so," Diana, the little traitor, agreed. "But he has managed to find the one woman, surely in all of existence, who is able to tolerate him—"

"Not merely tolerate him," Aunt Griselda observed, "but bring him to heel!"

Diana shook her head woefully. "Surely this saintly creature is his only hope of having a successful marriage. But it gets worse! Because, you see, he is a duke..." She dropped her voice low as if the words she was about to utter were almost too horrible to speak aloud. "And the man he is about to lose her to is a *blacksmith*!"

This was enough to shake Marcus from his silent brooding. "Nettlethorpe-Ogilvy is not a blacksmith. He is in trade, to be sure, but he is one of the richest men in all of England."

"A blacksmith," Diana repeated in a stage whisper.

There was a sloshing sound. Marcus glanced up and saw that the wherryman had suddenly begun to exert himself with the oars.

"Oh, thank you, sir!" Diana cried. "I knew such a feeling

gentleman as yourself would not be indifferent to matters of the heart."

The wherryman responded with a snort. "Matters of the heart. Matters of the pocketbook, more like." He jerked his chin toward Marcus. "Seeing as you're a duke, I'll be expecting something substantial for my efforts."

"And you will get it," Marcus said.

They fell silent as they continued their progress across the river. As the stairs finally came into view, a cry went up from just beyond the trees. Patches of light glowing in a myriad of colors slowly began to spread along the shoreline.

The lamp lighting had just commenced.

That meant that the fireworks would begin shortly.

Marcus was already on his feet, ready to alight the second the boat drew close to shore. He tossed a silver crown to the wherryman and sprang onto the stairs before the boat came to a full stop, then hurried toward the entryway. He did not pause to wait for Diana and Aunt Griselda. They would understand. It was imperative that he find Cecilia before Nettlethorpe-Ogilvy could tender his proposal, because if he was too late... if she accepted...

He knew Cecilia Chenoweth, and she would not go back on her word. If she agreed to marry Nettlethorpe-Ogilvy, he would lose her forever. And why would she possibly refuse an honorable proposal, one that would save her from ruination? Marcus had gone and told her that she would be *dead to him* if she defied his order and told Diana about the pending case against Ellery—a *brilliant* choice of words. To make matters worse, during the trial, he had done nothing but scowl at her.

No wonder she assumed his offer of marriage had been withdrawn. Well, it hadn't. The only thing more stubborn than the will of kings might be the will of this duke. But tonight, he was prepared to admit that he had been wrong, that he had been an idiot, and to beg Cecilia to marry him, anyway.

He flashed his season pass at the attendant manning the doors of the Spring Garden House, not slowing his stride. "My sister and my aunt are—"

"Right here," Diana said, jogging up beside him, pale blue skirts clutched in her hand.

Marcus turned his head and saw that Aunt Griselda was just behind her, keeping pace rather impressively for an eighty-two-year-old woman.

"Good," Marcus said, slowing to a brisk walk as they strode into the garden. "The Astleys usually take a supper box in the Chinese Arcade," he said, steering them to the left.

It didn't take long to find them, even in the crush. "Is Cecilia here?" he asked without preamble, stopping short just outside of the box.

Harrington Astley's face twisted into a grin as he took in Marcus's drawn expression and the gigantic bouquet of dahlias. "*Cecilia*, is it? Not sure she'll want you calling her that after the way you've treated her."

Marcus had already scanned every inch of the supper box. She wasn't there.

And neither was Nettlethorpe-Ogilvy.

"Where is she?" he snapped.

Fauconbridge had risen to his feet, his expression drawn. "We thought you'd changed your mind. When you didn't join us tonight, it seemed to confirm it."

"No, I didn't. I—" Marcus broke off with a sound of frustration. He didn't have time for this. "Where is she?"

"She went for a stroll with Nettlethorpe-Ogilvy."

He'd known this would be the answer, but it made sweat break out across his palms nonetheless. "How long have they been gone?"

"Ten minutes."

Fuck. He was probably too late.

Still, if there was any chance... For the sake of his future with Cecilia, he had to try.

"Where did they go?"

Fauconbridge exited the box, coming to stand beside him. "No idea. But I'll help you look."

Marcus turned on his heel and headed toward the back of the gardens, as that was the only place one might find a spot of privacy suitable for a proposal. As soon as he'd cleared the packed walkways of the Grove, he broke into a jog, which drew no small amount of stares and whispers. But he found he didn't give a fuck whether he looked ridiculous, nor what people thought of him. The only thing that mattered was that he find Cecilia before she went and agreed to marry Nettlethorpe-Ogilvy, and he had to spend the rest of his life without the woman he loved...

He stopped short in the middle of the pathway, causing Fauconbridge to plough into his back. *The woman he loved.* That... was right. He did love Cecilia Chenoweth.

And what brilliant timing, to figure this out when he was on the cusp of losing her.

His pause gave the rest of the Astley party the chance to catch up with him. "Everyone, fan out," Lady Cheltenham said. She turned to Diana, Lucy, and Isabella. "You three are to stay with Lady Griselda." She fixed Isabella with a pointed gaze. "And do not even *think* about heading for those dark walks."

"But, Mama—" Lady Isabella protested.

"*No*," Lady Cheltenham said, turning on her heel and stalking off toward the cascade.

Marcus hurried deeper into the gardens. God, where were they? Why couldn't he find her? The fireworks would probably start any minute.

He noticed he was drawing stares, which wasn't much of

a surprise. He was sure Ellery's court case had been on the front page of every paper. He'd expected whispers to follow him for months, but now that he was jogging through Vauxhall, a desperate look on his face and a huge bunch of flowers clutched in his hands, a literal crowd was trailing after him, not wanting to miss whatever spectacle was about to unfold.

Fuck it. Everyone was already talking about him.

And the only thing that mattered was that he found her before it was too late.

"Cecilia!" he shouted as he rounded a thick-trunked yew tree, only to find she wasn't behind it. "Cecilia!"

Fauconbridge, who was twenty yards to his left, recoiled in surprise, but recovered quickly. "Ceci," he called. "Ceci, where are you?"

All around him, he heard his friends take up the cry, from Morsley's deep bellow to Aunt Griselda's accented shout. And now he was really drawing a crowd, one that was following him in unabashed curiosity.

But it was all to no avail. Every time he burst out of a cluster of trees, it was only to find… another cluster of trees. How many fucking trees did they have at Vauxhall, anyway? And why had he once admired them? He was half-tempted to buy the pleasure gardens so he could raze them to the ground.

He burst clear of another cluster, stumbling into the graveled path of the South Walk.

And that was when the sky above him exploded in blazing bursts of red.

CHAPTER 42

*C*eci swallowed thickly as she watched Archibald Nettlethorpe-Ogilvy rise from where he'd been kneeling on the ground.

He had just proposed, as she had always known he would.

Ever since Marcus spurned her, she had known what she needed to do when this moment came.

And she had found the courage to do it.

But now, the trembling of her hands was nothing next to the fluttering of her heart.

God, how she hoped she hadn't just made a terrible mistake...

"Well." Mr. Nettlethorpe-Ogilvy gave her an awkward smile. He reached for her, then paused, as if he was unsure if it was now permissible for him to touch her. "I suppose we should, er..."

"*Cecilia!*"

They both turned. She would recognize that voice anywhere, even if it now contained a note of desperation rather than its usual disdain.

Her heart began to pound. It appeared that she and

Marcus would have things out much sooner than she had anticipated.

Well, no matter. She had planned exactly what she was going to say to him.

Marcus came bursting through a clump of fir trees, and the sight of him running toward her with his cravat askew, a bunch of pine needles in his usually meticulous hair, and an expression of wide-eyed desperation on his face was a thousand times more affecting than his usual polished perfection.

"Cecilia," he gasped, hurrying over to her.

It was then that she noticed the crowd that had been following him. Her shoulders stiffened as hundreds of people trickled into the clearing. They hung back a little way, fanning out in a circle around the edges of the glade and craning their necks to get a view of the spectacle.

Marcus seemed oblivious to the onlookers. His eyes sought nothing but her. "Did he propose?"

"He did, and—"

He made a sound of despair, then fell to both knees before her, the flowers he carried falling forgotten into the dirt as he seized her hands. "I know I have behaved abominably these past few days. You have every right to be angry with me. I know I must have given the impression that I no longer wished to marry you." His blue eyes were miserable. "But nothing could be further from the truth."

"Marcus," she breathed. "Please stop—"

"I will not. I *cannot*. Because I love you, Cecilia."

His eyes remained locked on hers as if he did not even hear the gasp that went up from the crowd. Ceci's vision blurred as her eyes filled with tears. She thought of all the nights she had lain awake in her bed, pining over this man. She had never dared to dream she would hear him say those words.

And here was her wildest dream, coming true, not five minutes after she had received another proposal.

"I love you," he repeated. "We are meant to be together. I know we are. I cannot even imagine marrying someone else, now that I have seen a glimpse of my future with you. And I am so, so sorry if I made you doubt that future, even for a second." He squeezed her hands. "Please tell me you'll give me another chance. That I'm not too late. I'll make it up to you. I swear it."

From over her shoulder, Archibald said, "Listen, Trevissick. It's all right—"

He wrinkled his nose as he glared at his rival. "It may be all right for you, but it is not all right for—wait, are you laughing at me? That is absolutely despicable! Here I thought you a man of character. I see now that—"

"It's all right because she refused me," Archibald clarified, cringing as a murmur of shock swept through the onlookers crowding the clearing, who by now had to number in the hundreds.

Marcus's eyes flew back to hers, suddenly filled with a cautious sort of hope. "Cecilia? Is… is that true?"

"It is." She pulled at his hands, trying to get him to rise, but he seemed too stunned to move. So, she knelt in the dirt with him so she could look him in the eyes. "As much as I esteem Mr. Nettlethorpe-Ogilvy, I cannot imagine marrying him when I am in love with you."

Relief washed over his face, raw and potent. "I thought I had ruined everything."

"You certainly gave it a good effort." She squeezed his hands. "Marcus, I know why you are so protective of Diana. But you have to stop. If you do not give her room to spread her wings, she will one day come to resent you."

His eyes were rueful. "You're right, of course. You should have heard the dressing down she gave me in the carriage."

He shook his head in disbelief. "I was so sure you were going to accept him. I was terrified."

"Do you know why I didn't?"

"I have no idea."

She reached out and plucked the cluster of pine needles from his hair. "For just the reasons you said. Because I love you. I belong with you, and you belong with me." Her voice was fierce as she added, "And because I knew that I could win you back."

He smiled at her, his real smile, the one he never used to use. He drew her hand up and pressed a kiss into her palm. "I like this confident side of you. It will serve you well once you are a duchess. I'm just sorry you'll find yourself married to a great arse like me."

She shook her head. "That is utterly untrue. You are a good man."

"Cecilia!" he hissed, for the first time sparing a glance at the crowd that surrounded them. "I am no such thing, and I will thank you to keep your voice down. I am a *Latimer*. We are not a nice sort of people. If we are to be married, you need to understand that."

"A very good man," she insisted softly. "It's also true, what you said in court yesterday, that you can be ruthless. But the difference between you and your father is that you are only ruthless for a good cause. That is the difference between a monster and a champion."

He cast his eyes to the fireworks exploding overhead. "You are going to ruin my reputation."

A laugh bubbled out of her. "Is this it, then? Your deepest, darkest secret? Worse even than the things you revealed in court yesterday? That you're *nice*?"

He rose from the ground, helping her up as he went. "Mark my words, Cecilia. I will have my revenge. You will *pay* for this." He leaned forward and in a hushed whisper enumerated the means by which she would pay, all of which seemed likely to end in multiple orgasms for each of them.

Ceci looped her arms around his neck. "Do you promise?"

He kissed her then, just on the forehead, as they were surrounded by a crowd, which responded with a cheer. Ceci could not help but note that the cheering of the gentlemen present was noticeably more enthusiastic than that of the ladies, but she didn't let it bother her.

When they broke apart, Archibald approached. He took her hand and bowed neatly over it. His voice was tremulous as he said, "I wish you every possible happiness, Miss Chenoweth."

He started to back away.

Marcus's mouth grew tight. He glanced around at the crowd, the one he had brought with him to intrude upon what Archibald had intended to be a private moment. "I say, Nettlethorpe-Ogilvy, I'm sorry about, er…"

Archibald waved this off. "It's all right. Excuse me." He threaded his way through the throng and disappeared into a cluster of trees.

Ceci squeezed Marcus's hand. "He'll be all right. Honestly, I think he was relieved when I said no." She leaned in to whisper, "I believe there is another young lady who is the true object of his affection."

"Good. Hopefully, he can settle things with her. And I will find a way to make it up to him."

Diana and Lady Griselda broke away from the crowd. "I suppose congratulations are in order," Lady Griselda said.

"Thank you," Ceci said.

"I was not congratulating you. I was congratulating *him*. He is getting the better end of this bargain, by far." She turned to her great-nephew. "You actually managed to choose a bride with some sense. Well done, Marcus.

Goodness knows you got little enough of that from your father's side of the family."

Marcus smirked, taking no offense. "Lord, is that the truth."

Diana came forward and clasped Ceci's hand. "I regret to inform you that you'll be taking on more than Marcus with this arrangement. You'll also find yourself in possession of a headstrong little sister and a deranged, but delightful, great-aunt."

The words were spoken in jest, but they settled over Ceci like a warm hug. She wasn't going to be alone anymore. She was going to have a *family*, and she didn't mind in the least that it would consist of a bullheaded duke, a woman who carried a blunderbuss beneath her skirts, and a young lady who looked as meek as a wood mouse but could gut you with her sword as fast as a fishmonger.

Her voice was thick as she replied, "I should like nothing better."

"Come," Marcus said, offering his arm. "We have an important errand to attend to."

Ceci accepted his arm and allowed him to lead her toward the front of the gardens, Diana and Aunt Griselda trailing behind. "What sort of errand does one perform at ten o'clock at night?"

Marcus gave her his signature smirk. "We're going to awaken the Archbishop of Canterbury."

Ceci gave him a sideways look. "Surely getting the special license can wait until tomorrow."

"It cannot. He's not only going to issue us a special license. He's going to marry us on the spot."

"Marcus! Don't be absurd."

His voice in her ear was deep and tempting. "If we marry tonight, then I can take you back home to Latimer House, and you can spend the night in my bed."

That did sound... tremendously appealing. But... "We can't rouse the Archbishop of Canterbury from his bed just so we can... so we can..."

"Why not? He owes me a favor."

"Mar-cus!"

By the time they reached the river, he had convinced her. Ceci mused that she was going to have her hands full keeping her obdurate duke of a husband in line.

She expected it would suit her marvelously.

Archibald stumbled through Vauxhall's wooded back reaches, scarcely seeing where he was going by the faint glow of the colored lamps that grew scarcer with each passing step.

He could not *believe* that had just happened. Not that Miss Chenoweth had refused him. He had known full well that Trevissick was the one who had captured her affections. He had been planning to bow out when he received news of her ruination and the duke's apparent rejection. This was the only reason he had proposed. He genuinely liked Cecilia Chenoweth. She was a good person, and they were friends. He would never allow her to face ruination. And surely there were worse foundations for a marriage than friendship and respect.

He was happy that she had worked things out with the man she loved, even if it meant that he had no idea who he was going to court now. His parents were determined for him to raise the family's standing by making a society marriage. But, excepting Cecilia Chenoweth, all of the eligible young ladies of his acquaintance looked down their noses at him for being *in trade*, and even worse, the grandson of a blacksmith.

Well, he had bad news for his future bride—his grandfather the blacksmith was Archibald's kindred spirit, not his parents, who cared only about clawing their way into the highest ranks of society.

To be sure, there was probably some proper young lady out there who would agree to marry him for his fortune, then wrinkle her nose every time he walked into the room. A depressing thought, to be sure.

So, Ceci declining his proposal was a heavy blow. At least she would've been nice to him. But what was worse was Trevissick storming into the clearing with half of Vauxhall trailing after him, forcing Archibald to admit that Ceci had rejected his offer of marriage in front of a crowd of three hundred.

Absolutely everyone would know of it by tomorrow. He would be the butt of yet another joke, the upstart blacksmith who was so detestable that even his outlandish fortune couldn't entice a woman to marry him.

He didn't want to do this anymore, had never really wanted to do it in the first place. If he had any say in the matter, he would marry the daughter of an industrialist, like himself. God knew there were plenty of companies eager to forge a connection with Nettlethorpe Iron. Then he would never have to set foot in another ballroom and feign an interest in the cut of Lady Hughley's dress or how much Mrs. Arbuthnot's new silk curtains must have cost. He could spend his days in his workshop, not giving a fig what anyone thought of him.

He might not find a love match, the way Ceci just had, but at least he would have a wife who didn't despise him.

Archibald sighed. But of course, he wasn't going to do that. His parents might not understand him at all and could not seem to grasp how utterly unsuited he was to the world they yearned to enter.

But they did love him, and he would never disappoint them.

He broke clear of the wooded area and found himself on one of the graveled paths. He must have been heading toward the dark walks, because the copse of trees ahead was pitch black, illuminated only by moonlight and the faint glow of the fireworks sparkling overhead. He should probably turn around, as he knew what people got up to in those dark walks, and it was nothing good. But he found he wasn't prepared to face the gossiping crowds he would find near the entrance.

He was contemplating where he could possibly go to wait a few hours for the throng to thin out when a rustling came from the underbrush on the far side of the path. He squinted in the moonlight as a young woman in a red dress came stumbling out of the bushes.

Just as she was about to burst onto the path, her foot caught on something and she careened forward. Archibald stepped forward reflexively, catching her about the waist as she crashed into his chest.

"Oh!" she gasped as she looked up, clinging to his shoulders for purchase.

Archibald froze.

It was *Isabella Astley*.

His mind, which was normally as precise in its workings as a Swiss timepiece, suddenly felt sluggish and fuzzy.

Isabella Astley had never said so much as a word to him.

Yet somehow, he was *holding her in his arms.*

He didn't know what to do. Well, that wasn't true. Obviously, he should release her. Except he wasn't going to release her, because this was *Isabella Astley*, and he could no more draw away from her than the tides could resist the pull of the moon.

She squinted up at him in the darkness. "Mr. Nettlethorpe-Ogilvy?" she asked uncertainly.

"Y-yes," he managed to sputter.

Strangely, instead of shoving him off, she gripped his arms more tightly. "Oh, thank goodness it's you!"

His lethargic brain managed to process a few facts—she had come from the dark walks, which were absolutely no place for a young, unaccompanied lady. She had been running... most likely, away from something. Or, rather, someone. Her breath was coming in pants, and her eyes were filled with consternation.

"Are you all right?" he asked.

She squeezed her eyes shut and tipped her head forward, so it was almost resting on his shoulder. "I am, now that you're here."

He had absolutely no idea what she was talking about, but that scarcely mattered. Isabella Astley was *glad he was there.*

He was prepared to stand rooted to that spot for the rest of his natural life if doing so would make her happy.

A rustling came from the trees behind her. Lady Isabella squealed, glancing over her shoulder. Without thinking, Archibald lifted her by her waist and turned, placing his body between her and whatever it was that had alarmed her.

She looked over his shoulder for a beat, then raised her eyes to meet his. "I must ask you for the most terrible favor."

"Anything," he breathed.

"Are... are you sure?" she asked, her blue eyes full of uncertainty.

"Anything," he said firmly.

"Oh, thank you," she breathed.

And then she looped her arms around his neck and pressed her lips against his.

~

Keep reading for two special previews—of Book Five in The Astley Chronicles, *Let Me Be Your Hero*, and of the novella *My Favorite Mistake*, which features everyone's favorite parasol-wielding lady's maid, Fanny Price!

If you thought that was spicy, you should read Ceci and Marcus's second epilogue! You'll get it for free if you subscribe to my newsletter. My newsletter subscribers receive a free bonus story for each of my books, as well as historical romance fun, giveaways, and goodies. You can sign up via my website, https://courtneymccaskill.com/.

PREVIEWS: LET ME BE YOUR HERO AND MY FAVORITE MISTAKE

Coming Soon: Book 5 in The Astley Chronicles, *Let Me Be Your Hero*

Being ruined is the least of Isabella Astley's problems.

Visiting the Dark Walks of Vauxhall seemed like a harmless adventure at the time. But ever since Lady Isabella overheard men plotting treason, someone has been trying to kill her!

Her only hope is Archibald Nettlethorpe-Ogilvy, a rich industrialist and engineering savant. Archibald fell hopelessly in love with Isabella the moment he clapped eyes on her. He has been scorned by so many women for being *in trade* that he knows such an ethereal beauty could never come to care for the likes of him. But now her life is in danger, and he happens to be one of the few men with enough wealth and power to protect her. Seizing his chance, he proposes marriage, an offer Isabella has no choice but to accept.

Passion flares between these unexpected lovers. For Archibald, putting his life on the line to keep Isabella safe is the easy part. But showing the woman who could crush him with a word his heart, and his true self? That is more terrifying than facing a thousand hired assassins...

~

The last thought to cross Archibald's brain before Isabella Astley's lips pressed against his was, *so she does know my name.*

He hadn't been sure. When he first made her acquaintance, at the wedding of one of her sisters to the Viscount Thetford, he was introduced not to Lady Isabella but to "the twins," which meant that her sister, Lady Lucy, had been the one to say all of the requisite greetings and carry the conversation while Lady Isabella stared off into space, her lips curved into a bemused half-smile and her thoughts clearly a thousand miles away.

It had been hard for Archibald to attend to the conversation as well. Seeing Isabella Astley for the first time had felt like getting run over by a brace of oxen. She was that beautiful. She had the large, dark blue eyes that were an Astley family trait. But, unlike most of her sisters, her hair was not blonde but a rich, dark brown, which, combined with her pale, creamy skin, made her eyes all the more striking. She was tall for a woman, only an inch shorter than him, and quite slim with only the barest hint of a bosom. She had a delicate quality about her that made him nervous even to bow over her hand out of fear that he might break her with his meaty paws.

All of this combined into an otherworldly quality. He remembered thinking that she did not look human. She looked like the daughter of the fairy king.

Up until that moment, Archibald had spent precisely zero minutes of his life thinking about *the daughter of the fairy king.* His thoughts tended to be consumed with more efficient ways to decarburize iron, or perhaps how to increase its tensile strength.

Yet, there he was, mooning over Isabella Astley like a lovestruck schoolboy.

But then, at the wedding breakfast, it had gotten a thousand times worse. Because that was when he finally heard her speak.

She was *so clever*. He had been seated at the next table over, a few feet away and at such an angle that he could just see her out of the corner of his eye. His assigned dining partner had decided to ignore him in favor of trying to flirt with Lord Graverley across the table. With nothing to distract him and seated in such close proximity, he hadn't been able to help but overhear Isabella Astley's every remark.

She was different from any young lady he had ever encountered. She stated her opinions with an assurance most women twice her age did not possess. She seemed to have little interest in the topics young ladies typically favored—fashion, the weather, and whatever had happened at last night's ball. Apparently, she read Gothic novels obsessively and was even trying her own hand at writing them.

When some of the matrons seated around her attempted to take her to task for her unorthodox opinions, it did not go well for them. When Mrs. Whitcombe informed her that the Gothic novels she loved were "tawdry," Lady Isabella innocently asked her to list the ones she had read and to describe their most tawdry elements.

Later, Lady Iveson pointedly told her that it wasn't decorous for young ladies to wear bold colors, a thinly veiled criticism of Lady Isabella's red gown.

"Thank God," she had returned. "How I should hate to be mistaken for a decorous young lady."

Then, during the dessert course, Lady Hering complained for ten straight minutes that the Ancient Egyptian artifacts decorating the bridegroom's family home were "ghastly." But when her ladyship began impugning the morals of anyone who would choose such a garish theme for their home, Lady Isabella sweetly asked, "Was it your intention to insult my sister's new family to my face? Or are you always this clumsy with your words?" While Lady Hering sputtered, Lady Isabella continued, "Egyptian artifacts might not be to my personal taste. But at least they're not a dead bore, unlike your conversation."

Archibald had to feign a bout of coughing to cover his laughter. She was like a solitary streak of oil paint, vivid and confident, on a sun-faded watercolor. Even though he knew next to nothing about her favorite topics, he could have sat listening to her all day, feeling nothing but surprise and delight at the extraordinary sentences that emerged from her rose-pink lips.

Over the months and years that followed, she never seemed to notice him, not even when he had come to stay as a guest at her family's home. He didn't blame her. How could he expect this ethereal creature to notice the likes of *him*, a glorified blacksmith who spent his days laboring either in his family's iron forge or his own machine shop? It was as ridiculous as expecting Aphrodite to notice Hephaestus.

Well, of course, Aphrodite *had* noticed Hephaestus. Hell, she had even married him.

But everyone knew how *that* had turned out.

So, Archibald had contented himself with admiring Isabella Astley from afar, and dreaming about her each night, never expecting her to look at him, much less speak to him.

So tonight, when she threw her arms around his neck and pressed her lips eagerly against his?

His brain ceased functioning, immediately and completely. That was the only explanation for the extreme impropriety of what he did next.

He did not kiss her in the way a gentleman should kiss a lady—a delicate, closed-mouth meeting of the lips designed not to unsettle her delicate sensibilities.

Instead, a primitive growl emerged from his throat. *Mine* was the word that echoed through his skull. He proceeded not to kiss her so much as devour her. She tasted of cherries, sweet and tart and utterly delicious, and he could not get enough of her. She felt so, so perfect in his arms. She was slight compared to his own hulking frame, but it would be a mistake to call her weak, for her kiss all but crackled with a vivacious energy that left him breathless.

He must have kissed her in thoughtless abandon for some minutes, for when Archibald was next aware of anything, he saw that he had pulled her flush against him, pressing his body against every inch of hers, from throat to thighs. One of his burly arms was wrapped around her waist and the other around her upper back. His meaty hand was tangled in her hair, depriving her of any chance to escape.

He pulled back, regret and shame flooding him. He was fifty times as strong as she, and he had just forced himself upon her. "Lady Isabella, I... I'm so sorry."

Her eyelids flitted open. At first, she looked almost drunk, she was so dazed, but her eyes slowly came into focus.

She stared at him for ten agonizing seconds as he sheepishly disentangled his fingers from her hair.

Just as he was preparing to step back, she said it.

"*I'm not.*"

And then she wrapped her arms around his neck and pulled him back to her.

Let Me Be Your Hero will be available in 2024 and is now available for pre-order. Keep reading for another special preview... Everyone's favorite parasol-wielding lady's maid, Fanny Price, gets her own happily-ever-after in the novella *My Favorite Mistake*!

$\sim$

Sixteen years ago, lady's maid Fanny Price believed in love at first sight. But that was before she met handsome horse trainer Nick Cradduck at a village fair. Nick swept her off her feet, then shattered her heart the very next day.

Fanny crossed all of England, finding a new post with the Astley family, just so she would never have to see that filthy blackguard again. But Nick isn't going down without a fight. He tracks Fanny down at the Cooper's Hill Cheese Rolling and Wake, of all places, on a bright, sunny spring morning not so different from the day they met. Now Fanny must decide if she'll send Nick packing... or take a second chance on the only man who's ever felt like her match.

$\sim$

May 1816
  Village of Brockworth, Gloucestershire, England

They say a bad penny always turns up again, and Fanny Price could tell you it was true.

How else could you explain how she came around a market stall at the foot of Cooper's Hill on a bright, sunny spring day, humming a tune and wondering which of the strapping lads parading themselves about the fairgrounds would be the one to win the famous cheese rolling event that afternoon, when who should she plough into but the man she had crossed all of England to avoid?

"Hearts alive!" she gasped. "Nick Cradduck!" Now, Fanny

wasn't usually the bumblesome sort, but she went stumbling back and would've fallen right on her rump had Nick not reached out and grabbed her about the waist.

She blinked up at him, momentarily befuddled. It had been sixteen years, but whereas the passage of time had left Fanny with crinkles at the corners of her eyes and a gray hair or two in her mane of red curls, Nick Cradduck had aged like a fine Scotch whisky. He was six feet tall and every bit as broad of shoulder and lean of hip as he'd been when last she saw him. He had hair as black as sin, the kind that felt like silk beneath your fingers (unfortunately for her, Fanny was in a position to know how Nick Cradduck's hair felt beneath your hand). His eyes were the color of a stormy sea. He hadn't shaved that morning; judging by the scruff on his chiseled jawline, it had probably been a day or even two. But—*starf take him!*—much like the bump on his nose and that little mole at the corner of his mouth, this "flaw" somehow only served to make him all the more handsome.

And, gracious, his arms! He must still be training horses, because only that sort of heavy work gave a man such sculpted, bulging muscles...

Fanny realized with a start that the reason she knew Nick's arms were bulging with muscles was because she'd grabbed onto them to catch her balance.

She remedied that right quick, letting go and taking a hasty step back.

Or at least, *attempting* to take a hasty step back. The fact that she'd disappeared in the dead of night didn't seem to have got it through Nick Cradduck's thick skull that she wanted nothing to do with him, because he didn't release her waist. Nor did he seem to have noticed the glare she was leveling his way.

"Fanny," he breathed. "At last, I've found you!"

And then the chuck-headed lout leaned down and *tried to kiss her*!

Well, she wasn't standing for that! "Unhand me, you... you..." Unable to summon words foul enough to say what she thought of him, she yanked at his big, warm, patient hands, desperate to get them off her before she remembered what they'd once felt like on her. She couldn't pry them loose, but she did manage to grab the handle of the parasol dangling from her wrist and brought it up to spear him in the stomach.

"Oof," he grunted, letting go of her at last and grabbing his belly. He cut his eyes to hers, resigned. "So, it's like that, is it?"

"How else could it possibly be?" she spat.

"You're not still angry about what happened in the church, are you?" His grey eyes softened. "That was all a misunderstanding."

"A misunderstanding?" Putting sugar in someone's teacup when they'd asked for cream, that was a misunderstanding. Arriving at four o'clock when you'd been meant to come at three, that was a misunderstanding.

This had been no *misunderstanding*.

"Well, see if you can understand this," she shouted, swinging her parasol for the side of his head.

One of those big hands shot up and caught the parasol, stopping it dead. She gaped at those tan fingers, clenched tight, and the familiar curl of black hair at his wrist, then slid her gaze back to his face, her eyes poisonous.

Nobody touched her parasol.

Nobody.

He might've had arms like a bloody Viking, but that didn't stop Fanny from giving a great bellow and starting to wrestle with him over the parasol. On any other parasol, the shaft would've snapped, but her mistress, Lady Caroline, had asked her brother-in-law to make this one especially for Fanny, and it had an iron rod hidden in its core, just thick enough to give it strength without making it overly heavy.

Speaking of her mistress, Fanny was glad her ladyship's young daughters weren't about, because she might've said a few words during the tussle that weren't entirely suitable for the daughters of an earl to hear.

But, to her eternal frustration, she didn't manage to wrench her parasol free.

She was trying to decide whether she should bite him on the hand to make him let it go when the sound of church bells rang out from over in the village.

Nick froze, listening, then sighed. "This isn't finished. I've got to speak to a man about some business. But as soon as I'm done, you and I are going to talk." He released her parasol, turned, and stalked off across the green.

"Don't bother, because I don't have a thing to say to you, Nick Cradduck!" she shouted after him. "And the only bit of you I want to see is your back part!"

He cast her a grin over his shoulder. "That can be arranged. You always liked my back part."

As he rounded a stall, Fanny had to own that he was right.

And that he still had an *excellent* back part.

Grumbling to herself, she spun on her heel. She wasn't going to give Nick Cradduck another thought. He could follow her all around the fair today, and he probably would. Why should she care?

He couldn't very well follow her home. Fanny served as lady's maid to the Countess of Ardingly—whom she still called Lady Caroline, as that had been her title when Fanny first came to be in her service. The Ardingly manor house was right in the middle of a twelve-hundred-acre estate.

He couldn't very well follow her there. So, no matter how

much of a bother he made of himself, after today, she would never have to see him again.

With that cheering thought, Fanny went to have a look around.

～

My Favorite Mistake is available now as part of the anthology *My Fair Regency*!

HISTORICAL NOTES

- The incident in which the future King George IV ordered an ornate piano from John Broadwood and Sons, changed his mind, and refused payment is a fabrication. This was one of the prince's signature moves, however. He famously ordered £54,000 worth of jewelry for Princess Caroline upon their marriage in 1795, only to refuse payment to jeweler Nathaniel Jeffreys upon discovering how much he disliked his new bride. This had the effect of bankrupting Jeffreys, who retaliated by publishing a pamphlet attacking the prince. The Prince of Wales was also famous for ordering one thing and then changing his mind, particularly when it came to architecture and furnishings. This is one of several reasons that the cost of the refurbishments to Buckingham Palace between 1820 and 1828 ran to £496,169, a breathtaking sum for the time. So, although I readily admit that this was a fabrication, I thought it in keeping with the prince's tendencies.

- The details of Ellery's trial probably seem bizarre to modern readers. But the notion that he should be capable of representing himself in court, even for capital charges, was accurate to the period. It was a common belief that an innocent man did not require a defense attorney. Judges would sometimes assign a barrister to represent the accused, but more often they would not, and it was not until 1836 with the passage of The Prisoners' Counsel Act that prisoners facing felony charges became *entitled* to a barrister. Often times, the judge would question witnesses directly, and jurors were also permitted to ask questions.

- The speed with which the trial takes place may also strike modern readers as strange, but this was also characteristic of the period. It is possible to browse old court cases on www.oldbaileyonline.org . If you care to do so, you will see that in London, where you didn't have to wait for the quarterly Assize Courts to come to town, a trial typically took place within a month or two of the crime being committed, and often was held in a matter of days. The swiftest trial I have come across was of a John Fray, who was charged with killing a man named Thomas Walkin on September 11, 1785. He was convicted of manslaughter just three days later on September 14, 1785. Most trials, even on capital charges, took less than an hour, and jury deliberations were usually short. The wheels of justice could turn quickly, indeed!

- Marcus has several habits that are presented as quirks that demonstrate his high level of concern about his appearance. These include his refusal to wear drawers out of fear that they would ruin the line of his breeches, his reluctance to remove his coat because he wears it so tightly that he can't get back into it without assistance from his valet, and the fact that he does not smile in public. I must confess that these practices were not so much quirks as habits common to all remotely fashionable men of the era. So, in reality, all of my heroes would have been doing these things, excepting Michael and Archibald (we all know how shockingly unfashionable they are, when left to their own devices!)

- During the Regency, there was not a single German language; indeed, Germany is known for having a number of regional dialects today, although these are on the decline. Mecklenburgish is a real dialect that was (and, to some extent, is) spoken in northeastern Germany. The University of Rostock has a Mecklenburg Dictionary project with the aim of putting a searchable dictionary of Mecklenburgish online. Alas, the project remains a work in progress and the dictionary is not yet available to the public. On the occasions when Aunt Griselda broke into German, I therefore used the equivalent term in Plattdeutsch, or Low German, a broader dialect spoken across northern Germany that remains more common today, with 6.2% of residents reporting they spoke it "very well" in 2016.

ACKNOWLEDGMENTS

I would like to thank everyone who has helped me bring this book into the world: my wonderful editor, Diana Bold; my indispensable beta readers Amy and Linda; and my brilliant cover designer Bailey McGinn. I'd like to thank my author buddies, both over in The Brazen Belles and at Regency Fiction Writers for always being there to commiserate with me about this crazy writing life! I would also like to thank all of the readers who go above and beyond to support me, especially my ARC readers and the members of my street team. Melinda, Gloria, Anne, Jessica, Mariah, Lindsay, Julie, Nicole, and Jocelyne: you are THE BEST, and I appreciate you more than I can say! Thank you to all of the Brazen Belles members who helped me brainstorm a name for my hellfire club, and particularly to Alison Franklin and Lisa Busenbark for pointing me toward Paradisium. Finally, as always, I want to give a shout-out to the University of Texas Library, which is pretty much the only thing standing between me and bankruptcy via research books.

Just ask Ceci and Marcus—the world is a much sunnier place with your mom by your side! I would therefore like to dedicate this book to my wonderful mother, Susan. Thanks for everything, Mom! I love you so much!

I would also like to thank my friends and family for all your love and support, especially my wonderful husband, my son, my sister, and my father. I am so fortunate to have you all in my life!

ABOUT THE AUTHOR

After reading *Black Beauty* for the 1,497th time, Courtney McCaskill was inspired to write her own stories. Reviews of her early work were mixed, with her fourth-grade teacher, Ms. Compton, saying, "Please stop writing all of your assignments from the point of view of a horse."

Today, Courtney lives in Austin, Texas with the hero of her own story, who holds the distinction of being the world's most sarcastic pediatrician. She is reliably informed by her son that she gives THE BEST hugs, "because you're so squishy, Mommy." In 2022, Regency Fiction Writers honored her with its Lady of the Realm award in appreciation of her volunteer work, both on its Board of Directors and as the Coordinator of the Regency Academe. When she's not busy almost burning her house down while attempting to make a traditional Christmas pudding, she enjoys playing the piano, learning everything there is to know about Kodiak bears, and of course, curling up with a great book! Visit her online at https://courtneymccaskill.com/.